T... ...IGED

It was thirty years ago that Mary Norton first created the Borrowers, and her four books which recount their adventures (all published in Puffins) have enchanted children and adults alike ever since.

Now there is a fifth book to delight in, and it is every bit as good as the first four. It tells how the resourceful Clock family – Pod, Homily and Arriety – find a new home after escaping from the wicked Platters, who wanted to put them on show in a model village. But safety is never guaranteed for the Borrowers, who must always guard against being seen by 'human beans'.

How Arriety and her family manage – just – to keep away from humans makes an exciting and entertaining story, ingeniously told, that will be enjoyed by all ages.

Also published in Puffins: *The Borrowers*, *The Borrowers Afield*, *The Borrowers Afloat*, *The Borrowers Aloft*, *Complete Borrowers Stories*, and *Bedknob and Broomstick*.

Other Puffins by Mary Norton

MARY NORTON

THE BORROWERS AVENGED

ILLUSTRATED BY
PAULINE BAYNES

PUFFIN BOOKS

To all our dear ones
Old Rectory, Monks Risborough

PUFFIN BOOKS

Published by the Penguin Group
Penguin Books Ltd, 27 Wrights Lane, London W8 5TZ, England
Penguin Books USA Inc., 375 Hudson Street, New York, New York 10014, USA
Penguin Books Australia Ltd, Ringwood, Victoria, Australia
Penguin Books Canada Ltd, 10 Alcorn Avenue, Toronto, Ontario, Canada M4V 3B2
Penguin Books (NZ) Ltd, 182–190 Wairau Road, Auckland 10, New Zealand

Penguin Books Ltd, Registered Offices: Harmondsworth, Middlesex, England

First published by Kestrel Books 1982
Published in Puffin Books 1983
9 10

Penguin Film and TV Tie-in edition first published 1992

Copyright © Mary Norton 1982
Illustrations copyright © Pauline Baynes, 1982
All rights reserved

Printed in England by Clays Ltd, St Ives plc
Set in Baskerville

CHAPTER ONE

Mr Pomfret, the village constable at Little Fordham, was a thin young man with very soft, brown eyes (Miss Menzies often said he looked 'wistful').

'Sometimes, I think –' she would say to Mr Pott, '– that Mr Pomfret does not really care for being a policeman.'

He was married to a small, bustling woman – as fair as he was dark – and they had one very large, quiet baby.

The windowsills of the flat above the police station were always strewn with furry toys. Miss Menzies usually found this disarming but as she walked down the path on this particular, drizzly autumn afternoon (October the third, to be exact) the glassy-eyed teddy bears and lop-eared rabbits staring down through the panes above somehow failed to comfort her. For some reason, her errand, which two days before had seemed the only right and sensible course, suddenly seemed less so. She felt a little shaky as she pressed the bell: dear Mr Pomfret had always been so kind, she dreaded now to forfeit his respect. Yet what she had to tell him was perfectly honest and straightforward: she pulled back her shoulders, regaining some of her courage, and pushed the bell.

It was Mrs Pomfret who opened the door, a little flushed, her hair awry. 'Oh, Miss Menzies, come in, do. You want to see my husband?'

A clothes-horse stood by the stove in the public side of the office; it was hung with towelling squares, steaming in the glow. Mrs Pomfret whisked this shut. 'Not much of a drying day,' she explained apologetically, as she made for an inner door.

'Do leave it,' said Miss Menzies but Mrs Pomfret had gone.

Miss Menzies carefully closed her umbrella and stood it beside the hearth. As she stretched out her hands to the fire, she noticed they trembled slightly. 'Oh, dear, oh dear . . .' she muttered; and thrusting them deep in her pockets she squared her shoulders again.

Mr Pomfret entered, quite cheerfully for him. Disturbed in the middle of his tea, he was wiping his mouth on his handkerchief. 'Good afternoon, Miss Menzies. Dreadful weather!'

'Yes, indeed,' said Miss Menzies faintly.

'Do sit down. Here, by the fire.'

Wordlessly, Miss Menzies sat down. Mr. Pomfret drew a chair from the far side of the desk and joined her by the stove. There was a short silence, then Mr Pomfret went on: 'Thought it might clear up around dinner time . . . quite a bit of blue sky . . .' The silence continued, and Mr Pomfret repeated 'around dinner time'. Then hurriedly blew his nose. 'The farmers like it, though,' he went on, stuffing his handkerchief into his pocket. Very cheerful and casual, he seemed.

'Oh, yes,' agreed Miss Menzies nervously, 'the farmers like it.' She moistened her lips with her tongue, staring across the hearth at his kind brown eyes as though beseeching them to be even kinder.

In the ensuing silence, Mrs Pomfret bustled in again with a cup of milky tea, which she set on a stool by Miss Menzies. 'Oh, how very kind,' gasped Miss Menzies as Mrs Pomfret bustled out again.

Miss Menzies stared thoughtfully at the tea, then, taking up the spoon, began very slowly to stir it. At last she raised her eyes. 'Mr Pomfret,' she said, in a clear and steady voice, 'I want to report a loss. Or it may be a theft,' she added as Mr Pomfret drew out his note-book. She laid down the spoon and clasped her hands together in her lap: the long, thin, curiously girlish face looked grave. 'Or missing persons – that might be more accurate.' Mr Pomfret unscrewed the top of his fountain-pen and waited politely for her to make up her mind. 'In fact,' she went on suddenly in a rush, 'you might even call it a case of kidnapping!'

Mr Pomfret became thoughtful, gently tapping his lower lip with his fountain-pen top. 'Suppose,' he suggested gently, after a moment, 'you just told me simply what happened?'

'I couldn't tell you simply,' said Miss Menzies. She thought awhile. 'You know Mr Pott and his model village?'

'Yes, indeed,' said Mr Pomfret. 'Quite a tourist attraction. They say that Mr Platter of Went-le-Craye is setting up some kind of model village, too.'

'Yes, I heard that.'

'A bit more modern, like, they say it's going to be, seeing as he's a builder.'

'Yes, I heard that, too.' Miss Menzies ran a nervous tongue across her lips again. 'Well –' she hesitated a moment and then went on boldly, '– to get back to *our* village, Mr Pott's and mine: you know we're sort of partners? That he makes all the

7

houses and I make the model figures – the people,
as you might say?'

'Yes, indeed, and very lifelike they are, too!'

'Yes.' Miss Menzies' hands tightened slightly, as
she clasped them together in her lap. 'Well, it's like
this – I didn't make all the figures. I didn't make
the ones that are missing.'

Mr Pomfret managed to look both concerned and
relieved at the same time. 'Ah, now I see it –' he

gave a small laugh. 'It's some of them that's missing, is it? I thought for a moment – I mean, when you said kidnapping –'

'That I meant live ones?' She looked at him steadily. 'I do.'

Mr Pomfret looked alarmed. 'Now, that's different.' Very serious suddenly, he poised his pen above his book. 'Person or persons?'

'Persons.'

'How many?'

'Three. A father, mother and child.'

'Name?' said Mr Pomfret, writing busily.

'Clock.'

'Clock?'

'Yes, Clock.'

'How do you spell it?'

'C-l-o-c-k.'

'Oh, Clock,' said Mr Pomfret, writing it down. He stared at the word: he seemed puzzled. 'Father's occupation?'

'Shoemaker, originally.'

'And now?'

'Well, I suppose he's still a shoemaker. Only he doesn't do that for a living –'

'What does he do for a living?'

'Well, I – er – I mean, I don't suppose you've heard of it: he's a borrower.'

Mr Pomfret looked back at her without any recognizable expression, 'Yes, I've heard of it,' he said.

'No, no, it's not in the sense you mean. It is an occupation. A rare one. But I think you *could* call it an occupation –'

'Yes,' said Mr Pomfret, 'I agree with you. That's

what I do mean. I think you could call it an occupation.'

Miss Menzies drew in a long breath. 'Mr. Pomfret,' she said, in a rush, 'I must explain to you – I thought you'd realized it – that these people are very *small*.'

Mr Pomfret laid down his pen: he studied her face with his kind brown eyes. He seemed more than a little bewildered: what could their height have to do with it? 'Do I know them?' he asked. 'Do they live in the village?'

'Yes. I've just told you. They live in *our* village, the model village, Mr Pott's and mine.'

'The model village?'

'Yes. In one of the model houses. They're as small as that.'

Mr Pomfret's gaze became curiously fixed. 'How small?' he asked.

'Five or six inches, something like that. They're very unusual, Mr Pomfret. Very rare. That is why I think they've been stolen. People could get a lot of money for a little family like that.'

'Five or six inches?'

'Yes.' Miss Menzies' eyes suddenly filled with tears; she opened her bag and felt around for her handkerchief.

Mr Pomfret was silent. After a moment, he said, 'Are you sure you didn't make them?'

'Of course I'm sure.' Miss Menzies blew her nose. 'How could I make them?' she went on in a strangled voice. 'These creatures are *alive*.'

Once again Mr Pomfret began to bang his pen against his lower lip: his gaze had become more distant.

Miss Menzies wiped her eyes and leaned towards him. 'Mr Pomfret,' she said in a steadier voice, 'I think perhaps we are talking at cross-purposes. Now, how can I put things more clearly . . .' She hesitated and Mr Pomfret waited patiently. 'With your experience of houses, have you ever had the feeling . . . the impression, that there are other people living in a house besides the human beings?'

Mr Pomfret looked even more thoughtful. Other 'people' – *besides* human beings: the terms were synonymous, surely?

'I can't say I have,' he admitted at last, almost apologetically.

'But you must have wondered about the mysterious way small objects seem to disappear. Nothing of great value – small things, like pencil stubs, safety-pins, stamps, corks, pill-boxes, needles, cotton-reels – all those sort of things?'

Mr Pomfret smiled. 'We usually put it down to our Alfred. Not that we'd ever let him get at a pill-box –' he added hastily.

'But you see, Mr Pomfret, factories go on making needles and pen-nibs and blotting paper, and people go on buying them, and yet there never is a safety-pin just when you want one, or the remains of a stick of sealing-wax. Where do they all go to? I'm sure your wife is often buying needles and yet all the needles she ever bought in her life can't be just lying about this house . . .'

'Not about this house, no,' he said: he was rather proud of his neat, new residence.

'No, perhaps, not this house,' agreed Miss Menzies. 'They usually like somewhere older and

11

shabbier – with loose floorboards, and age-old panelling, and all that sort of thing; they make their homes in the oddest nooks and crannies. Most of them live behind wainscots, or even under the floor . . .'

'Who do?' asked Mr Pomfret.

'These little people. The ones I'm trying to tell you about –'

'Oh? I thought you said –'

'Yes, I said I had three of them. We made a little house for them. They call themselves "borrowers". And now they've gone –'

'Oh, I see,' said Mr Pomfret, tapping his lip with his pen. But, Miss Menzies realized, he did not see at all.

After a moment, in spite of himself, Mr Pomfret asked in a puzzled voice, 'But why would they *want* these kind of things?'

'They furnish their houses with them: they can adapt anything. They're very clever. I mean, for little people like that, a good piece of thick blotting paper makes an excellent carpet and can always be renewed.'

Blotting paper was quite obviously not Mr Pomfret's idea of 'an excellent carpet'. He became silent again and Miss Menzies realized unhappily that she was getting herself into even deeper water.

'It's not so extraordinary, Mr Pomfret, although it must sound so. Our ancestors spoke openly about "the little people". In fact, there are many places in these islands where they are spoken of even today . . .'

'And *seen*?' asked Mr Pomfret.

'No, Mr Pomfret, they must never be seen. Never to be *seen* – by any human being – is their first and most serious rule of life.'

'Why?' asked Mr Pomfret (he wondered afterwards what had induced him to go even this far).

'Because,' explained Miss Menzies, 'to be seen by a human being might be the death of their race!'

'Oh, dear,' said Mr Pomfret: he hardly knew what else to say. After a moment a thought occurred to him. 'But you say you've seen them?' he ventured.

'I have been very privileged,' said Miss Menzies.

Again there was silence. Mr Pomfret had begun to look worried and Miss Menzies, too, felt she had said too much: this conversation was becoming more than a little embarrassing. She had always liked and respected Mr Pomfret as he had always liked and respected her. How could she get things back on a less uneven keel? She decided to adopt a more normal and decisive tone, and somehow lighten the atmosphere. 'But please don't worry, Mr Pomfret, or go out of your way, or anything like that. All I'm asking you to do, if you *would* be so kind, is just to record the loss. That's all. In case,' she went on, 'they might turn up somewhere else . . .'

Still Mr Pomfret did not write. 'I'll make a mental note of it,' he said. He closed his book, and slid a black elastic round the covers. He stood up suddenly as though more easily to put it in his pocket.

Miss Menzies stood up too. 'Perhaps,' she said, 'you might like a word with Mr Pott?'

'I might,' said Mr Pomfret guardedly.

'He'd bear me out about the size and everything.'

'You mean,' said Mr Pomfret, eyeing her almost sternly, 'that Mr Pott has seen them, too?'

'Of course he's seen them. We talk of little else. At least –' suddenly, she faltered. Was it she, perhaps, who talked of little else? And had Mr Pott ever really seen them? Looking back, in a sudden kind of panic, she could think of no occasion when he had actually admitted to having done so: she had been so strict about not having them disturbed; about leaving them alone to live their lives. Even on that one day, when she had persuaded him to make a vigil near the little house, none of the family had appeared, she remembered, and Mr Pott, nodding drowsily in the sunshine, had fallen off to sleep. Perhaps, through all these months, Mr Pott – never really listening – had simply tried to humour her: he was a kind, good man with manias of his own.

Mr Pomfret, she realized, was still gazing at her, half expectantly, with his warm brown eyes. She gave a little laugh. 'I think I'd better go now,' she said rather hurriedly, looking at her watch, 'I'm due at the church at six to help Mrs Whitlace with the flowers.' As he opened the door for her, she lightly touched his arm. 'Just report the loss, Mr Pomfret, that's all. Or make a mental note as you said . . . Thank you so much. Look, it's stopped raining . . .'

Mr Pomfret stood in the doorway for a moment, staring after her as she loped away along the shining asphalt with those long-legged, girlish strides. How old would she be now, he wondered, forty-eight? fifty? Then he went inside.

'Dolly –' he called tentatively. Then, seeming to change his mind, he went beside the stove and gazed unseeingly into the fire. He appeared to be thinking deeply. After a while, he took out his note-book again, unloosed the elastic and stared down at the almost blank page. He thought again for a while, before licking his pencil. 'October 3rd, 1911'. After writing these words, he licked his pencil again and underlined them heavily. 'Miss Menzies,' he wrote next, and hesitated. What to write now? He decided at last to put a question mark.

Miss Menzies walked down the path to the church holding her umbrella close to her head as if to cover her embarrassment. She was thinking hard about her little people (people . . .? Of course they were people. Pod, Homily, and her young Arrietty) for whom she had made a home (a safe home, she had thought) in Mr Pott's model village. Pod and Homily she had only observed from a distance, as it were, as she crouched down to watch them from behind a waving clump of thistles, but Arrietty – fearless, bright-eyed Arrietty – had almost become a friend. And then there was Spiller. But Miss Menzies had never seen Spiller. No one ever saw Spiller unless he willed it: he was a master of concealment; could melt into any background; lurk near, when thought to be far; arrive when least expected and disappear as fast. She knew he was a loner who lived wild in the hedgerows; she knew he could navigate streams; had built a boat out of an old wooden knife-box, caulked at the seams with beeswax and dried flax; and that for shorter trips he used the battered lid of an old tin soap-box . . . Yes, Arrietty had talked a lot about Spiller, now Miss Menzies came to think about it. Arrietty's mother thought him dirty but, to Arrietty, he had smelt of the whole wide out-of-doors.

Miss Menzies sighed. Perhaps Spiller would find them and help them if they were in trouble . . . wherever they were.

CHAPTER TWO

When Miss Menzies reached the church, she found Mrs Whitlace and Lady Mullings in the vestry drinking tea.

'I'm so sorry to be late,' said Miss Menzies hurriedly, hanging up her mackintosh.

'Don't worry, my dear,' said Lady Mullings. 'There was little to do today except to change the water. Bring up a chair and sit down. Mrs Whitlace has brought us some drop scones.'

'How delicious,' exclaimed Miss Menzies, taking a seat between them. She looked a little flushed from her walk.

Lady Mullings was large and statuesque (and given to floating veils). She was a widow and lived alone, having lost two sons in the Boer War. She had a sweet, sad face, always heavily powdered (a habit which in those days was considered rather worldly). Miss Menzies, on occasion, had even suspected a touch of lip-salve, but one could never be sure. All the same, Miss Menzies was devoted to Lady Mullings, who was kindness itself and who, some years before, had cured Miss Menzies' arthritic hip.

For Lady Mullings was a faith-healer. She took no credit for it: 'Something or someone works through me,' she would say, 'I am only the channel.' She was also, Miss Menzies remembered suddenly, a 'finder': she could locate lost objects or, rather, visualize in her mind the surroundings in which such objects might be found. 'I see it in a dark place . . .' she had said of Mrs Crabtree's ring, '. . . sunk sideways, there's kind of mud . . . no, more like jelly . . . something is moving now . . . yes, it's a spider. Now, there's water . . . oh, the poor spider!' The ring had been found in the S-trap of the sink.

'I came a little early,' Lady Mullings was saying now, reaching for her gloves, 'and must leave a little early, I'm afraid, because someone is coming to see me at six-thirty . . . someone in trouble, I'm afraid – so I'd better hurry. Oh dear, oh dear, what about these tea things . . .?'

'Oh, I'll see to those,' said Miss Menzies, 'and Mrs Whitlace will help me – won't you, Mrs Whitlace?'

'I will, of course!' exclaimed Mrs Whitlace, jumping up from her seat. She began to collect up the plates and Miss Menzies, in spite of her present worries, found herself smiling. Why, she wondered, did Mrs Whitlace always seem so happy? Well, perhaps not always, but nearly always . . .

Miss Menzies had a very warm regard for Kitty Whitlace who, before her marriage, had been a Kitty O'Donovan who had come over from Ireland at the age of fifteen to be kitchen-maid at Firbank Hall – in the 'good old days' as they were called now. Lonely and homesick as she had been at first, her winning ways and eagerness to please had gradually won over the sour old cook, Mrs Driver. After several years, these same winning ways had also won the heart of Bertie Whitlace, an under-gardener. Whitlace later left to become sole gardener at the rectory and, after their marriage, Kitty had followed him, and become cook-general in the same old house.

18

Alas, the old rectory was empty now, but the Whitlaces had stayed on as caretakers. The Tudor rectory was listed as 'an historic building' to be preserved by the parish, as was the church, with its famous rood-screen. Mr Whitlace was appointed verger and Mrs Whitlace cleaner of the church. They lived very happily in the deserted old house – in the kitchen annexe, which was almost a cottage in itself.

There was a sink for the flower-arrangers in the far corner of the vestry. As she filled the battered kettle which stood on the draining-board, lit the somewhat rusty gas ring which, for safety's sake, stood on the stone flags beneath it, Miss Menzies had a sudden thought: should she, *dare* she, confide in Lady Mullings, who after all was meant to be a 'finder'? Waiting for the kettle to boil, she washed out a few spare flower-vases in cold water, still thinking hard. But how, she wondered unhappily, could she explain the borrowers to Lady Mullings? She was still smarting from that embarrassing interview with Mr Pomfret. He had clearly thought her quite mad. Perhaps not *quite* mad, but he had obviously been very puzzled. What, she wondered, had he said afterwards to Mrs Pomfret? Up until now – and she knew it well – Miss Menzies had been a much respected member of the village community. And yet, and yet . . . should any stone be left unturned?

'Perhaps,' thought Miss Menzies, as she dried up the crockery, 'we are all a little "touched"?' Lady Mullings with her 'findings', Mr Pott with his model village, herself with her 'borrowers'. Even sensible Mrs Whitlace, brought up as she had been on the

far coast of West Cork, was apt to go on about
'fairies'.

'I've never seen one myself,' she would explain.
'But they're all about, mostly after dark. And, say
you offend them, like, there's not a dirty trick they
wouldn't stoop to.'

'I'll be coming down the village with ye,' she was
saying now. 'Whitlace will be wanting his evening
paper.' Mrs Whitlace always called her husband

'Whitlace': it was the name he had been known by at Firbank. She had tried 'Bertie' a few times after they had first married but somehow it wouldn't fit. He had always been called 'Whitlace' and 'Whitlace' he seemed to remain.

'Oh, good –' said Miss Menzies, putting a small piece of net edged with blue beads over the top of the milk jug, which she placed in a bowl of cold water. This was for Mrs Whitlace's elevenses next morning, after she had cleaned the church.

Mrs Whitlace gathered up the leaves and flower stalks and put them into the waste-paper basket, with a half-eaten drop scone. These she would transfer to the larger dustbin next morning. She tidied up the piles of hymn-books which stood on top of the disused harmonium. The sugar bowl she put in the cupboard among the chalices, candlesticks and offertory plate. She turned the key of the great oaken cupboard, and locked the vestry door.

As the two women walked down the aisle, to let themselves out through the main entrance, Miss Menzies was struck by the beauty of the little church and again by the cleverness with which Mr Pott had constructed its exact replica in his model village: the way the light fell through the intricate carving of the famous rood-screen, making patterns on the pale flagstones of the aisle. Their footsteps struck hollow sounds into the silence, the door groaned loudly as they opened it and clanged to when they shut it behind them with a sound which sent its echoes crashing down the nave. Even the turning of the key in the lock seemed to grate on the silence.

Before they reached the lychgate, they felt the

first few drops of rain. Mrs Whitlace hesitated, her hand to her new straw hat trimmed with velvet violets. 'My umbrella,' she exclaimed, 'I've left it in the vestry.' Selecting the vestry key from the bunch she carried, she sped away around the church.

'I'll wait for you here by the lychgate,' Miss Menzies called after her.

The rain became heavier as Miss Menzies stood under the thatch of the lychgate, and she was glad of its shelter. Pensively she watched the puddles filling in the rutted lane beyond. She thought of Lady Mullings and of how she might approach her. Not again would she betray herself as she had with Mr Pomfret. But she knew that for this interview she must take some intimate belongings for Lady Mullings to get her 'feeling'. She could not take clothes, their size would arouse wonder: Lady Mullings would, of course, mistake them for dolls' clothes. She must take something which a human being might have used. She thought suddenly of bedclothes – their sheets: these could be taken for handkerchiefs (and one *was*, she remembered). Yes, that was what she should take. But should she go at all? Was it wise? Was it fair on Lady Mullings to seek her help and hold back so much vital information? Yet, if she told all, might she not (in some way unforeseen) betray her little people? Would Lady Mullings believe her even? Might she not see, in Lady Mullings' face, the same odd blank expression she had seen on Mr Pomfret's? No, she thought, that would be beyond bearing. And supposing Lady Mullings *did* believe her, might not she get too excited, too involved, too enthusiastic? Taking over the search herself, for instance? A search which, for the sake of the borrowers, should be quiet, methodical and secret?

Miss Menzies sighed and looked towards the church. From the lychgate, she could not see the door of the vestry, only the main door under the porch. Mrs Whitlace seemed to be taking her time. Had she slipped through the small wicket gate which led straight into the rectory? Perhaps she had left her umbrella there? Ah, here she was at last . . .

Mrs Whitlace hurried down the path. She seemed a little upset and the umbrella wobbled slightly in the speed of her advance. When she reached Miss Menzies she did not open the gate but closed her umbrella and stared into Miss Menzies' face. 'Miss Menzies,' she said, 'there's something after happening you might call odd.' Miss Menzies noticed the usually rosy face looked strangely pale.

'What was it, Mrs Whitlace?'

'Well,' Kitty Whitlace hesitated, 'I mean –' again she hesitated, then went on with a rush, '– you wouldn't call me fanciful?'

'No, indeed,' Miss Menzies assured her. 'Anything but that!' (Except, Miss Menzies reminded herself suddenly, about fairies.)

'I could have sworn on my sacred oath that we'd left the church empty –'

'Yes, of course we did,' said Miss Menzies.

'Well, when I turned the key in the lock and began to open the door, didn't I hear voices . . .?'

'Voices?' echoed Miss Menzies. She thought a moment. 'Those jackdaws in the belfry sometimes make an awful racket. Perhaps that was what you heard.'

'No. This was in the vestry itself. I stood there

23

quite silent at the door. And somebody seemed to say something. Quite clear, it was. You know how sound carries in that church?'

'What did they seem to say?' asked Miss Menzies.

'They seemed to say "What?" '

'What?' repeated Miss Menzies.

'Yes – "what?", just like that.'

'How odd,' said Miss Menzies.

'And the curtain, you know the one, between the vestry and the Lady Chapel, was moving slightly as though someone had touched it. And there was a rustle of paper. Or something.'

'Perhaps,' said Miss Menzies, 'it was the draught from the open door.'

'Perhaps,' agreed Mrs Whitlace uncertainly. 'Anyway, I gave the church a good going over. Except the belfry. Whatever I heard was quite close. I mean, it – whatever it was – couldn't have got up into the belfry. Not in the time.'

'You should have come back for me. I'd have helped you.'

'I thought of mice. I mean, the paper rustling and that. I went all through the waste-paper basket.'

'There are mice in that church, you know,' said Miss Menzies. 'Field mice. They come in from the long grass in the churchyard. You remember that time of the Harvest Festival?'

'Strong mice, then,' said Mrs Whitlace, 'I threw half a drop scone into that basket. Everything else was there, but devil a bit of a scone.'

'You mean it had gone?'

'Clean gone.'

'You're sure you threw it in?'

'Sure as I stand here!'

24

'That is odd,' agreed Miss Menzies. 'Would you like me to go back with you? Perhaps we could get Mr Pomfret –' Mrs Menzies blushed as she said his name, at the thought of her recent embarrassment. No, she would not like, quite as soon as this, and under these circumstances, to enlist his help again.

'You know what I think, Mrs Whitlace?' she said after a moment. 'That since the robbery – those candlesticks on the altar were very valuable, Mrs Whitlace, more valuable than any of us really knew – that we have all become a little nervous. Not alarmed exactly, but a little nervous. And things do speak, you know – inanimate things. I had a fretsaw once which every time I used it seemed to say "Poor Freddie". You couldn't mistake it – "Poor Freddie, poor Freddie" . . . It was quite uncanny. And there was a tap that dripped which seemed to say "But *that* . . . But *that* . . ." With a terrific emphasis on the "that". I mean to say,' explained Miss Menzies, 'that a tap, that tap over the sink in the vestry, for instance, could easily say "What".'

'Maybe,' said Mrs Whitlace opening her umbrella again (she still looked preoccupied). 'Well, if you'll excuse me, Miss, we'd better be getting on. Whitlace will be a-waiting for his tea.'

Later that evening, after tea, when Whitlace was ensconced by the stove with his evening paper, Kitty Whitlace told her story again. She told it more fully, as he barely listened when working out the racing odds, and she was free – as it were – to think aloud. 'I told her,' she said, in a worried, slightly hurt voice, 'that I heard something, or somebody, say "What?". The thing I didn't tell her – because nobody, least of all you, Whitlace, would deny I'm a good cook and, as you might say, you can't have too much of a good thing – what I didn't tell her was what the other voice said.'

'What other voice?' asked Mr Whitlace, absently.

'I told you, Whitlace, that I heard *voices*, not just one voice.'

'What did it say, then?' asked Mr Whitlace, laying down his paper.

'It said, "Not drop scones AGAIN!" '

In February, Miss Menzies went away to stay with her sister in Cheltenham, returning on the second of March. She found Mr Pott very busy with his model village, preparing for the summer season. The snows of winter had inflicted a certain amount of damage to the little houses, so that most of her spare time was spent in helping to put things right.

Almost her first action in the garden had been to lift the roof off the borrowers' house and sadly stare inside. A little bit of damp had got in and Miss Menzies prevented further damp by digging a small channel to carry off the rainwater which had collected in puddles on many of the miniature roads. If – oh, IF! – her little people ever returned, they must find their toylike house as neat and dry as when they had left it. This was the least she could do. The roof when she put it back seemed sound and firm. Yes, she had done her best: even to the extent (in an embarrassed and roundabout way) of reporting the loss to the police. That, perhaps, had been the greatest ordeal of all!

By mid March, in spite of several days of rain, the model village began to look more like itself. Once she had cleaned it out, it did not occur to Miss Menzies to examine the little house again: it had been deserted for so long and, if they were to open in time for Easter, there was so much else to do: new figures to make, old ones to refurbish, rolling stock to be oiled and painted, roofs to mend, gardens to be weeded . . . Mr Pott had been clever with his drainpipes and such water as there was now flowed smoothly into the stream. Miss Menzies was especially proud of her oak trees – stout stalks of curly parsley, dipped in glue and varnished over.

It was Miss Menzies, too, who persuaded Mr Pott to put up the pig-wire fence along the river bank. She felt sure that whoever had stolen the borrowers had approached the model village from the water. 'Don't seem much point to me,' Mr Pott had protested, 'seeing as they've gone now . . .' But he hammered in the stakes all the same and wired them up securely. He had never quite believed in the borrowers himself but realized, in his quiet way, that the idea of these creatures had meant a great deal to Miss Menzies.

And so the long winter passed. Until – at last, at last! – came the first intimations of spring. And (for all the characters concerned) a strange spring it turned out to be . . .

CHAPTER THREE

At a house called Ballyhoggin, at Went-le-Craye, Mr and Mrs Platter sat staring at each other across their kitchen table. They appeared to be in a state of shock – they *were* in a state of shock. Words had now utterly deserted them.

Mr Platter was a builder and decorator, who sometimes acted (under certain conditions) as the village undertaker. He had a dry, shrivelled, somewhat rat-like face and rimless glasses through which, when the light caught them, one could not see his eyes. Mrs Platter was large and florid but, at this moment, florid no longer. Her heavy, rather lumpy face had turned to a curious shade of beige.

On the table three small saucers were set out in a row. They contained something gooey. It looked like over-cooked rice, but Mrs Platter called it 'kedgeree'.

At long last, Mr Platter spoke. He spoke very slowly and deliberately in his dry, cold, rasping voice. 'I shall take this whole house to pieces brick by brick,' he said. 'Even –' he went on, '– if I have to hire a couple of extra men!'

'Oh, Sidney –' gasped Mrs Platter. Two tears rolled down her pendulous cheeks. With a fumbling hand, she reached for a tea-towel and wiped them away.

'Brick by brick,' repeated Mr Platter. Mrs Platter could see his eyes now: they were round and hard, like blue pebbles.

'Oh, Sidney –' gasped Mrs Platter again.

'It's the only way,' said Mr Platter.

'Oh, Sidney –' Mrs Platter had covered her face with the tea-towel. She was really crying now. 'It's the nicest house you ever built . . .' Her sobs were barely muffled by the tea-towel. 'It's our *home*, Sidney.'

'Considering what's at stake,' went on Mr Platter stonily. He hardly seemed to notice his wife's distress. 'We had a fortune in our hands. A fortune!'

'Yes, Sidney, I know . . .'

'Houses!' exclaimed Mr Platter. 'We could have built all the houses we should ever want. Bigger and better houses. Houses such as you have never even dreamed of! We could have shown these creatures all over the world. And for any money. And now' – his pupils became pinpoints – 'they've gone!'

'It's not my fault, Sidney,' Mrs Platter wiped her eyes.

'I know it's not your fault, Mabel. But the fact remains – they've gone!'

'It was I who gave you the idea of getting hold of them in the first place.'

'I know that, Mabel. Don't think I'm not grateful. We committed a felony. It was very brave of you. But now –' His face was still stony. 'Someone or something has stolen them back.'

'But nobody knew they were here. No one, Sidney, except· us.' She gave her face a final clean-up with the tea-towel. 'And we always went up to the attic together, didn't we, Sidney? To check on the locking of the door. In case one of us forgot. And there was that piece of zinc at the bottom of the door, in case they bored through, like –'

'We found the window open,' said Mr Platter.

'But how could little things like that open a window?'

'I've explained to you how they opened it, Mabel. The cord and the pulley and all that . . .' He thought awhile. 'No, someone must have come up with a ladder. They must have had help –'

'But nobody knew they were here. *Nobody*, Sidney. And they were there at breakfast time, when we took up their porridge. You saw them yourself. Now, didn't you? And who'd bring a ladder in broad daylight? No, if you ask me, Sidney, they can't have got far. Not on those little legs of theirs . . .'

'They must have had help,' repeated Mr Platter.

'But no one's even seen them, only us –' She hesitated. 'Except –'

'Yes, that's what I do mean –'

'You mean that Miss Menzies, or whatever she's called. And that Abel Pott? I can't see Abel Pott climbing a ladder. Not with his wooden leg, I can't. And that Miss Menzies, she's not the type for a ladder. And how would they know to come here?'

'There's that Lady Mullings down at Fordham. Ever heard tell about her?'

'Can't say I have.' She thought for a moment. 'Oh, yes I have – I tell a lie – didn't you do her roof once?'

'That's right. They say she's a "finder".'

'A finder?'

'Finds things. Sort of sees where they are. They say she found Mrs Crabtree's ring. And she found those burglars that took the candlesticks . . .'

'What candlesticks?'

'Those silver-gilt candlesticks out of the church. Said she saw them in a pawnshop, next to two china dogs. Gave the address and all. And that's where they were. You wouldn't credit it . . .'

'No, you wouldn't, would you?' said Mrs Platter slowly. She was looking thoughtful. 'Oh, well – we mustn't give up hope. Suppose we go up now and have just one more look . . .?'

'Mabel,' Mr Platter glanced at the clock on the wall, 'we've been looking for four hours and thirty-five minutes. And not a sign of them. If they're still in this house, they'd be inside the walls, under the floor . . . anywhere! Remember that bit of loose floorboard I hitched up?'

'Where they could see into our room? Yes.'

'Well,' said Mr Platter, as though that settled the matter. 'And talking of houses,' he went on, 'in my opinion, the best house I ever made in my life was that showcase I made for *them* for our model village. The trouble I took over that showcase. The trouble. Stairs, ventilation, drainage, furniture, real carpet, electric light . . . And that plate-glass front, slotted, so you could lift it up for cleaning. Real home-like it looked and yet – this was the trick – there wasn't a corner they could get themselves into where the public couldn't see them. Day or night –'

'There wouldn't be public at night, Sidney.'

'Evenings,' said Mr Platter, 'winter evenings. This wouldn't have been no tourist summer show, girl. Not like the Riverside Teas, or Pott's model village. And there it sits' – there was real grief in his voice now – 'a perfect miniature house out in the tool-shed, covered with a blanket.'

There was a gloomy silence. After a while, Mrs Platter said, 'I been thinking, Sidney, before you start taking our home to bits – brick by brick, as you say – that it might be a good idea to take a run down to Abel Pott's . . .'

'The model village?'

'Yes, that's where they'd aim for, wouldn't they?'

'Maybe. Yes. But it's a pretty good step. At their kind of pace, it might take them a week to get there.'

'All the better. Let them settle in and feel safe, like.'

'Yes, you've got a point there.' He thought for a moment. 'And yet, on the other hand . . .'

'What, Sidney?'

He began to smile. 'We got the boat, haven't we? Say we went down ahead and laid in wait for them?'

'What? *Now?*'

Mr Platter looked irritated. 'Not *now*, this minute. As I say, it'll take them a bit of time to get there. Tomorrow, say, or the day after . . .'

CHAPTER FOUR

'I don't know where your father's got to,' exclaimed Homily for about the fourth time that evening as she and Arrietty sat by the fireless grate in the far too tidy room, 'Spiller said he'd found a place . . .'

Although through the tiny glass panes they could see the neat roofs of Mr Pott's model village, here indoors a grey dimness had stolen all the colour from their bright and toylike home. Home? Was it really 'home'? This miniature village made by Mr Pott? More of a hide-away, perhaps – after that long, dark winter in the Platters' attic.

Arrietty glanced at the neatly strapped bundles ranged against the farther wall. 'We'll be ready when they do come,' she said. We were all right here, she thought, before those Platters stole us. All the same, it lacked something – it was, perhaps, too ordered, too perfect and in some way too confined. Improvisation is the breath of life to borrowers, and here was nothing they had striven for, planned or invented: all had been 'given', arranged by a kind but alien taste.

'When they *do* come? They've been gone two days!'

'Perhaps,' said Arrietty, 'it's a good sign really: it may mean they've found somewhere.'

'Pity that old mill wasn't any good. But, anyway, we couldn't have lived on corn.'

'Nor could the miller,' Arrietty pointed out, 'that's to say, when he was alive.'

34

'All tumbled down, they said it was. And the rats something fierce.'

'Spiller will find somewhere,' said Arrietty.

'But where? What sort of place? I mean, there's got to be human beans or we'll have nothing to live on! And this idea of everywhere by boat! Something could easily have happened to them! Or suppose those Platters got them again?'

'Mother –' began Arrietty, unhappily. She got up suddenly and went to the window and stared out at the fading sky. Then she turned, a dark outline against the dim light. Homily could not see her face. 'Mother –' she said again in a more controlled voice, '– don't you see that you and I, sitting here in this model village, the very place the Platters stole us from, are in far more danger than Papa or Spiller?'

'There's that pig-wire along the river bank.'

'They'd be through that in a trice. They'd get some things called wire-cutters. And if you want to take *all* our stuff, we've *got* to go by water.'

'That knife-box of Spiller's! Suppose it sank? You and your father can swim, but what about me?'

'We'd fish you out,' said Arrietty patiently. 'And it never has sunk yet.' She knew her mother in this mood. After all, Homily had been brave enough in their other escapes: in their home-made balloon, brave enough in the boot and, come to think of it, extremely courageous in the kettle. A worrier she might be but she would always rise to an emergency.

'Spiller will find somewhere,' she said again. 'I know he will. And it might be somewhere lovely . . .'

'I've liked it here,' said Homily. Glancing round the room she shivered, crossing her arms. 'I wish we could light the fire . . .'

35

'But we can't!' exclaimed Arrietty. 'Someone might see the smoke – we promised Papa!'

'Or put the light on,' Homily went on.

'Oh, Mother!' cried Arrietty. 'That would be madness! You know it really . . .'

'Or have something to eat that wasn't Spiller's nuts . . .'

'We were lucky to have those nuts.'

'They take such an age to crack,' said Homily.

Arrietty was silent: she had heard these kind of grumbles so many times before. And yet, she thought (coming back to her stool as the room grew slowly dark) that perhaps in her heart Homily understood the need for this speedy removal better than she pretended. Three human beans, at least, perhaps four – perhaps even more – knew they had been here, knew they had departed but (unless they gave the game away) there was no one, as yet, who knew they had returned.

It was for this reason Pod had forbidden them the use of light or fire, had kept them away from the windows and, throughout the daylight hours, confined them to the miniature house. Such days, with Pod and Spiller away, could sometimes seem very long. It was late March and three days had passed since their dramatic escape by home-made balloon from the Platters' attic. Looking back on it now, Arrietty realized what a wonderful feat this had been. 'Why do things always happen to us in March?' she wondered. She came back to her stool and, curling her legs round slightly, laid her head on her knees. Both she and Homily were very tired: the packing had not been easy – beds taken down, mattresses rolled, arm-chairs clamped together; each bundle arranged in such a way that everything would fit into Spiller's boat. And still Pod and Spiller had not come.

She remembered her father's face on their first arrival back: the way he had glanced about the tidy little room, with its doll's-house furniture and polished wooden floor. How he had looked up with a rueful shrug at the pocket-torch bulb hanging from the ceiling. Battery controlled, this contraption meant more to him than any other of Miss Menzies' inventions ('Clever . . . she's bright, you know'). He wished he had thought of it himself. And Arrietty remembered he had sighed a little. No, it hadn't been easy for any of them.

'Hark!' said Homily suddenly. Noiselessly Arrietty sat up, holding her breath in the silence. A faint scrape on the door – a breath of nothing. Neither moved: it might be a passing vole, a beetle or even a grass-snake. Homily stole from her stool and melted into the shadows beside the threshold. Arrietty could just perceive her bent head and the stooped, listening outline.

'Who's there?' Homily whispered at last, just above her breath.

'Me,' said a familiar voice.

As Homily opened the door, a waft of air flew into the room, scented with spring and evening, and there against the pale sky was the solid outline.

Eagerly Homily pulled him by the arm. 'Well, what news? Where's Spiller? Did you find anything?' She pushed forward her own stool. 'Here you are. Sit down. You look all out.'

'I am all out,' said Pod. Sighing, he laid his borrowing bag on the floor. There was something in

37

it, Arrietty noticed, but not much. 'Walking, walking, climbing, climbing . . . it takes it out of you.' He looked round wearily at the stacked furniture in its neat piles. 'Would there be a drop of something?' he asked.

'There's a few tea leaves,' suggested Homily, 'I could warm them up over the candle.' She bustled towards the luggage, 'If I can find them –' She pulled at a few bundles. 'What with everybody packing, you don't know what's in what . . .'

'I could do with something a bit stronger,' said Pod.

'There's that sloe gin,' said Homily. 'But you don't like it . . .'

'That'll do,' said Pod.

She brought it to him in part of a broken nutshell. It was some of Miss Menzies' making. 'I was going to leave it behind,' Homily said: she had always been a little jealous of Miss Menzies as a provider.

Pod sipped the drink slowly. Then slowly he began to smile. 'You'll never guess,' he said. They could not – in that dusky half-light – see his expression but his voice sounded amused.

'You mean you've found somewhere?'

'Could be.' He took another sip of gin. 'But I've found *someone*. At least, Spiller has . . .'

'Who, Pod? Who?' Homily, leaning forward, tried to see his face.

'And what's more,' Pod went on stolidly, 'he's known about them all the time.'

'Them!' repeated Homily sharply.

'The Hendrearies,' said Pod.

'No!' exclaimed Homily. The little room became

tense with shock. Thoughts raced shadow-like around it from floor to ceiling, as Homily sat with clasped hands, head and shoulders in rigid outline against the half-light of the window. 'Where?' she asked at last, in an oddly colourless voice.

'In the church,' said Pod.

'The church!' Homily's head swung sharply round towards the window.

'Not the model church,' said Pod, 'the real one –'

'The human church,' explained Arrietty.

'Oh, my goodness,' cried Homily, 'what a place to choose!'

'There wasn't all that choice,' said Pod.

'Oh, my goodness me,' muttered Homily again, 'what a thing! But how did they get there? I mean, the last we saw of them, they were locked up in that gamekeeper's cottage, with just enough food for six weeks. I never did quite take to Lupy, as you well know, but many a time I've thought of them, wondering how they made out. Famine! That's what they were facing. You said it yourself, remember? When the humans go and the place gets locked up (and locked up it was – every crevice, didn't we know it? – against the field mice!). And that ferret, sniffing about outside . . .'

'How did they get out?' asked Arrietty, listening intently. She had edged her way along the floor and was sitting by her father's feet. 'I'd love to see Timmus,' she added. She hugged her knees suddenly.

Pod patted her shoulder. 'Yes, he's there. But not the two bigger boys. Seems they went back to the badger's sett. And Eggletina went to keep house for

them. Well –' Pod moved uneasily, '– seems they got out the same way as we did.'

'By *our* drain?' exclaimed Homily. 'In the scullery?'

'That's right. Spiller went for them.'

'And brought them down by our stream?' There was slight affront in her voice.

'That's right. Just like he did us. And a nice dry run he said it was, too. No bathwater and no floods. It was when we was shut up in the attic. You see, Homily, as the weeks went by and turned into months, Spiller never thought he'd see us no more. It was his escape route, not ours: he'd a perfect right to use the drain.'

'Yes, but you know the way Lupy talks . . .'

'Now, Homily, who's she got to talk to? And you wouldn't have wanted them to starve – now, would you?'

'No,' said Homily grudgingly, 'not starve exactly. But Lupy could well lose a fair bit of weight.'

'Maybe she has,' said Pod.

'You mean, you didn't see them?'

Pod shook his head. 'We didn't go into the church.'

'Why ever not?'

'There wasn't time,' said Pod.

'Then where are we supposed to live? Not that I hold with a church. Not for borrowers. Arrietty's read all about churches: they're one of the places that get absolutely chock-a-block of human beans. Where they congregate, as you might say, like starlings or something . . .'

'Only at regular hours, like. A church can be a good sort of place to be. Say there's a stove that heats the water. For the radiators, like –'

'What are radiators?'

'Oh, you know, Homily! Those things they had at Firbank –'

'You forget, Pod,' said Homily, with some dignity, 'that at Firbank, I never went upstairs.'

'Radiators –' said Arrietty, '– I remember: those things that bubbled?'

'That's right. Full of hot water. Keeps the house warm in winter . . .'

'And they've got those in the church?'

'That's right. And the stove they have burns coke.'

Homily was silent, for almost a full minute. After that, she said slowly, 'Coke's as good as coal, wouldn't you say?'

'That's right,' said Pod. 'And they've got candles.'

'What sort of candles?'

'Great long things. There's a drawer that's full of them. And they throw away the candle ends.'

'Who do?' asked Homily.

'The human beans.'

Homily was silent again. After a while, she said slowly, 'Well, if we've *got* to live in a church . . .'

Pod laughed. 'Who said we'd got to live in a church?'

'Well, you did, Pod. In a manner of speaking . . .'

'I said no such thing. The place that Spiller and I had in mind is somewhere quite different.'

'Oh, my goodness,' said Homily, 'whatever next?' Her voice sounded frightened.

'There's an old empty house, not a stone's throw from the church. Spiller and I have been all over it . . .'

'Empty!' exclaimed Homily. 'What would we live on then?'

'Wait!' said Pod. He took another sip of sloe gin. 'When I say "empty", I mean no one lives in it, except –' he drained the nut-shell, '– the caretakers.' Homily was silent. 'Now, these caretakers, name of Witless, they live in the very far end of the house, which used to be the kitchen. There's the kitchen, the scullery and the larder . . .'

'A larder . . .' breathed Homily. Awe-struck, she sounded as though granted a heavenly vision.

'Yes, a larder,' repeated Pod, 'with slate shelves. And,' he added, 'a mite of lovely stuff laid out on them.'

'A larder . . .' breathed Homily again.

'And that reminds me,' went on Pod. He stooped down and opened his borrowing bag. He drew out a fairly large piece of rich plum cake and a rather hacked-off morsel of breast of chicken. 'I guess you and Arrietty have been on pretty short commons these last two days . . . Fall to,' he went on, 'Spiller and I had our fill. There was some stuff called "brawn" but wasn't sure if you would like it . . .'

'I remember it at Firbank,' said Homily. She tore off a morsel of chicken and handed it to Arrietty. 'Here, child, try this. Go on, Pod –'

'There's a small staircase that goes up from the scullery and some bedrooms above. Not the main staircase that goes curving up and up –'

'How do you know all this, Pod?' Daintily, she tore off a piece of chicken for herself.

'I told you: Spiller and I went all over.'

'How could you, Pod, without your climbing pin? I mean, how could you get up the stairs?'

'You don't have to,' he said. She could tell he was smiling. 'The house is covered with creeper – ivy, jasmine, clematis, honeysuckle – everything you can think of. You can get just about anywhere.'

'Were the windows open?'

'Some were. And some of the panes were broken. It's all that crisscross stuff. Lattice, I think they call it.'

'And in the main house, you're sure there's no one?'

'No one,' said Pod. He thought for a moment. 'Except ghosts!'

'That's all right,' said Homily, breaking off another piece of chicken. With little finger crooked, she took a ladylike bite. She would have preferred to unpack a plate.

'She comes through now and again, this Mrs Witless, with a broom and a duster. But not often, she's frightened of the ghosts.'

'They always are, human beans,' remarked Homily. 'I can't think why.'

'She calls them "fairies",' said Pod.

'Fairies! What nonsense! As if there were such things!'

Arrietty cleared her throat: she felt her voice might tremble. 'I would be,' she said.

'Be what?'

'Frightened of ghosts.' (Her voice *did* tremble.)

'Oh, Arrietty,' exclaimed Homily irritably, 'it's nice you can read and that, but you read too much of all that human stuff. Ghosts is air. Ghosts can't hurt you. Besides, they keep human beans away. My mother lived in a house once where there was a headless maiden. Real good times they had with her, as children, running through her and out the other side – kind of fizzy it felt, she said, and a bit cold. It's human beans that can't abide them, for some reason. Never occurs to them that ghosts is too self-centred to take a blind bit of notice of human beans . . .'

'Let alone borrowers,' said Pod.

Homily was silent. She was thinking quietly of the larder – of cold smoked ham, or half-eaten apple tarts, of cheddar cheese, of celery in glass jars, of early cherries . . .

44

As if reading her thoughts, Pod said, 'He keeps up the kitchen garden, this Witless. Grows everything, Spiller says . . .'

'Where's Spiller now?' asked Homily.

'Down by the stream. Making the boat fast –'

'What to?'

'The pig-wire, of course.' Pod stretched out his legs wearily, 'Finish up that bit of cake. We got to start loading.'

'Tonight!' gasped Homily.

'Of course, tonight. While there's a bit of light left . . .' He rose to his feet. 'Then we just lie low awhile till the moon rises. Then we'll be off: Spiller's got to see to navigate . . .'

'You mean we're going to that place tonight!'

Pod, from where he stood, leaned forward, placing two tired hands on the shelf above the fireplace. He bowed his head. Then, after a moment, he slowly raised it. 'Homily,' he said, 'I don't want to scare you. Nor you neither, Arrietty. But you got to realize that every minute – any minute – that we're here, we're in grave danger.' He turned round and faced them. 'You don't want to be taken back to that attic. Now, do you? Nor to be put on show for the public to stare at? In a glass-fronted cage, like they were making – those Platters? For the rest of our lives . . .' He paused a moment. 'For the rest of our lives . . .' he repeated slowly.

There was a long silence. Then Arrietty whispered huskily, 'No.'

Pod straightened up. 'Then let's get busy,' he said.

CHAPTER FIVE

It was not easy to get all the bundles through the squares of the pig-wire; even with Spiller's help. The bedsteads were the worst. They had to dig away the earth on the bank of the stream with their bare hands and slide the bedsteads underneath. The squares of mesh were wide enough for most things but not wide enough for the beds. 'I wish we still had our old mustard spoon,' Homily grumbled, 'it would have come in useful here . . .'

'If you ask me –' panted Pod, as, stooping, he pushed the last bundle through to Spiller in the boat, '– if you ask me –' he repeated, standing upright to relieve his aching back, '– we shan't use half this junk.'

'Junk!' exclaimed Homily. 'All these lovely chairs and tables, made for us special! And all our very own, as you might say – to take or leave –'

'What have you *left*?' asked Pod wearily. Irritated as they were, they kept their voices down.

'Well, the kitchen sink, for one thing – being a fixture, like. And think of all those lovely clothes, washed and ironed, and fitting us a treat . . .'

'And who's to see us in them?' asked Pod.

'You never know,' said Homily. 'I've always kept a good home, Pod. And fitted you and Arrietty out proper. And it hasn't always been easy –'

'I know, I know,' Pod whispered more gently. He patted her on the shoulder. 'Well, we'd better be getting aboard –'

Arrietty took one last look round at the miniature

46

village. The slate roofs glinted palely under the rising moon, the thatched ones seemed to disappear. There was no light in the window of Mr Pott's house, he must have gone to bed. A tinge of sadness mingled with the feeling of tired excitement. Why, she wondered? And then she thought of Miss Menzies. Miss Menzies would miss them. How she would miss them! And, in Miss Menzies, Arrietty knew she was losing a friend. Why, she thought, did she, a borrower born and bred, succumb to this fatal longing to talk to human beans?

It always brought trouble: she had to admit that now. Perhaps, as she grew wiser and older, she would grow out of it? Or, perhaps (and this was a strange thought) this hidden race to which she belonged once *had* been human beans themselves? Getting smaller and smaller in size as their ways of life became more secret? Or, perhaps even (as she remembered The Boy at Firbank had hinted), their race *was* dying out . . .

She shivered slightly and turned towards the pig-wire and, with Spiller's help, climbed down into the boat.

Homily was arranging down quilts and pillows in what had been the teaspoon compartment of Spiller's old knife-box. 'We'll have to get some sleep,' she was saying.

'You'll get that right enough,' said Pod. 'We'll have to lay up till morning.'

'Where?' Homily's voice sounded startled.

'Where the stream turns into the rectory garden. It comes from the pond, like: there's a spring. We aren't none of us going up across that lawn in the moonlight. Owls galore, they say there are. No, we'll hole-in against the bank under the alders. Nothing'll see us there . . .'

'But what about crossing that lawn in the daylight? Carrying all this stuff?'

'The stuff stays in the boat – until we've got our bearings. Some corner of the house that's safe. Safe to settle down in, as you might say.'

Spiller was fixing the shabby leather gaiter over the cargo. Once this was done, except to very sharp eyes, the knife-box would look like some old floating log. 'And we'd not be needing – not even a quarter of this stuff – say I'd got my tools.'

'Yes,' agreed Homily, in a sad whisper, 'that's a real shame, that is. To lose your tools . . .'

'They weren't lost, not in the meaning of the word. What did we take away from that gamekeeper's cottage, except one hard-boiled egg?'

'That's right,' said Homily. She sighed. 'But needs must.'

'I could make anything, *anything* we really needed, like, say I had my tools.'

'I know that,' said Homily. There was real understanding in her voice as she thought of the partitions, the gates, and the passages under the floor at Firbank. 'And that cigar-box bedroom you made for Arrietty! There's not a soul alive who wouldn't call that a triumph . . .'

'It wasn't bad,' said Pod.

Arrietty, who had been helping Spiller with the last lashings-down of the gaiter (a leather legging such as in those days most of the gamekeepers wore), heard her own name and became suddenly curious. Edging her way along the side of the knife-box, she heard her father saying, 'Wouldn't be surprised if the Hendrearies had got them . . .'

'Got what?' she asked, leaning towards them.

'Keep your voice down, girl.'

'We was talking about your father's tools,' explained Homily, 'he thinks the Hendrearies may have taken them. Not that they hadn't a right to, I suppose, seeing as we left them behind . . .'

'Left them behind – where?' Arrietty's voice sounded puzzled.

'In that gamekeeper's cottage. When we escaped down the drain. Where,' she added rather acidly, 'you used to talk to that boy. What was his name now?'

'Tom Goodenough,' said Arrietty. She still sounded puzzled. After a moment, she said, 'But the tools are here in this boat!'

'Oh, don't be silly, girl! How could they be?' Homily sounded really impatient. 'All we took away from that cottage was one hard-boiled egg!'

Arrietty was silent for a moment. Then she said slowly, 'Spiller must have rescued them.'

'*Now* what are you on about, girl? You'll only worry your father . . .' Pod, she noticed, had kept strangely silent.

Arrietty slid down from her perch and came between them. 'When we were loading, Spiller and I,' she had dropped her voice to a whisper, 'there was a blue bag, like one of Uncle Hendreary's – I sort of knocked against it, and it nearly fell into the water. Spiller jumped forward and saved it. Just in time.'

'Well, what about it?'

'When we stowed it, I heard something rattle inside.'

49

'That could be anything,' said Homily, thinking of her pots and pans.

'And it seemed fairly heavy. Spiller seemed quite angry. As he grabbed hold of it, I mean. And he said –' Arrietty swallowed. She seemed to hesitate, as though to recall the words.

'What did Spiller say?' asked Pod, in a strained voice. He had been standing very still.

'He said "Look out what you're doing! Them's your father's tools!" '

There was a stunned silence. Then Homily spoke: 'Arrietty, are you *sure* he said that?' She glanced across at her husband. His head and shoulders were outlined faintly in the moonlight. Still he had not moved.

'That's what it sounded like. I didn't give it two thoughts. Not with the bag nearly falling into the water . . .' As neither parent spoke, she went on, 'Yes, that's what he said all right. He nearly shouted it: "Them's your father's tools!" '

'You're sure he said "tools"?'

'Yes, *that* was the word he shouted. Never seen Spiller cross like that. That's what I was thinking of most . . .' She looked from one dim shape to the other. 'Why? What's the matter?'

'Nothing's the matter!' Arrietty thought she heard a short sob. 'Everything's wonderful! Wonderful . . .' Homily was really crying now. 'Oh, Pod –' she rushed forward, flinging her arms around the still figure. 'Oh, Pod,' she sobbed, 'I think it's true!'

He held her closely, patting her back. 'Seems like it,' he said gruffly.

'I don't understand,' faltered Arrietty. 'Spiller must have told you . . .'

50

'No, lass,' said Pod quietly, 'he didn't tell us nothing.' He felt around for something with which to wipe Homily's face. But she broke away from him and rubbed it on the small pillow she had been holding in her hand. 'You see, Arrietty,' she said, still gasping a little, 'church or rectory, or whatever it is, we can begin to live now. Really live. Now we've got his tools . . .' She threw down the pillow, and seemed to be straightening her hair. 'But why, Pod, *why* didn't he tell us?'

CHAPTER SIX

It was pleasant to be on the water again. Spiller's boat, fastened securely at the prow, swayed softly – drawn and released by the current of the stream. Fragile wisps of cloud drifted across the moon, and sometimes obscured the stars. But not for long: a gentle radiance seemed to quiver upon the water, and a faint hint of wind stirred the rushes on the farther bank. All was silent – except for Homily's humming. Brisk and light-hearted once more, she was making up the beds. A difficult business this was, as the teaspoon compartment in which she and Arrietty were to sleep was only partly under the gaiter. It meant a lot of crawling back and forth for careful tuckings-in of Miss Menzies' flannel blankets and handmade, quilted eiderdowns. If it rained, their heads and shoulders would be dry: but what about their feet, Arrietty wondered?

She stood in the one free place in the stern, breathing in great draughts of the welcome night air, and idly watching Pod and Spiller moving about in the prow. Spiller, stooping, was drawing out his punt pole, the long yellow knitting needle which once – so long ago – had belonged to Mrs Driver. Out it came from under the gaiter, inch by inch, and he laid it down across the thwarts. He stood up cheerfully and rubbed his hands; then turned towards Pod who, stooping towards the fence, was fumbling with the twine. Then, suddenly – swift as whiplash – Spiller swung round, staring upstream. Pod too, rather more slowly, straightened himself and followed the direction of Spiller's eyes.

Arrietty leant quickly forward and laid a warning hand on her mother's arm, as Homily, a little dishevelled, emerged once again from under the gaiter. 'Hush!' she whispered. Homily stopped her humming. They both listened. It was unmistakable – not very near, as yet – the sound of oars!

'Oh, my goodness . . .' breathed Homily. She stood up, peering bleakly ahead. Arrietty's hand on her arm tightened to a painful grip. 'Quiet, Mother! We mustn't panic . . .'

Homily, hurt (in more senses than one), turned reproachfully towards her daughter and Arrietty knew that she was about to protest that she never panicked, that all her life 'calm' had been her watchword, that she had never been one to fuss, that – But Arrietty pinched her arm more tightly and, grumpily, she remained silent, staring blankly ahead.

Spiller had moved quickly beside Pod. Somehow, the twine had got wet or someone had tied the knots too tightly. There was something desperate about the two bent backs. Arrietty, suddenly contrite, released her grip and laid a comforting arm about her mother's shoulders and drew her closer. Homily took Arrietty's free hand and squeezed it gently. This was no time for quarrels.

At last, the twine slid free. They saw Spiller snatch up his punt pole and, driving it hard into the bank below the fence, he spun the boat into mid-stream. Homily and Arrietty clung more closely together as, with strong rhythmic strokes,

Spiller propelled them against the current. Upstream? Towards the sound of oars? Towards danger? Why?

'Oh, my goodness gracious . . .' breathed Homily again.

But on they went, stroke after stroke, the knife-box shuddering slightly on the shallow ripples of the current. The sound of oars became clearer and, with it, another sound – a kind of scrape and a splash. Homily, wild-eyed but silent, clung more closely to Arrietty and Arrietty, twisting in her mother's grasp, cast a desperate glance backwards. Yes, they had left the wire fence behind – the fence, the model village and all that their 'home' there had stood for. But where, oh where, could Spiller be making for now?

They soon saw: the knitting needle swung up in a moonlit flash across the boat and down on the other side. Two swift, deep strokes from Spiller and they were plunged among the rushes of the farther bank. Not plunged exactly, more crashing into them, the head of Spiller's boat being square.

There was no longer any sound of approaching oars. Whoever was rowing had heard the noise. A frightened frog plopped out of the rushes. Then all was silent again.

The sudden, sharp, unexpected swerve had bowled Homily and Arrietty over. They lay where they had fallen, listening hard. There was no sound except for the murmur of the gently flowing stream. Then an owl hooted, answered faintly by its mate across the valley. Silence again.

Arrietty rose stealthily to her knees and edged

her way towards the stern of the boat. She could just see over.

Moonlight fell fully on her face and (she realized unhappily) on the exposed stern of the boat. She turned and glanced forward: Pod and Spiller, lost among the deeper shadows, were scarcely visible now but she could see they were moving, moving and leaning. And then the boat began to stir: steadily, silently, inexorably, Pod and Spiller were pulling them more deeply into the rushes. A strong scent of bruised spearmint drifted back to her, and a faint smell of cow dung. Then the knife-box became still. Once more there was silence.

Arrietty, in shadow now, looked back over the stern. Between the bent and flattened rushes, she could still see the open stream and still she felt exposed.

'Could have been an otter . . .?' said a voice. Startlingly close it sounded, and it was a voice she recognized.

All the borrowers froze. Again there came the sound of a scrape and a splash.

'More likely a water-rat,' said another voice drily – nearer still now.

'Oh, my goodness . . .' breathed Homily again in Arrietty's ear, 'it's them! Those Platters . . .'

'I know,' whispered Arrietty, barely above her breath. 'Keep still . . .' as Homily made an instinctive move towards the gaiter.

Then the boat came into view, drifting down on the current. It was a small dinghy – the one the Platters had used at Riverside Tea for children's trips round the island – and the two figures in it, outlined against the moonlit bank, looked top-heavy and enormous. The oars, pulled in from the rowlocks, stuck up against the sky. The larger figure leaned forward. Again there was the scrape and a splash.

'I never thought we'd spring leaks like this, Sidney,' said the first voice.

'Stands to reason. Boat's been laid up all winter – she'll soon settle down once the timbers begin to swell.'

Another scrape, another splash. 'Oh, drat, something's gone into the bilges. I think it's the mutton sandwiches . . .'

'I told you, Mabel, this wasn't going to be easy.'

'I made them so nice, Sidney, with chutney and all.' There was a short silence and Arrietty held her breath, watching intently as the other boat drifted by. 'It's all right, Sidney,' she heard the first voice say. 'It was only the hard-boiled eggs . . .'

Again there was silence, except for the scrape and the splash. Arrietty turned her head, and there was Pod climbing towards them along the curve of the gaiter. He put his finger to his lips and she kept obediently still.

As he let himself down beside her, they heard the sound of oars again. Pod cocked his head, listening quietly. After a moment, under cover of the splashings, he said, 'They've gone past?' Arrietty nodded. Her heart was still beating wildly.

'Then *that's* all right, then.' He spoke in almost his normal voice.

Arrietty groped for his hand. 'Oh, Papa –'

'I know, I know,' he said, 'but it's all right now. Listen! They'll be tying up soon . . .'

Even as he spoke, they heard the clatter of the oars withdrawn from the rowlocks, and Mabel's voice, more distant now but carrying tremulously across the water. 'Oh, please, Sid, gently! You'll wake old Pott!'

'Him?' they heard Mr Platter say. 'He's deaf as a post. And his light's out. Been asleep this good couple of hours, I shouldn't wonder . . .' And again they heard the sound of baling.

'Could they sink?' whispered Arrietty hopefully.

' 'Fraid not,' said Pod.

Once more Mabel's voice came to them across the water: 'Have I got to keep this up all night?'

'Depends,' said Mr Platter. Then there were some murmurings and slight creaks and scufflings. They made out a few words like 'Can't seem to get my hand on the painter . . . mixed up with the umbrellas . . .' Then Mrs Platter complaining about 'too much stuff . . .'

'Too much stuff!' they heard Mr Platter repeat indignantly. 'You'll thank your stars for some of it before the night's out. I warned you what we were in for, didn't I, Mabel?' There was no reply, and they heard the hard voice rasp on. 'A vigil! That's what we're in for – a vigil! Tonight, tomorrow night and, if need be, many a night to come . . .'

'Oh, Sid –' (The borrowers, listening intently, caught the note of dismay.)

'We'll get them back, Mabel, if we die for it.

Or –' here Mr Platter's tone became less certain, '– somebody else does . . .'

'Somebody else . . .? Oh no, Sidney. I mean, vigils and felonies – those I can get used to. But what you're suggesting now . . . well, that wouldn't be very nice, not murder, dear. Might involve the police –' As he did not reply at once, she added lamely, 'If you see what I mean . . .'

'It may not be necessary,' said Mr Platter loftily.

There were more creakings, faint scrapes of wood on wood, an occasional watery plop . . . 'Careful, Sidney, you nearly had me out!' and other small, half frightened exclamations.

'They're tying up,' whispered Pod. 'Now's our moment!' He was speaking to Spiller who, silent as a shadow, had joined them in the stern, punt pole in hand. 'Get hold of the rushes – you, too, Homily. Come on, Arrietty . . . that's right, that's right. Pull – gently now, gently . . .'

Slowly, slowly, they slid out – stern foremost – into more open water but, suddenly, it became dark, as dark as it had been among the rushes. 'I can't see,' whimpered Homily, 'I can't see nothing, Pod.' She stood up, cold hands dripping water. She sounded very frightened.

'No more can they,' Pod whispered back – very confident, he sounded. 'Stay where you are, Homily. Now, Spiller –'

As the boat shot forward, Arrietty looked up. The stars were bright but a cloud had come over the moon. Turning, she looked back but could see very little: all was dimness down by the fence. She felt the boat turn, sharply, against the stream.

59

Oh, blessed cloud! Oh, blessed Spiller! Oh, blessed, silent knitting needle, driving them swiftly forward in Spiller's nimble hands! Upstream, stern foremost – it didn't matter: they were getting away!

Gauzily, magically, the last traces of cloud drifted away across the moon and the gentle radiance shone down again. She could see her parents' faces and looking back she could see the wire fence, silver in the moonlight, and the moving shadows beside it. If I can see them, she thought, they could see us. Her father, too, she noticed, was staring at the fence. 'Oh, Papa,' she faltered, 'suppose they see us?'

Pod did not reply for a moment, his eyes on the moving figures. 'They won't look,' he said at last. Smiling, he laid a hand on her shoulder and all fear suddenly left her. After a moment, he went on – in the same low, confident voice, 'The stream curves about here, and then we'll be out of sight . . .'

And so it was. In a few minutes Arrietty, looking back, saw only the peaceful water: the fence had disappeared from view. They all relaxed, except for Spiller steadily poling ahead.

'There's a butter-knife somewhere,' said Pod. 'I left it handy . . .' He turned, as though to climb back over the gaiter and then he hesitated: 'You and your mother better go to bed. You'll need all the sleep you can get. It'll be a busy day tomorrow . . .'

'Oh, Papa, not yet –' pleaded Arrietty.

'Do as I say, girl. And you, too, Homily. You look all out –'

'What on earth do you want with the butter-knife, Pod?' Her voice did sound very tired.

'What it was meant for,' said Pod, 'a rudder. Now, creep along under, the two of you, and get tucked in.' He turned away. They watched him as he made his careful way over the gaiter. 'A born climber,' breathed Homily proudly. 'Come along, Arrietty, we'd better do as he says. It's getting chilly and there's nothing we can do to help . . .'

Still Arrietty hesitated. To her, it seemed the fun was just beginning. There would be things to see on the banks – new things – and the joy of the great out-of-doors. Ah, there was a bat! And another one. There must be midges about. No, not midges so early in the year. And it was chilly. But spring was just round the corner. Lovely spring! And a new life . . . But it *was* chilly. Homily had disappeared from view.

Reluctantly, Arrietty felt her way under the gaiter. Very stealthily, she extracted the small pillow and drew it to the end of their bed. At least, she would sleep with her head out of doors!

Creeping between Miss Menzies' home-made bedclothes, she soon began to feel warmer. Lying flat on her back, she could only see the sky. And there was the moon again, sometimes obscured by a sudden tangle of overhanging branches, sometimes by filmy cloud. Now and again, there were strange night noises. Once, she heard a fox bark.

To what kind of new life were they going, she wondered? How long would it take them to reach this unknown house? A large human house, this much she knew. Larger than Firbank – this she had gathered from Pod – and Firbank had been large enough. There was a lawn, it seemed, which sloped down towards a pond – a pond with its own spring which fed this very stream up which they were so silently travelling. Oh, how she loved ponds! She remembered the one at the bottom of the field, that time they had been living in the boot. What fun she had had with that pond. Fishing for minnows, paddling about in Spiller's old tin soap-dish, learning to swim . . . How long ago it all seemed now! She thought of Mild Eye and his caravan; the succulent smell of his pheasant stew as she and her parents, terrified and hungry, crouched under the dubious shelter of Mild Eye's tousled bunk; and of that fierce-faced woman, who was Mild Eye's wife. Where were they now? Not too near, she hoped.

She thought again Firbank, and of her childhood under the floor; the darkness, the dusty passages between the joists. And, yet, how clean and bright Homily had kept the tiny rooms in which they actually lived! What work it must have been! She should have helped more, she realized uncomfortably . . .

And then that glorious day when Pod had taken her 'upstairs' and her first delirious glimpse of the Great Outdoors and her meeting with The Boy (her first real sight of a living human bean!) and what trouble it had caused . . .

But – how much she had gleaned from reading aloud to him; how strange were some of the books he had brought down into the garden from the great house above. How much she had learned about the mysterious world in which they all existed – herself, The Boy, the old woman upstairs – strange animals, strange customs, peculiar ways of thought. Perhaps the strangest of all creatures were the human beings themselves ('beings' not 'beans', as her father and mother still called them). Was she a 'being'? She must be. But not a human one, thank goodness! No, she would not like to be one of those: no borrower ever robbed another borrower; possessions did slide about between them – that was true – small things left behind or discarded by previous owners (or things just 'found'): what one borrower did not make use of, another one could. That made sense: nothing should be wasted. But no borrower would deliberately 'take' from another borrower: that, in their small precarious world, would be unthinkable!

This was what she had tried to explain to The Boy. She would always remember his scornful voice when he had cried out in sudden irritation: ' "Borrowing" you call it! I call it "stealing"!'

At the time, this had made her laugh. She had laughed and laughed at his ignorance. How silly he was (this great clumsy creature) not to know that human beans were made for borrowers, as bread for butter, cows for milking, hens for eggs: you might say (thinking of cows) that borrowers *grazed* on human beans. What else (she had asked him) were human beans *for*? And he had not quite known, now she came to think of it . . .

'For us, of course,' Arrietty told him firmly. And he had begun to see her point.

All the same, as she lay there – gazing up at the moon – she found all this very puzzling. Looking back, she saw how long it had taken her to realize how many millions of human beings there were in the world, and how few borrowers. Until those long days of reading aloud to The Boy, she had thought it the other way round. How could she think otherwise, brought up, as she had been, under the floor at Firbank – seeing so little and hearing less? Until she met The Boy, she had never laid eyes on a human bean. Of course, she had known they existed, or how else could borrowers exist? And she had known they were dangerous – the most dangerous animals on earth – but she thought they must be rare . . .

Now she began to know better.

Somewhere, far in the distance, she seemed to hear the sound of a church clock. Drowsily, she counted the notes: they seemed to add up to seven.

CHAPTER SEVEN

Looking back to that morning of their first arrival, the thing that Arrietty remembered most clearly was the long, long walk: an impossible walk it had seemed at times.

They had all slept well, even Pod and Spiller had slipped in an hour or two of rest: the journey, it seemed, had taken less time than any of them had expected. She had not woken, nor had Homily, when Spiller eventually ran them aground on what turned out to be a small pebbly beach under a cliff-like overhang of roots and mud. This was where the vast rectory lawn joined the curve of the out-flowing stream. She had not seen the lawn at first, only the dim tangled branches of a juniper bush which cut out all view of the sky and shed its darkness over this hidden anchorage. Could this be *it*? Had they really arrived? Or was this cavernous place just a resting place on what might turn out to be a much longer journey?

No, this *was* it! They had arrived: she heard the church clock, much nearer now, striking the hour of nine. She could see Pod and Spiller splashing about in the shallows among the pebbles and, between them, was Spiller's soap-box lid, bobbing emptily as Pod made it fast to a root. He turned and saw her as she stood, shivering slightly, wrapped in her eiderdown quilt. Homily, looking dazed and dishevelled, was emerging from under the gaiter. 'So you've stirred yourselves, at last!' said Pod cheerfully. 'Well, here we are! What do you think of it?'

Arrietty did not quite know what she thought of it: except, perhaps, that it was secret, dark, and felt, somehow, safe. Homily, now standing uncertainly beside her, also wrapped in a quilt, nodded her head towards the soap-dish. 'Where are we supposed to be going in that?' she asked suspiciously. Spiller, Arrietty noticed, had begun climbing up the bluff: the tangled roots gave a wide choice of handholds.

'We're not going anywhere in that,' Pod told her. 'We're going to pack it up with a few things for the night. Where we're going, we're going on our own two feet . . .'

'Where *are* we going?' asked Homily.

'Up to the house,' said Pod. 'You'll see in a minute . . . And we'd better get going – while there's no one about: Spiller says they're out for the day . . .'

'Who are?'

'Witless and Mrs Witless, of course: he does jobbing gardening, and she's gone to town on the bus. Now then, Homily,' he went on, coming up just below them, 'pass me down them eiderdowns and any other bedclothes. And, Arrietty, you'll find a bit of twine up for'ard . . .'

Reluctantly, they divested themselves of their warm coverings and Arrietty went for'ard to find the twine.

'What about some cooking pots?' asked Homily as, half-heartedly, she began to fold up the quilts.

'There won't be no cooking tonight,' said Pod briskly.

'We got to eat –'

'Spiller's seen to all that. Now come on –'

Arrietty came back with the twine and they began to work more quickly, passing the folded bedclothes

67

down to Pod who splashed back and forth loading up the soap-dish. 'Stream's risen a bit,' he remarked, 'it rained in the night . . .'

'Not here,' said Homily, laying a hand on the gaiter. 'This Thing's as dry as a bone . . .'

'Stands to reason,' he glanced up at the thick leafage above them, 'we're good and sheltered here. Better take your boots and stockings off, and I'll help you over the side –'

As Arrietty, still shivering a little, sat down to undo her boots, she thought of the Platters and almost pitied them, crouched by the fence all night in their leaky small boat under their dripping umbrellas. Spiller, she noticed, had disappeared over the bluff.

'Did you get any sleep, Pod?' asked Homily, one leg over the edge of the boat. 'You and Spiller?'

'Enough,' said Pod, reaching up as she leaned forward and catching her under the arms, 'we got in well before midnight – didn't you hear the clock? That's the way . . . let yourself go. That's right!'

'Oh,' squealed Homily, as she splashed down on to the pebbles, 'this water's cold!'

'Well, what do you expect at this time of year?'

Arrietty had slid down by herself, boots and socks in her hand; she was longing for a climb up the roots. Homily seemed less enthusiastic.

'Now up you go, you two!' said Pod (he was untying the soap-dish). 'There's nothing to it, Homily: you can do it easy . . . No need to fuss –'

'I haven't said a word,' remarked Homily coldly. She eyed the small cliff with distaste. 'Will you take my boots, Pod?' she asked after a moment.

'Yes, give them here,' said Pod. He took them

rather roughly, and pushed them under the lashing which secured the bedclothes in the soap-box. 'Now, up you go!'

Arrietty, already climbing, held out a welcoming hand. 'It's lovely! It's easy! Come on . . . I'll help you –'

Stolidly, Homily began to climb. If it is possible to climb up a mass of overhanging, tangled roots with dignity, Homily managed it that morning – steadily, calmly, and with no hesitation. Pod, following her up – one end of the mooring string in his hand – smiled to himself with an amused, grim kind of pride. There was no one like her – not once she had set her mind to a thing!

Reaching the top, Arrietty looked round for Spiller but she could not see him. This was nothing new: he could melt into any background provided (this she remembered) that background was out of doors. Instead, she gazed at a vast expanse of lawn, not mown to a velvet smoothness (as once it must have been) but roughly cut with a scythe. She knew about scythes: her father's was made from a razor-blade; and she knew about mowing-machines: there had been one at Firbank. But what caught her sharp attention and made her heart beat faster was the sight she saw in the distance – a long, low, gabled house, whose roofs caught the morning sunshine but whose front seemed vague and windowless. It must (as her father had told them) be covered with creeper – creeper gone wild. The Old Rectory – oh, what climbings there would be, what hidings, what freedom! And then she noticed that between the place on which she stood and the distant-seeming house, there was a pond – a rush-bound pond with an island in the middle. She could see the flat, round leaves of still unopened water lilies . . .

Then she was aware of some sort of commotion behind her: Spiller, Pod and Homily on the edge of the bank seemed locked in some sort of struggle. Panting and heaving, they were pulling on the mooring string of the soap-dish. She ran to help them, and Spiller slipped over the edge to disentangle some part which had been caught up among the roots. He managed to get it free and, guiding it with one hand, followed its progress upwards as the others pulled and steered it from above. At last it was beside them and they could all sit down. Pod rubbed his face on his sleeve and Homily flapped at hers with her apron; Spiller lay flat on his back. Anybody who had felt chilly down below, now felt chilly no longer.

Arrietty sat up on her elbow and looked at Spiller as he lay spread-eagled on the ground. Odd that she had never thought of Spiller as one who could be tired. Or even as one who slept. And yet somehow, during the night, he and Pod (on that packed, uncomfortable boat) had found a place in which to close their eyes – while she and her mother had lain so cosily tucked up in Miss Menzies' bedclothes. How kind Spiller had always been to them! And yet, in a way, so distant: one could never talk to Spiller except about the barest essentials. Oh well, she supposed one could not have everything . . .

She rose to her feet to have another look at the distant house. After a moment, the others got up too. They all stared, each with a different thought.

'The tower of that church,' said Homily wonderingly, 'is the spitting image of the one down in the model village –'

'Or vice versa,' said Pod, laughing. Arrietty was pleased to hear her father laugh: it seemed like a good omen. Homily tossed her head: Pod sometimes used words she failed to understand, and this always seemed to annoy her. 'Well, I'm going to put my boots on,' she announced, and sat down among the dry leaves under the juniper bush. 'And you'd better do the same, Arrietty. That grass will be wet after the rain . . .' But Arrietty, always admiring of Spiller's horny feet, preferred to go barefoot.

And then began the long, long walk.

CHAPTER EIGHT

They had to keep close to the pond (more like a lake it seemed to them) where the sedges and water plants provided cover. On the end of its towing-line, the soap-dish slid easily over the wet grass. Spiller went first, then Pod, Arrietty next, and Homily bringing up the rear; the cord passing from shoulder to shoulder. At first they barely felt the pull of it.

A more direct route would have been straight across the lawn but, in spite of Pod's assurances that the great house would be empty, they could never quite lose the inborn fear of prying, human eyes.

The tiredness came on slowly at first. Some of the grasses were coarse and tiresome, and sometimes they came across some of last year's thistles, beaten down by weather, but prickly just the same. The little new ones, pushing up among the grass stems, were soft and silvery, and furry to the touch. All the same, Arrietty began to miss her boots. But as Spiller showed no sign of stopping, pride kept her silent.

On and on they plodded. Sometimes a shrew mouse would dart away at their approach, woken at last from its long winter sleep. Frogs were there in plenty, plopping here and there, and there were aconites among the grasses. Yes, spring was here . . .

At last, (after hours it seemed) Pod called, 'We'll take a break, Spiller.'

And they all sat down, back to back, on the tightly packed soap-box.

'That's better,' Homily breathed, stretching out

her aching feet. Arrietty put on her shoes and the rough warm stockings Homily had knitted so skilfully on a pair of blunted darning needles.

'How did Spiller know, Pod,' Homily asked after a while, 'that there'd be no one in the house?'

'I told you, didn't I? That black thing in the hall –'

'What black thing?' Homily did not like the sound of this.

'It's a black thing they have in the hall. They turn a handle and tell it things. They grind the handle round and round, like, and tell it where they're going and this and that . . .'

'And who hears them?'

'Well, Spiller does, for one – say he's about. Spiller knows that house backwards. You'll see . . .'

Homily was silent for some moments. She could not visualize 'that black thing in the hall'. How black? How big? Which hall?

'That black thing – do they tell it the truth?' she asked at last.

Spiller gave his small grunt of a laugh. 'Sometimes,' he said.

Homily was silent again: she was not reassured.

Pod rose to his feet. 'Well, if you're rested, we'd better get going again.'

'Just a minute, Pod,' pleaded Homily. 'My legs ache something dreadful.'

'So do mine, if it comes to that,' said Pod. 'And Arrietty's, too, I shouldn't wonder. And you know for why? We're out of condition – that's for why. Nigh on six months cooped up in an attic – it stands to reason. Exercise, that's what we need . . .'

'Well, we're getting it now,' said Homily wearily as she rose to her feet.

And on they plodded.

There was one place where they had to leave the pond and cross the open grass. Here, they broke the procession, leaving Spiller to tow the soap-dish, as they made for the shelter of a small shrubbery. This was a group of overgrown azalea bushes, whose tender twigs were glinting into bud. It seemed like a forest to them. Here they rested again. The crumbly ground was covered with last year's dead leaves, and the branches above them hung with tattered spiders' webs.

'I wish we could spend the night here,' said Homily, 'camping, like . . .'

'No, girl,' said Pod. 'Once we get the soap-dish through this lot, we'll be right up by the house. You'll see . . .'

It was a struggle to get the soap-dish through the low-hanging, rootlike branches; but at last it was done and they found themselves in the open again, at the foot of a grassy bank. To their left, they could see a flight of mossy steps. Only the lower treads were visible, spreading fanlike into what had once been lawn.

'We're not going up *them*, Pod,' complained Homily, 'are we?' They were shallow steps, but not that shallow; and Pod was walking towards them.

'No, you and Arrietty stay where you are,' he called back quietly. 'Spiller and I'll go up by the coping and pull the soap-dish up from above.' He turned round again. 'Or you *could* start climbing the bank . . .'

'Could we!' exclaimed Homily, and sat down

firmly, wet grass or no wet grass. After a moment, Arrietty sat down beside her: she too could do with the rest. 'They won't take long,' she told her mother.

Homily laid her weary head on her clasped knees. 'I don't care if they take forever,' she said.

They did not take forever. It seemed quite a short time before they heard the soft call from above. Arrietty rose slowly to her feet. 'Are you there, Arrietty?'

Arrietty said, 'Yes . . .'

'Pick up the string and start climbing.'

'Is it long enough?'

'What do you say?'

'I said, "Is it long enough?" '

'Plenty. We'll come down to meet you –'

Homily raised her head from her knees and watched as Arrietty, the tow-line in one hand, picked her way up the bank, occasionally pulling on the grasses. Then the grasses hid her from view. But Homily could hear the sound of subdued voices:

'Give it here, girl . . . that's right . . . that's splendid . . . where's your mother?'

Slowly and stiffly, Homily rose to her feet. She
stared at the bank: the climb had not looked too
bad and, unlike Arrietty, she would have both hands
free. But she did not intend to hurry . . . did them
no harm to rest. She could still hear the mumble of
their voices.

At last, she pushed through the last of the grasses
and found herself standing on weedy gravel; and
there was the great house towering above her.

'Good girl!' said Pod, taking her hand. He turned
and looked up at the house. 'Well, here it is – we're
home!'

'Home?' echoed Homily wanly, looking across
the uneven gravel to the iron-studded front door.
Ivy everywhere and other kinds of creepers. Some
of the latticed windows were almost hidden.

'You'll see,' said Pod. 'Wait till I take you inside.'

'How do we get in?' asked Homily.

'Come on. I'll show you –' He turned to the right,
away from the direction of the front door. The soap-
dish, dragged by Spiller, made a scraping noise on
the stones. Homily glanced fearfully at the dark
latticed windows: might there be other eyes looking
out from within? But all seemed peaceful: the house
had an empty feeling. Perhaps that 'black thing' in
the hall had been told the truth for once . . .

The sunlight fell slantingly on the front of the
house but when they turned the corner they suddenly felt its rich warmth: this side of the house
must face full south. And the windows here were
different, as though added at a later date – tall, great
windows with low sills and squared panes, dimmed

a little by time and weather. Homily's home-making instincts rose to the surface: if somebody cleaned them, she told herself, those panes would look 'lovely'.

They passed by three of these long windows, the soap-dish scraping behind them, until the wall of the house ended in a built-out erection of glass. Homily peered in through the dingy panes, some of which were cracked. 'It's the conservatory,' Pod told her, 'where they used to grow the flowers in winter. Come on –' Spiller led them on to the corner, where they turned again at right angles: glass panes again, peeling white paint, and a shabby glass door, cracked and rotten at the base where the wood met the weedy gravel. Here they halted.

'This is where we get in,' Pod told them, 'and you don't want to disturb them weeds: they hide the entrance, like . . .'

Very carefully, he parted a clump of ragwort and dead-looking grass stems. 'Careful of the nettles,' he said. 'Spiller keeps them down – much as he can – but they spring up again fast as he cuts them . . .'

'I thought you said this Witless was a gardener,' remarked Homily as, gingerly, she followed Pod through the gap.

'He only keeps up the kitchen garden. The main garden's gone too far. And he keeps up the church-yard as well.'

Arrietty, preparing to follow, glanced about her. What she had taken to be trees, she saw were box hedges run up to a great tangled height. Cover! Cover everywhere. What a place, she thought, what a wonderful place!

Stooping a little, she followed Pod and Homily

through a jagged hole under the door. When she touched the wet wood to steady herself, a piece came away in her hand. 'Careful,' said Pod, 'we don't want this hole any bigger.'

Inside, the place felt gloriously warm, with the sun pouring down through the sloping glass roof. It smelt of dead geranium leaves and a cindery smell like coal dust. Old cracked plant-pots stood about, some in piles. There were several bits of sacking. There were one or two rusty stands which must have held plants. The floor was tiled in a pattern of dull reds and browns but many of the tiles were broken.

Pod had gone back through the hole to help Spiller with the soap-dish and Homily, standing still just inside the door, gazed about her in a kind of dazed bewilderment. Every few seconds, they heard a soft plop. It came from a tap in the corner. Below the tap, set in the tiles, Arrietty saw there was a grating. By the sound of the plop, Arrietty guessed that there was water below the grating. In the opposite corner stood a curious brick stove whose pipe went up through the roof. It had a door like an oven door, which stood half open, stuck fast on its rusty hinges.

'What a place!' said Homily.

'I think it's lovely,' said Arrietty. 'Water and everything. You could cook on that stove . . .'

'No, you couldn't,' said Homily, looking at it with distaste, 'someone 'ud see the smoke.' And she sat down suddenly on a piece of prised-up tile. 'Oh, my legs . . .' she said.

On the farther wall, opposite the shabby door under which they had entered, there were double glass doors built in the style of french windows. These, Arrietty realized, must once (perhaps before the conservatory had been added) have led straight into the garden, like those drawing-room doors she remembered at Firbank. They stood slightly ajar. One door, Arrietty noticed, was handleless. She tiptoed towards it and pushed it gently. With a faint creak of rusted hinges, it slid open a few more inches. Arrietty peered inside.

She saw a long room (vast, it seemed to her) panelled with bookshelves in faded oak and there, too, on her left, she saw the three long windows, through which the great squares of sunlight streamed across the floor. Opposite the middle window, in the right-hand wall, she made out a fireplace, rather a small one: to Arrietty's eyes it looked more modern than the rest of the room. Each of the three windows had deep window seats of oak, faded now by years of glass-warmed sunlight.

So entranced she was, that she did not hear Pod come up beside her, and started slightly when she felt his hand on her shoulder. 'Yes,' said Pod, 'this was the library.' Arrietty looked up at the bookshelves: there indeed were a few old dilapidated books, some untidy piles of tattered magazines, and one or two other objects of the kind no longer needed or cared for by a previous owner: old tin boxes, a broken riding whip, a cracked flower-vase or two, a noseless bust of some Roman emperor, a dusty pile of dried-up pampas grass.

'Doesn't look to me as though anybody ever comes in here,' said Homily, who had crept up behind them.

81

'That's just the idea,' said Pod. 'It's perfect. Perfect!' he repeated happily.

Arrietty thought so too, but turned back reluctantly to help Spiller with the unlashing of the soapbox. Pod and Homily turned back as well and Homily, still looking exhausted, sank down limply on her piece of prised-up tiling. 'Perfect, it may be,' she said, 'but where are we going to sleep tonight?'

'In the stove,' said Pod.

'What – among all that ash!'

'There's not much ash on the bars,' said Pod, 'it's all underneath.'

'Well,' said Homily, 'I never thought I'd be asked to sleep in a stove . . .'

'You slept *under* one at Firbank.'

'Oh, Firbank –' moaned Homily, '– why did we ever have to leave . . .'

'You know quite well why we had to leave,' said Pod. 'Now, Arrietty,' he went on, 'get a bit of something – a strip of old sacking will do – and clean a bit of dust off them bars.' He moved towards the door. 'And I'll get a few green leaves –'

'Where's Spiller?' asked Homily, looking about her. He had been there a moment before.

'Slipped round to the larder to get a bite to eat, I shouldn't wonder.'

There was a sudden whirring sound and they all looked up as (very close it seemed now) the church clock began to strike. Pod raised his hand: he seemed to be counting. Homily and Arrietty watched Pod's trance-like expression: they seemed to be counting, too. 'Eleven,' said Homily as the last chime died away.

'Twelve,' said Pod. 'What did you get, Arrietty?'

'I got twelve, too.'

'That's right. Your mother missed a stroke. Well,' he went on, with an odd little smile, 'now we know: takes a good three hours to cross that lawn on foot . . .'

'Seemed more like three years to me,' said Homily. 'Hope we don't have to do it often.'

'There are ways and means,' said Pod darkly, as he made his way towards the entrance hole.

'Ways and means!' repeated Homily, as he disappeared from view. 'What can he mean? Ways and means . . . he'll be teaching us to fly next!'

Arrietty wondered, too, as she tore off a piece of loose sacking. Soon Pod was back with a bundle of leaves – box, they were, dark green and springy – soon the soap-dish was empty and the beds made up.

'Could be worse,' said Homily, dusting her hands together. It had really looked quite cosy: the blankets and quilts spread out on the springy leaves. 'Wish we could close the door . . .'

'Well, you couldn't call it open,' said Pod. 'Just room to get in and out –'

'I think I'll get in,' said Homily, moving back to the stove.

'No,' said Pod.

'What do you mean "no"?'

'Well, don't you want to see round the house?'

Homily hesitated. 'Well, after I've had a bit of a lie-down. We've been going all morning, Pod.'

'I know that. We're all a bit weary, like. But –' he went on, '– we may never get another chance like this. I mean, they're all out, aren't they? The human beans? And won't be back for hours . . .'

Still Homily hesitated. A bell shrilled. They all turned, like figures moved by clockwork, and stared at the double doors. The bell became silent.

'Whatever was it?' breathed Homily, moving backwards towards the stove, nervous hands feeling for the door.

'Wait!' said Pod sharply.

They waited, still as statues, and the bell shrilled out again. Three times it rang, and still they did not move.

'Well, that's all right,' said Pod, after a moment. 'Proves what I say.' He was smiling.

'How do you mean?'

'That black thing in the hall: when the bell goes, the human beans always come running –'

And then Arrietty remembered. Something The Boy had told her . . . What was it called now? A telegraph? No that was something else. What had he called it? The word seemed on the tip of her tongue. Ah, yes . . .

'I think it's a telephone –' she said uncertainly. She spoke rather shyly: sometimes it embarrassed her to know more about the great human world than either of her parents. 'Miss Menzies had one,' she added as though to excuse her startling knowledge.

It took a lot of explaining – wires, poles, speaking from house to house . . .

'Whatever will they think of next!' exclaimed Homily at last.

Pod remained silent for a moment, and then he said, 'Difficult to get the hang of it. At least, the way you explain it, Arrietty. But there's one thing I'm certain of –'

'What's that?' asked Homily sharply.

'That thing out in the hall – we're going to thank our stars for it!'

'How do you mean, Pod?'

'For what it tells us,' said Pod.

Homily looked bewildered. 'I never heard it say a word –'

'That the house is empty. That's what it told us, plain as plain. You mark my words, Homily, that black thing in the hall is going to be a . . .' (in his happy excitement, he seemed at a loss for the word) . . . 'a . . .'

'Godsend?' ventured Arrietty.

'Safeguard,' said Pod.

But, in the end, they did not explore the house that day. Homily seemed uneasy at the thought of being left on her own, and Spiller arrived with a tempting feast of titbits garnered from the larder. So they all sat down on bits of broken tile and ate a delicious luncheon. There were goodies they had not seen or tasted for what seemed like years: smoked ham, pink and tender; anchovy butter; small scraps of flaky pastry; grapes – to be carefully peeled; something wrapped in a lettuce leaf which Homily hailed as pigeon pie; a whole slice of home-made bread and a small, uneven chunk of rich plum cake.

After this meal, as sometimes happens, they all began to feel sleepy. Even Pod seemed aware of a sudden tiredness. Homily gathered up the leftovers and wondered where to put them (leftovers – they had forgotten there could be such things!). 'I'll get you a dock leaf,' said Pod, moving towards the door. But he moved rather slowly and Spiller forestalled him and was soon back with a selection of rather rusty-looking leaves. But Spiller, Arrietty noticed, had not eaten anything: he had never been one for eating in company.

But where to put the food where no stray eye might discover it? Even the broken tiles, Pod had explained, must be put back exactly as they had found them: there must be nothing to arouse attention or suspicion.

'We could put it outside among those weeds,' suggested Homily.

'No,' said Pod, 'it 'ud only attract the rats. And that we don't want . . .'

At length, Homily decided to take the leftovers to bed with her. 'They'll make a nice breakfast,' she told them, as she climbed up into the nest of eiderdown quilts.

Arrietty helped her father replace the bits of tiling (Spiller, in his sudden way, had silently disappeared). After this, there seemed nothing more to do so, feeling tired, she decided to join her mother in their comfortable, make-shift bed. Before she fell asleep, she heard the church clock strike four. Only four o'clock! But all the same, it had seemed a long, long day . . .

CHAPTER NINE

Arrietty was the first to wake in the morning. It was almost too warm under such a mound of quilts as all three had gone to bed fully dressed. She had awakened once in the night, disturbed by a strange noise – a banging, a tapping, a shuddering sort of noise followed by a silence and then by a series of gurgles. Pod and Homily awakened too. No one had spoken. 'What is it?' asked Arrietty after a moment. Pod had given a short grunt and had turned back on his side. 'It's the pipes,' he had muttered, 'the hot water pipes. Keep quiet, now, there's a good girl: we were up a bit late, me and Spiller . . .' and he pulled the bedclothes over his ears.

'Oh yes,' Arrietty remembered those radiators . . . 'A bit old-fashioned,' Pod had told them, but she supposed any caretaker must keep the house aired: that was what caretakers were for.

Carefully, she crept out through the narrow gap by the barely opened stove door, the hinges of which had become so rusted that it was quite immovable. It had been a clever place, she realized, in which to take shelter. She let herself down on to the shallow cluttered tiles, still strewn with the ashes she had brushed from the bars above, and took cover between the bricks on which the old stove had been built. She stared out cautiously, much as she and Pod had stared out from under the clock at Firbank.

All looked just as it had done the day before: the piled plant-pots, the cracked panes of glass, the garden beyond. The tap dripped rhythmically at its long intervals. No, this was different: a slightly thinner sound, more a plink than a plonk. Arrietty leaned forward, still careful to keep under cover. There seemed to be something blue on the grating under the tap. She narrowed her eyes, straining to see better. Something very blue. Some kind of utensil, something in which when the drop fell it went plink instead of plonk.

Filled with curiosity, she took a careful step forward. And then she saw what it was – they had had one in their storeroom at Firbank – it was a glass eye-bath. Homily had never used the one they had at Firbank because of its weight and its awkward shape: she hadn't patience with it. Well, here must be somebody who did have patience with it and somebody (Arrietty realized with beating heart) must be another borrower.

For one moment, she was tempted to turn back and waken her parents. Then she decided against it. No, she would stay here and watch and wait. After a while the eye-bath would be filled to the brim and, sooner or later, whoever had put it there would come back and fetch it. Arrietty sat down and, leaning against the brick support, she drew up her legs and clasped them in her arms. Chin on knees, she could watch in comfort.

Her thoughts began to stray a little. She thought of Spiller. Of his kindness and his wildness, of his reserve and independence. Of his deadly bow and arrow. He only shot for the pot. She herself would like to learn to use a bow but never, never, she realized, could she bring herself to kill anything living: in her case, it would be just for 'self-defence' as, when in danger, Pod might use his hat-pin. And yet, and yet – she remembered uncomfortably – how often, hungrily and gratefully, they had devoured the game which Spiller had procured for them. No questions asked – at least, none that she had been aware of – just a savoury dish on their table. Would Spiller come and live in this house with them, she wondered? Helping them to borrow and taking Pod's place perhaps when Pod got older? Would she herself ever learn to borrow? Not a cautious bit here or there, but fearlessly and well, learning the rules, knowing the tools . . . The answer, she felt, to the first question was 'no': Spiller, that outdoor creature, would never live in a house, never throw his lot in with theirs. But he would help them – always help them, of that she was sure. The answer to that second question was 'yes': she knew in her bones that she would learn to borrow, and learn to borrow well. Times had changed: there would be new methods, new techniques. And, as part of the rising generation, some of these she might even invent!

Suddenly there was a sound. It was quite a small sound and seemed to come from the library next door. Arrietty stood up and, keeping her body covered by the brick support, peeked her head forward.

All was quiet. She watched and waited. From where she stood, she could see the tap and, to the left of this, the place where the tiles ended and the library floorboards began. She could see a little way into the library, part of the fireplace and the light from the long windows but not the windows them-selves. As she stood there under the stove, still as the crumbled bricks which supported it, she could feel the quickening pulse of her own heartbeats.

The next sound was very slight. She had to strain her ears to hear it. It was a faint continuous squeak. As though, she thought, someone was working a machine, or turning some miniature handle. It grew – not louder exactly, but nearer. And then, with a catch of the breath, she saw the tiny figure.

It was a borrower – no doubt of that – a borrower with a limp, dragging some contraption behind him. Whatever the contraption was, it moved easily – almost magically – not like Spiller's soap-box which was rather apt to bump. In this case, it was the borrower who bumped. One of his shoulders went right down with each step taken: he was very lame. And fairly young, Arrietty noticed, as he came on towards the tap. He had a soft mop of tow-coloured hair and a pale, pale face. The thing he dragged was on wheels. What a wonderful idea, Arrietty thought: why had not her own family ever owned such a thing? There had been plenty of old toys, she had been told, pushed away in the playroom cupboard at Firbank and some of them must have had wheels. It was these four wheels, she realized, which produced the fairylike squeaking.

When the young borrower reached the drain, he turned his truck so the rear end faced the eye-bath. Then, stooping down, he took a drink of water. Arrietty drew back a little when, wiping his mouth on his sleeve, he moved towards the glass door which led to the garden. He stood there for some moments, his back to Arrietty, gazing out through the panes. 'He's watching the birds,' she thought, 'or seeing what sort of day it is . . .' And it was a lovely day. Arrietty could see that for herself. No wind, pale sunlight, and the birds were starting to build. After a while he turned and limped his way back to the eye-bath. Stooping, he tried to lift it. But it seemed very heavy and was slippery with water. No wonder Homily had had no patience with such an object: there was nothing you could get a grip on.

He tried again. Suddenly, she longed to help him; but how to announce herself without giving him a fright? She coughed, and he turned quickly, then remained frozen.

Their eyes met. Arrietty kept quite still. His heart, she realized, must be beating just as hard as hers was. After a moment, she smiled. She tried to think of something to say. 'Hallo!' might sound too sudden. Perhaps she should say 'Good morning'? Yes, that was it. 'Good morning,' she said. Her voice, to her ears, sounded tremulous, even a little husky, so she added quickly on a brighter, clearer note. 'It's a lovely day!'

He was still staring at her, as though unable to believe his eyes. Arrietty returned his stare and kept quite still. She tried to hold on to her smile. 'Isn't it?' she added.

Suddenly, he gave a half laugh, and sat down on the edge of the drain. He ran his hand rather ruefully through the mop of his hair, and laughed again. 'You gave me a fright,' he said.

'I know,' said Arrietty, 'I'm sorry . . .'

'Who are you?'

'Arrietty Clock.'

'I haven't seen you before.'

'I – we only came last night.'

93

'We?'

'My mother and father. And me . . .'

'Are you going to stay here?'

'I don't know. It depends –'

'On what?'

'On whether it's safe. And nice. And – you know . . .'

'Oh, it's nice,' he said. 'Considering –'

'Considering what?'

'Considering other places. And it used to be safe . . .'

'Isn't it now?'

He gave her a small, half-rueful smile and shrugged his shoulders. 'How can one tell?'

'That's true,' said Arrietty. 'You never know –' She liked his voice, she realized: he spoke each word so clearly, in a clipped kind of way, but the general tone was gentle.

'What is your name?' she asked.

He laughed, and tossed his hair back out of his eyes. 'They call me Peagreen,' he said, still smiling – as though she might find it ridiculous.

'Oh,' said Arrietty.

'It's spelt P-E-R-E-G-R-I-N-E.'

Arrietty thought for a moment. 'Peregrine,' she said.

'That's it.' He stood up then, as though suddenly aware that all this time he had been sitting. 'I'm sorry . . .' he said.

'What for?'

'For flopping down like that.'

'You had a bit of a shock,' said Arrietty.

'A bit,' he admitted, and added, 'who taught you to spell?'

94

'I –' Arrietty hesitated: suddenly it seemed too long a story. 'I just learned,' she said. 'My father knew a little. Enough to start me off . . .'

'Can you write?'

'Yes, very nicely. Can you?'

'Yes.' He smiled. 'Very nicely.'

'Who taught you?'

'Oh, I don't know. All the Overmantels can read and write. The human children used to have lessons in that library,' he jerked his head towards the double doors. 'It goes back generations. You only had to listen, and the books were always left on the table . . .'

Arrietty moved forward suddenly from between the bricks, her face alight and interested. 'Are you one of the Overmantels?'

'I was until I fell off the chimneypiece.'

'How wonderful! I don't mean falling off the chimneypiece. I mean – that you're an Overmantel! I never thought I'd meet a real Overmantel. I thought they were something in the past –'

'Well, they are now, I suppose.'

'Peregrine Overmantel,' breathed Arrietty, 'what a lovely name . . . Peregrine Overmantel! We're just Clocks – Pod, Homily and Arrietty Clock. It doesn't sound very grand, does it?'

'It depends on the clock,' said Peagreen.

'It was a grandfather clock.'

'Old?'

'Yes, I suppose so.' She thought a moment. 'Yes, it was very old.'

'Well, then!' said Peagreen laughing.

'But we mostly lived under the kitchen.'

Peagreen laughed again. 'Ah-ha,' he said, and

there was mischief in his face. Arrietty looked
puzzled: had she made some sort of joke? Peagreen
seemed to think so.

'Where do you –' she began and then put her
hand to her mouth. She remembered suddenly that
it was not done to ask strange borrowers where they
lived: their homes, of necessity, must be hidden and
secret – unless, of course, they happened to be one's
relations.

But Peagreen did not seem to mind. 'I don't live
anywhere just at present,' he said lightly, answering
her half-asked question.

'But you must sleep somewhere –'

'I'm moving house. As a matter of fact, you could
say I've moved. But I haven't slept there yet.'

'I see,' said Arrietty. Somehow suddenly the day

seemed less bright and the future more uncertain. 'Are you going far?'

He looked at her speculatively. 'It depends what you call "far" . . .' He turned back to the eye-bath and laid his hands on the rim. 'It's a bit too full,' he said.

Arrietty was silent for a moment, then she said, 'Why don't you tip a bit out?'

'That's just what I was going to do.'

'I'll help you,' she said.

Together they tilted the eye-bath. It had a lip on either side. As the water gurgled down the drain, they set it back on its base. Then Peagreen moved to his cart to push it nearer. Arrietty came beside him. 'My father would like this truck,' she said, running a finger along the curved front: the rear was open like a lorry without a tailboard. 'What's it made of?'

'It's the bottom half of a date box. I have the top, too. But that hasn't got wheels. It was useful though, when they had carpets.'

'When who had carpets?'

'The human beings who lived here. The ones who took down the overmantel. That's when I fell off the chimneypiece.' He went back to the eye-bath. 'If you could take one lip, I'll take the other . . .'

Arrietty could and did, but her mind was reeling with what she had just heard: the overmantel gone, a whole lifestyle destroyed! When did it happen, and why? Where were Peagreen's parents now? And their friends and, perhaps, other children . . . She kept silent until they had set the eye-bath down on the lorry. Then she said casually, 'How old were you when you fell off the chimneypiece?'

'I was quite small, five or six. I broke my leg.'

'Did somebody come down and rescue you?'

'No,' he said, 'I don't think they noticed.'

'Didn't notice that a little child had fallen off the chimneypiece!'

'They were packing up, you see. There was a kind of panic. It was night, and they knew they had to get out before daylight. Perhaps they missed me afterwards . . .'

'You mean they went without you!'

'Well, I couldn't walk, you see.'

'But what did you do?'

'Some other borrowers took me in. Ground-floor borrowers. They were going too, but they kept me until my leg got better. And when they went, they left me the house, though, and some food and that. They left me quite a few things. I could manage.'

'But your poor leg!'

'Oh, I can climb all right. But I'm not too good at running, so I don't go out of doors much: things can happen out of doors, when you have to run. It was all right, and I had the books . . .'

'You mean the books in the library? But how did you get up to the shelves?'

'Oh, it's easy: all those shelves are adjustable. There are knotches cut out in the uprights, it's like climbing a rather steep staircase. You just prise out the book you want, and let it drop. But you can't put it back. My house got full of books.'

Arrietty was silent, thinking all this over. After a while she said, 'What were they like, those human beings – those ones who pulled down the overmantel?'

'Dreadful. Always pulling things down and putting things up. You never knew where you were from one day to another. It was a nightmare. They blocked up the old open fireplace and put a small grate there instead . . .'

'Yes, I saw it,' said Arrietty. Even she had thought it spoiled the look of the room, with its glazed tile surround painted with writhing tulips – very snake-like, those tulips.

'Art-nouveau,' Peagreen told her, but she did not know what that meant. 'They said the old one was draughty, and it was rather: if you stood inside you could look up and see the sky. And sometimes the rain came down. But not often. In the old days, they burned great logs in it – logs as big as trees, the grown-ups used to tell us . . .'

'What sort of other things did they do? I mean, those human beings –'

'Before they went, they put in the telephone. And the central heating. And the electric light. Very newfangled they were: everything had to be "modern".' He laughed, 'They even put a generator into the church.'

'What's a generator?'

'A thing that makes electric light. All the lights in the church can go on at one go. Not like lighting the gas jets one by one. But all the same . . .'

'All the same what?'

'They went, too. Said the place was creepy. In this house, you never know what you're going to get in the way of human beings. But there's just one thing you can be sure of –'

'What's that?' asked Arrietty.

'They may *come* – but they always *go!*'

'Why's that, I wonder?'

'It's because of the ghosts. For some silly reason, human beings can't abide them.'

Arrietty swallowed. She put out a hand as though to steady herself on the rim of the date box. 'Are there – are there many ghosts?' she faltered.

'Only three that I know of,' said Peagreen carelessly. 'And one of those you can't see: it's only footsteps. Footsteps never hurt anybody.'

'And the others?'

'Oh, you'll see for yourself in time.' He smiled at her and picked up the cord attached to his truck. 'Well, I'd better be getting along: those Whitlaces will be up by seven.'

Arrietty increased her grip on the edge of the truck, as though to detain him. 'Can you speak to ghosts?' she asked him hurriedly.

'Well, you could. But I doubt if they'd answer you.'

'I wish you weren't going,' said Arrietty, as she removed her hand from the truck. 'I'd like you to meet my father and mother: there's so much you could tell them!'

'Where are they now?'

'They're asleep in that stove. We were all very tired.'

'In the stove?' He sounded surprised.

'They've got bedclothes and everything.'

'Better let them sleep,' he said. 'I'll come back later.'

'When?'

'When the Whitlaces have gone out.' He thought for a moment. 'About two o'clock, say? She goes down to the church and He'll be up in the kitchen garden, by then . . .'

'That would be wonderful,' and she stood there watching as he pulled his truck towards the double doors and into the library beyond. The fairylike squeaking became fainter and fainter until she could hear it no longer.

CHAPTER TEN

'Arrietty!'

It was a hoarse whisper. Arrietty broke out of her dream and turned quickly towards the stove. Yes, of course, it was her mother: Homily stood peering out of the stove, her hair tousled and her face drawn and worried. Arrietty ran towards her. 'Oh, Mother, what is it?'

Homily leaned a little further forward, still speaking in the same tense whisper: 'You were talking to somebody!' Her frightened eyes flicked round the sunlit conservatory as though, thought Arrietty, some monster might appear.

'Yes, Mother, I know.'

'But, Arrietty, you promised –' Homily seemed to be trembling.

'Oh, Mother, it wasn't a human bean! I was talking to a *borrower*!'

'A borrower!' Homily was still trembling. 'What sort of a borrower?'

'An Overmantel, to be exact.'

'An Overmantel!' Homily's voice now became shrill with incredulity. 'But how – I don't see . . . An Overmantel!' Her eyes flicked about again. 'Besides,' she went on, her voice becoming firmer, 'I never heard, not in my whole life, of an Overmantel bothering to talk to the likes of us.'

Arrietty remembered only too well her mother's dislike of Overmantels. 'A stupid stuck-up lot!' she had called them, who only lived for pleasure and were careless of their children. Pod had pointed out that somehow they always managed to get their children educated. 'Only to show off!' Homily had retorted.

'This one was quite young. Only a boy, Mother—'

'Don't tell me any more,' said Homily, 'I'm going to get your father—' As she disappeared through the crack, Arrietty heard her mutter, 'What with Hendrearies down at the church . . . and now, of all things, an Overmantel!'

Arrietty, once again, leaned against the brickwork thoughtfully biting a thumbnail. What was going to happen now, she wondered? She could hear their voices: a good many exclamations from Homily, a few quiet words from Pod. He came out first, combing his tousled hair with the little silver eyebrow comb they had borrowed from the showcase at Firbank. 'What's this,' he said mildly, 'you've met another borrower?' He climbed down (a little awkwardly for him) on to the tiles.

'Yes,' said Arrietty.

'What's he like?'

'Quite young. Well, at first, I thought he was not much older than me. His name is Peagreen.'

Pod was silent. Thoughtfully, he pushed the comb back into his pocket as Homily appeared. She, too, Arrietty noticed, had tidied her hair. She came beside her husband and both stood quietly, looking at Arrietty.

'Your mother tells me he's an Overmantel,' Pod said, at last.

'Well, he *was*,' said Arrietty.

'Once an Overmantel, always an Overmantel. Well,' he went on, 'there's nothing wrong in that: they come in all kinds!'

'Not really –' began Homily excitedly. 'You remember those ones in the morning room at Firbank? They –'

Pod raised a quiet hand to silence her. 'Does he live alone?' he asked Arrietty.

'Yes, I think so. Yes, I'm sure he does. You see, it's like this . . .' And she told him, perhaps a little too eagerly, of Peagreen's accident, his early life, all the troubles and dangers and hungers and loneli-nesses she had imagined for him (not that he had ever mentioned these himself)' . . . it must have been too awful!' she finished breathlessly.

Homily had listened silently: she had not known quite what to think. To feel pity for an Overmantel: that would be a development for which she would need time.

'You don't know where he lives?' asked Pod.

'No,' said Arrietty, 'he's just moved house.'

'Oh, well,' said Pod, 'he's a grown man now: it's none of our business. We've more important things of our own to go into now – Spiller and me, we was talking late last night: we got decisions to make and we've got to make them quickly.' He pulled out a piece of tile and sat down on it. 'What about that bit of breakfast, Homily? We can talk as we eat . . .'

'It's like this,' said Pod, when they were all seated and had opened up the dock leaf, 'with this weather and a full moon, we could unload the boat tonight.'

'Oh, Pod,' groaned Homily, 'not across that lawn again! Not so soon!' She was holding up a piece of limp ham which, during the long night, had become a good deal paler.

'Who said anything about walking across lawns?' Pod retorted. 'Just you listen quietly, Homily, and

I'll tell you Spiller's idea.' He broke off a corner of dry bread and laid a sliver of ham across it. 'You know that pond? – well, you might call it a lake –' They waited anxiously until he had finished his first mouthful. At last, he swallowed. 'That lake, as you might have noticed, comes right up to the steps. If you didn't notice, it was because we cut away from it, through those bushes, to the bank, remember?'

Homily nodded. Arrietty, her eyes fixed on her father, stretched out her hand for a grape. She had begun to feel excited and was more thirsty than hungry.

'Now,' Pod went on, 'Spiller, with his punt pole and with the help of the paddle –'

'What paddle?' asked Homily.

'The butter-knife,' whispered Arrietty.

'– Can turn his boat into the stream and take it into the main lake, across the lake, and right up to the steps. Once on the lake, the going is smooth as silk, no currents there once he's out of the stream . . .'

'Then why didn't he do it yesterday?' complained Homily, 'instead of all that walking?'

'Because,' said Pod patiently, 'it was broad daylight. What sort of cover, I ask you, could you expect to find in the middle of a lake? No, Homily, moving our stuff by boat is a night-time job. Though I wouldn't say no to a bit of a moon . . .'

'That lake doesn't come right up to the bank, Pod,' said Homily after a moment.

'Near enough for us to unload and bring the stuff up the bank.'

'That'll take us all night,' said Homily, 'if all we've got to help us is Spiller's soap-box.'

'The first things I'll need out of that boat is me tools and the ball of twine.'

'What about my cooking pots? Say we wanted a drink? Now, with our breakfast? There's that tap in the corner, dripping away, but we've nothing to put under it.'

'You must use your cupped hands,' said Pod, in the same patient voice, 'for the time being.'

They were not quarrelling, Arrietty realized, this was a 'discussion': later on, even she might venture to join in.

'There's an awful lot of stuff, Pod,' Homily pointed out, 'tables, chairs, beds . . .'

Was Pod going to remind her, Arrietty wondered, of his repeated warnings not to bring too much? No, she realized, he wasn't: he was too kind (and what good would it do now?).

'This move,' he said, 'must be done in two operations: everything up the bank and on to the gravel. And then, piece by piece, we bring it along here.'

There was a short silence. Then Arrietty swallowed nervously. 'Papa –' she began.

'Yes, Arrietty?'

'Where are we going to put all this stuff when we get it along here?'

Homily look about her at the vast, empty conservatory. Then she looked back at Pod. 'The child's got a point, Pod. Where *are* we going to put it? Seeing as we have to put every tile back just where it was, so nothing should look out of place . . .'

Pod was silent a moment. Then he said gravely, 'You're right: that is a bit of a problem.'

They were all silent. After a while, Homily said,

'Seems like we have to find some sort of place first.'
She looked towards the library.

'There's nowhere in there,' said Pod, turning his
head to follow her gaze, 'barring the shelves and
they're all open to view, as you might say.' He
turned back and linked his hands together across
his bent knees. He stared down at them thoughtfully.
'Yes, now I come to think of it, this is more than a
bit of a problem.'

'You've been in the hall, Pod. What about those
other rooms, as you go along the passage?'

'They keep them locked,' said Pod.

'What do you come to when you get to the end of
the passage?'

'The old kitchen,' said Pod.

'What's that like?'

'Empty,' said Pod. 'They don't use it. Except for
the cooking stove in the corner. They keep that
alight for hot water. And She simmers on it,
Spiller says. They've got their own little kitchen
beyond. Well, not a kitchen, exactly. It's a little
place with a small sink and gas stove. The gas
stove is very small – only takes one dish, Spiller
says, and boils a kettle. And they get the hot
water for the sink from the stove in the old
kitchen. As I say, She simmers things on it and it
keeps the place warm.'

'Might be useful for us,' said Homily thoughtfully.

'Might be,' said Pod.

'That old kitchen – there wouldn't be a place for
us? To live in, like?'

'There could be,' said Pod, 'but say you've got a
choice, better not choose a room where human
beans are always coming in and out, bringing coal,

107

carrying dishes . . . She cooks a lot for other people,' he added, 'takes it on as a job.'

Again there was silence: all were thinking hard.

'Are there any cupboards in the old kitchen?' Homily asked after a while.

'Plenty,' said Pod, 'and down at floor level underneath the dressers.'

'Suppose,' suggested Homily, 'we just stored the stuff in one of those? For the time being, say, till we found somewhere permanent?'

Pod thought this over. 'No,' he said, after a moment, 'it wouldn't do. Who's to say someone might not open that cupboard door? And that stuff – though it's safe enough now down in Spiller's boat – is all we've got in the world, Homily. Furthermore,' he went on (rather pleased with the word), 'there's so much of it. More than we need,' he sighed. 'But we'll let that pass now. As I see it, it's against the law of –' he paused.

'Averages,' suggested Arrietty.

'That's the word: it's against the law of averages that we could cart all that stuff all the way down that long passage, across the old kitchen, and stack it in an empty cupboard – and mind you, Homily, that kitchen is just below the place where they sleep, those Witlesses – without making a sound!'

'I suppose you're right,' said Homily, after a moment.

'I know I'm right,' said Pod. 'You can picture it: this house is dead quiet at night. One of them, Him or Her, would wake up, think it was rats or something, and there we'd be – caught red-handed!'

Homily was quiet for a moment, and then she

said, 'Yes, I – I see what you mean.' Her voice sounded rather faint.

'And not only us,' Pod went on, 'all our possessions!'

A kind of burglary in reverse, Arrietty thought to herself, but she felt sorry to have had to be the one to point out all these difficulties. But difficulties they certainly were, and very grave ones.

'Then what are we going to do?' Homily said at last, after a long unhappy silence.

Pod stood up. 'It's obvious,' he said. He took a few restless steps across the tiles and then came back and sat down again. 'Go on as we are for the time being,' he announced firmly.

'What, live in that stove!' exclaimed Homily. But Arrietty felt a wave of relief: she had thought he might say that they must go away again. Suddenly she realized that she loved this house, the garden, the sense of freedom, and she felt that somehow, by some means yet to be discovered, they would find happiness here.

'Our stuff is safe enough where it is,' Pod went on, 'in Spiller's boat under that bank. And there it can stay, until we find some corner for ourselves . . .'

'But there doesn't seem to be one,' said Homily, 'not here on the ground floor. And I can't go climbing creepers at my age.' She was thinking of the rooms upstairs.

'Give me a few days,' said Pod.

Once Homily had made up their bed, there seemed nothing much else to do. Pod went off to make another exploration of the library but came back just as frustrated. They were waiting for Spiller who, at some point, was bound to appear, but time dragged very heavily. Once, the telephone rang. It rang three times, and they all rushed under the stove at the sound of scurrying footsteps in the passage. They heard Mrs Whitlace say, 'Hallo!' Then there was a pause, and she said, 'Yes – Yes.' There was another pause, and they heard her say, 'I will, of course!' in her cheerful, ringing voice. There was a click, and the footsteps scurried away again.

'I wonder what that was about,' said Homily, as they came out from under the stove. She was brushing herself down. 'Pod,' she went on, 'we've got to do something about these ashes . . .'

'I'll get you a wisp of box. You can sweep them to the side, like.'

'And how are we going to wash, I'd like to know? Drip by drip under that tap . . .'

'It may only be for a few days,' said Pod.

'How do we know?'

'Now, Homily, you be your old self: we've been through a lot worse than this, remember?'

'I was only asking,' said Homily as Pod turned towards the garden door. Arrietty jumped up and forestalled him. She held him back by clinging to his arm. 'Oh, Papa, could I go? It needn't be box: I saw a thistle head – a thistle head makes a lovely broom. Please, Papa!'

He let her go, rather unwillingly, but remembering his promise that, very soon now, he would teach her to borrow. All the same, he watched her anxiously through the dim glass panes as she darted about among the weeds and grasses. Soon she was back with two dried-up thistle heads, both a little damp with dew but, as she told Homily, they would sweep all the better for that. 'Are there any crumbs?' she asked her mother. 'There's a robin in that bush . . .'

'Plenty,' said Homily, and handed her the crumpled dock leaf.

'Now, Homily –' warned Pod. But Homily said, 'Oh, let her go, Pod. It's a lovely day and we can watch her from here . . .'

But, alas, as she crossed the path, the robin flew away. But she scattered the crumbs all the same and threw away the dock leaf. She went on to the untidy box hedge on the far side of the path and looked up into the branches. Very dark it looked up there, hemmed in by the think clumps of leaves at the outer edges. It was a hollow kind of darkness but crisscrossed with a myriad sinewy twigs and branches. It was an easy climb and a hidden one. Arrietty barely hesitated: such a climb was beyond resistance . . . It was wonderful – no thorns, no scratchy pieces, only, here and there, soft curls of paper-thin bark. Up and up, she went: this climb was child's play, she thought, and, what was more, completely secure and hidden. Perhaps the leaves on the outside might rustle a little but what did that matter? Bushes were apt to rustle a little – birds could cause it, or even a puff of wind. But there was no wind today and as she got higher the surroundings became lighter until, at last, on a topmost branch she found herself in sunshine.

Oh, the view! There was the stable yard, with its mellowed roofs and beyond that the walled garden – the kitchen garden, Pod had called it. The walls were too high to see very far inside, but she could see the iron gate, with its upright bars: just wide

enough, that gate, to take a wheelbarrow. It appeared to be padlocked.

On the other side, so close that it surprised her, was the squat tower of the church, with its small, low parapet and, just below this, the clock face. Around the church, obscured here and there by trees and bushes, the churchyard lay dreaming in the sunshine. Very peaceful it looked with its medley of gravestones. Some graves looked carefully tended, others old and forgotten, but they did not lie in rows. If anyone had asked her about the layout of the churchyard, she would have described it as 'higgledy-piggledy', but somehow, she thought, this made it seem beautiful. It made her long to explore it, to read the names on the headstones, and learn something of those who, when their time had come, had been so gently laid to rest. She had not quite realized how near the church was to the rectory, barely a step for a human being and not many more for a borrower.

Gazing at the church, she found herself comparing it with Mr Pott's miniature counterpart in his model village. Looking at it now (as she swayed rather dreamily on a little seat she had found for herself between two upcurving boughs) she realized with what loving care Mr Pott had copied the original, almost – it seemed to her now – stone by stone. Was it true that her cousins, the Hendrearies, were living there? Spiller had said so, but her father had not seen them. Perhaps because he had not yet been inside the church? She had never liked Aunt Lupy, with her stout, important figure and her heavy, plummy voice. Nor, for that matter, had she particularly cared for her Uncle Hendreary, with his wispy beard and rather shifty eyes. She had never got to know the elder boys very well during those uncomfortable months she and her parents had stayed in their home: they were always out borrowing and seldom spoke at meals. And Eggletina had always seemed strange and withdrawn ('Never been the same, poor child,' Aunt Lupy would say, 'since that adventure with the cat . . .'). But she had liked Timmus, their youngest child.

Little Timmus, with his rosy cheeks and great, round, wondering eyes. Liked? No, that was not the word: she had loved Timmus! During those dull, long winter evenings in Aunt Lupy's house, she had kept him happy telling him stories (many of them the same stories she had read aloud to The Boy at Firbank). 'Quite the little mother, aren't you?' Aunt Lupy used to say, with her patronizing laugh. But Aunt Lupy, after all, had been kind enough to take them in – when they were homeless and what Homily called 'dessitute'. But, after the first rapturous reunion between Aunt Lupy and her mother the kindness had soon worn off. When danger threatened all of them, they had been made to feel unwelcome. Perhaps, Arrietty thought now, that was understandable. Too many mouths to feed, that had been the trouble . . .

Oh, well . . .

Yes, perhaps she had been 'a little mother' to Timmus; perhaps she had made his dull young life a little less dull? Curled up together on the foot of her uncomfortable bed, she had carried him into other worlds, and strange made-up adventures. But she had taken herself off, too. The chilly, twilit room had no longer contained them: they had flown away into fairy places and mysterious realms unknown. Yes, this was what she was realizing now: if perhaps she had helped Timmus, Timmus – with his loving, grateful ways – had certainly helped her.

And how seldom she had thought of him since. Imprisoned in the Platters' attic, they had been too busy planning their escape. And now they had this journey, the business of packing up for it, this exciting arrival at the rectory, the meeting this morning with Peagreen. In all this time, it never once occurred to her how Timmus must have missed her in his shut-up lonely life. How old would he be now? She tried to think, but all she could think of was that she must see Timmus again.

She looked back again towards the kitchen garden. It would (Pod had told them) be filled with good things in summer: they would never want for fruit or vegetables. And herbs for Homily's cooking. Not just the wild ones from the hedgerows (as had been the case so often before) but of rarer kinds and greater variety. But where would poor Homily do her cooking? Where, in the end, would they make their permanent home?

A sudden whirring from the church tower announced the clock was about to strike. She turned quickly, swaying slightly on her slender branch. The clock struck two. Two o'clock! It couldn't be! Where had the morning gone? Her parents must be out of their minds with worry. And Spiller must have arrived by now to bring them their luncheon. *And*, what was worse, she had forgotten to tell her parents that Peagreen might appear.

Down she went in careless haste, sliding, dropping, missing footholds. Why had she thought there was nothing 'scratchy' in this bush? There seemed plenty of scratchy things now.

Once on the ground, she dashed across the path, too hurriedly to notice that not one robin but two were feasting on her crumbs. They flew away at her approach into the bushes. She hardly bothered to avoid the nettles and nearly got stung several times (and a nettle sting was a big sting to a borrower) before she reached the hole under the door; dashing through it in her dew-wet boots she came to a sliding stop and looked around wonderingly at the silent, seated group.

CHAPTER ELEVEN

Her entrance did not cause the stir she had expected. Only Homily said, 'No need to come in like a thunderbolt,' but her voice sounded dispirited as though she had other matters on her mind. Arrietty had a feeling that, when she entered, they had all been sitting in silence. No. Spiller was not sitting exactly, he was lounging against the wall, idly running a lump of beeswax along the string of his bow.

She prised out a bit of tile and sat down facing them, her back towards the garden. A little tray of food lay, untouched, on the ground between them: why had nobody eaten? The tray, she realized, was a rather battered tin ashtray. No one spoke and no one seemed to notice her dishevelled appearance. What had been happening, she wondered? To what decision had they come?

At last Pod said, 'Well, that's how I see it,' and gave a great sigh.

'I suppose you're right,' said Homily glumly.

'I don't see what else there is to do. We can't keep on holding up Spiller's boat for ever . . . he'll be needing it soon. It's his livelihood, as you might say, borrowing for others.' Homily did not reply and Spiller, having raised his eyes for a moment, looked down again at his bow. 'And there should be a good bright moon tonight . . .' Pod added, as though to introduce a more cheerful note, '. . . and we've practically nothing to pack.'

So that was it: they were going! This lovely house,

this dear house, had been found wanting. Although at first it had seemed so promising, for some reason now it would not 'do'. Arrietty felt the tears pricking into her eyes, and bowed her head so that they would not show.

'We might try the church of course,' said Pod. 'The Hendrearies seem to have managed to get along there . . .'

Homily threw up her head, her eyes flashing. 'Nothing,' she exclaimed, 'absolutely *nothing*, Pod, would persuade me to stay with Lupy again! Not wild horses, with wings of fire, down on their bended knees! Remember the last time we stayed with them!'

'Well, I didn't rightly mean stay with them,' said Pod, 'that church is a big place, Homily.'

Homily's eyes were still angry. 'Not even under the same roof!' she said firmly. 'However big . . .'

Pod knew when he was beaten. Once more, there was silence. Homily now sat again with her head bowed; very depressed she looked, and very tired. Why, Arrietty wondered, did all these decisions have to be made so quickly? Her mother's next listless words seemed to echo her thought.

'Why don't we just sleep on it tonight, Pod?' she suggested wearily.

'Because the weather might change,' said Pod.

Arrietty brushed a hand across her eyes and raised her head again and then, suddenly, she began to smile. She was looking at the double doors which led into the library: it was Peagreen! He stood there, hesitating a little shyly. He seemed ready to slip away again.

'Peagreen!' she exclaimed, and jumped to her feet.

Pod and Homily turned sharply: even Spiller straightened himself against the wall.

'Papa, this is Peagreen! We met this morning. Peagreen, this is my father and mother. And our friend Spiller . . . Peagreen, come in. Do . . .'

'Yes,' said Pod, slowly rising, 'come in and sit down. Arrietty, get him a piece of tile . . .'

Peagreen bowed and as he limped shyly forward his usually pale face looked faintly flushed. 'How do you do?' he said, as Arrietty placed a tile for him. He sat down on it a little uncertainly and rather towards the edge. There was a short surprised silence, and then Pod said, 'It's a lovely day, isn't it?' Homily just stared.

'Yes,' said Peagreen.

'Not that I've been out of doors yet,' Pod went on.

'I have,' Arrietty put in conversationally. 'I climbed that bush outside. It was lovely. You can see for miles . . .'

Peagreen smiled, 'So you've found my look-out?' he said.

'Your look-out?' repeated Pod. He sounded interested.

'Yes,' said Peagreen, turning courteously towards him. 'You'll find it very useful. Almost indispensable, in fact. I'm not much of a walker, but luckily I can climb.'

Homily was still looking amazed. So this was an Overmantel! Nothing like those she had ever heard about, except perhaps the voice, which she thought rather affected.

'Have you lived here long?' asked Pod politely.

'All my life,' said Peagreen.

'So you know all the ins and outs?'

'You could put it like that,' said Peagreen, smiling, 'but in my case, it's more "ins" than "outs". I'm not an open-air type – except by necessity.'

'And it's a nice old house,' Pod said. 'We're sorry to be leaving it.'

Peagreen looked surprised. 'But this young lady here . . . your daughter . . . well, I gathered from her you had only just come?'

'That's true,' said Pod, 'but there are difficulties . . .' He sighed.

'I'm sorry,' said Peagreen, still looking puzzled. He was too polite to ask what these difficulties might be.

'Well, it's like this –' began Pod, and hesitated, but looking back into that simple, boyish face he felt encouraged to go on. 'It's just this: there seems no place on this ground floor, no place at all, where it would seem safe for a family of borrowers to live. Not settle down in, like. Not to start a new life in. I like the house, no doubt about that, but you've got to face facts. Hard as it may be. And it *will* be hard for us . . .'

Peagreen leaned forward on his seat. 'I – I could make a suggestion,' he said, after a moment.

'I'd be glad if you would,' said Pod, but there was not much hope in his voice.

'I don't know what you'd think of it. It isn't much. And it's rather inconvenient, I'm afraid, but my old house is free now. And you'd be very welcome to it. For the time being, at least . . . I mean, until you can find somewhere better.' His flush had deepened and he seemed rather embarrassed. Nevertheless, his face looked eager and smiling.

'That's very kind of you,' said Pod, wary of committing himself, 'very kind indeed. But you see, my missus and I, we'll soon be getting on a bit and any house we settled in would have to be on the ground floor, like.'

'But my house *is* on the ground floor,' said Peagreen.

'I can't think where,' said Pod.

Peagreen jerked his head towards the double doors. 'In there . . .'

'In the library? Impossible!' exclaimed Pod.

Peagreen smiled. 'I can show you, if you like. It isn't far . . .' He rose to his feet.

'If it isn't too much trouble,' said Pod. He still looked very mystified, having searched – several times over – every crack and cranny in the library.

'No trouble at all,' said Peagreen. 'I'd better lead the way . . .' he added, and began to limp ahead.

Spiller, Arrietty noticed, had slung his bow over his shoulder and was making for the garden door. She took a few steps towards him. 'Aren't you coming, too, Spiller?'

He turned as he reached the door and shook his head. Then he slipped away through the hole.

Feeling slightly disappointed, Arrietty followed the others into the library; they were grouped, she noticed, in front of that strangely modern fireplace. Why had not Spiller come, she wondered? Was he shy? Was he a little suspicious of Peagreen? Or, being an outdoor borrower, was he just not interested in any kind of indoor home?

As Arrietty came up to them she noticed, where Peagreen was standing, a wide dark stain on the lighter wood of the floorboards. Peagreen glanced down. 'Yes,' he said, 'they used to put a rug over that. I'll explain later . . .' He turned again to Pod. 'The thing to remember,' he said, 'is that it's the third tile from the end.' Crossing the hearth, he gave the tile in question a slight kick. Nothing happened, so he kicked it again, slightly harder.

This time, the top of the tile slid forward a little from the base of the tile just above it. Peagreen, stretching his arms, got his fingers on the protruding edge and, with an effort, managed to pull it forward. Pod hurried up, anxious to save the tile from falling, but Peagreen said, 'It's all right: it won't fall; these tiles were made to fit exactly.' He tugged once more and with a grating sound the tile came free, Pod supporting it in front and Peagreen at the side. They paused a moment for breath. Then Peagreen said, 'Now, we just have to push it along a little . . .' This they did, and leaned it gently against the tile beside it. A gaping hole was revealed, very dark and somewhat forbidding.

'I see,' said Pod, 'very clever.' He ran his hand along the edge of the tile. 'You scraped off the cement?'

'Yes. At least the Wainscots did. There wasn't much cement –'

'No, there wouldn't be,' said Pod, 'not with tiles that fitted like these.'

'Who were the Wainscots?' asked Arrietty.

'The borrowers who took me in. Shall I go in first?' he said to Pod, who was peering into the hole. 'It's a bit dark at the entrance . . .'

'Thanks,' said Pod. 'Come along, Homily –' and he put out a hand to guide her. Arrietty brought up the rear.

They all trooped in through the cavern-like hole. Arrietty noticed it had been hacked out by hand and was almost a short tunnel. They found themselves in a vast dimly lit space, draughty and cold after the warmth of the sunlit conservatory. Looking up, to find out the source of light, she saw a patch of blue sky. They were somewhere inside the old chimneypiece.

'There should be a bit of old candle-end about,' Peagreen was saying. 'I usually left one here, and a few safety matches. To tell you the truth,' he went on, as he fumbled about in the semi-darkness, 'I don't use this entrance much myself.'

'Is there another?' asked Pod.

'Yes. But that's not too easy either. Ah!' he exclaimed in a satisfied voice: he had found the candle and was striking a light.

What a strange place it was! A cathedral sort of place, the soot-blackened walls going up and up, with the sky as a far distant canopy. The cracked floor was littered with twigs and sticks and, in one corner, a neat but high pile of ash beside which, to Arrietty's surprise, she recognized the eye-bath. But Peagreen now was moving the light towards the farther wall, so dutifully she followed its gleam. 'This is really what I wanted to show you,' Peagreen was saying, holding the candle high: and Arrietty saw, propped up at either end by two piles of slatey-looking stones, the prongs of a narrow hand-fork minus its handle: it was the kind of weeding fork, Arrietty realized, which a lady-gardener might use – someone like Miss Menzies, for instance; and now, when she came to think of it, Miss Menzies *had* owned such a fork but hers had a handle; and she kept it very clean. This one, in the flickering candlelight, looked very worn and blackened.

'You can cook on these prongs,' Peagreen told them. 'They found it in the conservatory –' he added, '–makes a kind of grill.'

Homily, hearing this, ventured a little closer; the expression on her face was one of extreme distaste: this was not her idea of a cooking stove, nor was this vast, dusty cavern her idea of a kitchen.

'What about the smoke?' she whispered to Pod.

'There wouldn't be any smoke,' Pod told her, 'at least not that anyone would notice, with this great hearth and the chimney so high. What little there was the walls about'd absorb it, like. Think of the size of our fire compared with the ones this was built for!'

'*Our* fire?' echoed Homily. Her whisper was bitter: was Pod really thinking she would consent to live in this awful place?

'What on earth did they use to cook in?' It was only the second time Homily had addressed Peagreen directly.

'Tin lids mostly.' He nodded his head towards a deeply shadowed wall, 'There are some shelves over there.' He turned away from the grid, holding the candle high. 'Well, then, I'll show you the rest – such as it is. Careful of the wood,' he warned them as he kicked some branches aside. 'The jackdaws drop it down: every spring they try to nest on the corner of the chimney and every spring they fail,' he was leading them towards the entrance hole. 'As long as those jackdaws keep on building, you'll never be short of fuel. And keep on building they will . . .'

Pod paused for a moment to look at the tottering pile. 'Could do with a bit of stacking,' he said.

Peagreen paused too, and glanced at the untidy mess. 'I didn't bother,' he said. 'You see, I can't cook – at least, not much. I just used that grid to heat up water. For my bath,' he added, 'or an occasional cup of tea.'

Yes, thought Arrietty, looking at Peagreen in the candlelight, that was what had struck her at their first meeting: that he looked so very clean. How she longed for a bath herself: perhaps later it could be managed?

Peagreen had paused by the hole which led to the library. He turned to Arrietty. 'Would you take the candle for a moment?'

She took it from him and tried to hold it high as she watched him kneel down on the cracked stone of the floor. Some flat thing lay there: something that when they had entered in nearly pitch darkness she had taken for a kind of door-mat. Now she saw it was the back cover of a leather-bound book. He pushed it aside and there was another hole, one that led downwards. Arrietty drew back from it with a little gasp of dismay. Was the rest of Peagreen's house somewhere under the floor? If so, it would be beyond bearing. She thought of those early years at Firbank, the dusty passages, the dimly lit rooms, the long monotonous days, the sense of imprisonment, intermingled with fear. She had grown used to it, that she realized now, but only because she had known no other life. But now she had tasted freedom, the joy of running, the fun of climbing; the sight of birds, butterflies, flowers – of sunshine, rain and dew . . . No, not that again, not under floor!

Peagreen took the candle from her gently and held it over the hole. She felt he had sensed her dismay and had mistaken it for fear. 'It's all right,' he assured her, 'only a few steps down . . .' and slowly he disappeared from view. Pod went next and, after him, Homily – with almost as much unwillingness as Arrietty herself was feeling. There were about six steps made of stone and neatly set together.

It was just as she had feared: a long dark passage between the joists which supported the floor above, the library floor it must be; it was quite straight and it seemed to go on and on. It was as dusty as the passages had been at Firbank, and smelt of mice droppings. Bringing up the rear of the procession, she felt there were tears on her cheeks. No good feeling in her pocket for a handkerchief: she had left it in the stove. Her only ally, she felt, was going to be her mother, and that not because of darkness but because of the awful kitchen. Pod seemed unconcerned.

At last, Peagreen paused at a second set of steps – these seemed to go upwards. He held the light steady until they had all caught up with him, and then he went on ahead.

'These steps are well made,' remarked Pod, 'can't think how the stones bind together.'

'Wainscot made them,' Peagreen called down from above. 'He was a better stone-mason than carpenter. Some kind of sticky stuff he used,' he went on, as Pod's head emerged to his level, 'something he mixed with resin from the fir trees.'

'Resin . . .' echoed Pod, as though to himself. In

all the alterations he had made at Firbank, he had never thought of resin! And fir trees there had been there in plenty . . .

Peagreen had passed the candle to Pod and seemed to be busy with his hands. Suddenly the small staircase was lit up by a stream of light from above. And, to Arrietty's surprise and joy, the light was daylight! Pod blew out the candle.

One by one, they emerged into what seemed, to them, a very long room. It was (Arrietty suddenly realized) the enclosed space below one of the window seats. It must be the one (judging by their long walk under the floorboards) below the window which faced the fireplace. The space was even longer than it had seemed at first because one end of it was filled with a stack of books which rose almost to the ceiling. Otherwise, it was empty. And spotlessly clean. Chequered sunlight fell across the floor from what appeared to be a grating let in to the outside wall. It was a grating very like the one she remembered at Firbank: the one which she used to call *her* grating, and through which she would gaze for hours at the forbidden world outside. Her spirits lifted: perhaps, oh perhaps, everything was going to be all right . . .

Pod was staring up at the wooden ceiling. 'You could get another storey in here,' he said, 'plenty of height . . .'

'Yes, Wainscot thought of that,' Peagreen told him, 'but decided in the end it would take too much material. He couldn't think of a way to get the stuff in.'

'We'd hit on something,' said Pod.

Arrietty's spirits began to rise even higher. She

could tell from her father's voice and the way he was looking about him that he was already making plans. He had now walked into the alcove which enclosed the grating. Heavy curtains, now drawn back, fell down on either side. In winter, Arrietty realized, these would cut off the draught.

'I'm leaving the curtains,' said Peagreen as he came beside Pod. 'I've no need for them where I'm going.' Where *was* he going, Arrietty wondered?

'I'm not looking at the curtains,' said Pod. He was staring upwards at the low ceiling of the alcove. Some sort of pulley hung there, from the inner ridge of which there hung down a piece of twine.

'Oh, that!' said Peagreen. He did not sound very enthusiastic. Arrietty moved close to see better. At Pod's feet she saw an old-fashioned iron weight, with a handle on top for lifting. To this the twine was fastened. The other end of the string, she saw, ran across the ridge of the pulley and was attached to the top of the grating. Whatever could this contraption be for?

'It works,' said Peagreen rather gloomily, 'I don't know where he found the pulley.'

'I do,' said Pod, smiling. 'He found that pulley in an old grandfather clock.'

'How do you know that?' asked Peagreen.

'Because,' said Pod, still smiling broadly, 'at Firbank, our house was under a clock. There's not a bit of mechanism in a grandfather clock that we don't know inside out: the times I've studied it all from below. Our name is Clock, by the way . . .'

'Ah, yes,' said Peagreen, suddenly remembering.

'The string from that pulley – in our clock, it was wire not string – was attached to one of two weights.

Pulled the weight up and down, like.' He was silent a moment. 'Where's the rest of the clock now?'

'Stashed away somewhere,' said Peagreen. 'Most likely in the old game larder. There's a pile of old junk in there. But the clock never worked.'

'It wouldn't,' said Pod. 'Not without that pulley.' He seemed to be deep in thought. After a while he said, 'I gather that grating isn't fixed?'

'It used to be fixed,' said Peagreen, 'but Wainscot got it free. Now it just stands by its own weight.'

'So you can open and shut it? I mean with the help of that pulley?'

'Yes,' said Peagreen. 'You push on the top to free it, then you take hold of the string and gradually let it go. It opens out flat on to an old brick outside.'

'Very clever,' said Pod, 'quite a one, your friend, for scraping out cement. Although,' Pod went on, peering downwards through the grating, 'I'm not sure about that great brick outside . . .'

'You need the brick,' explained Peagreen, 'for the ventilaty to rest on. Otherwise you might not get it up again. It's quite heavy: cast iron, you see.'

'Yes, I see that,' said Pod. 'It's just that we were brought up to think that a borrower should never use – when he's constructing his house, say – anything that a human bean might move.'

'No one ever has moved it,' said Peagreen, 'at least, not in my lifetime. It's a mossy kind of old brick: you'd hardly notice it, among all the weeds and things . . .'

'All the same –' said Pod.

'And I never did open it right down,' Peagreen went on, 'I'd just open it a little way so I could slip out sideways. Except, of course, during these last few days, when I had to get my things out.'

'Yes, that must have been quite a business,' said Pod.

'Oh, Papa –' Arrietty broke in, 'he has a little truck! Quite a big truck, really, it's half a date box. With wheels,' she added eagerly. 'Four wheels!'

'A truck, eh?' said Pod, looking at Peagreen with increased respect. 'With wheels?'

'I didn't make it,' Peagreen hastened to assure him, 'it belonged to the Wainscots. I'm not very good with my hands.' He glanced at the weight and pulley. 'I loathe that contraption. That's why I'm moving, partly.'

Pod turned back to the grating. 'Well, let's try it,' he said. 'What do you say, Homily?'

'No harm in trying,' she said timidly. Although she had kept so quiet, she had been watching closely. Arrietty could not quite make out her expression: it was an odd mixture of anxiety, hope and fear. Her hands were so closely clasped together against her chest that the knuckles looked white.

Pod went close up to the grating and, raising his arm above his head, he struck the top of it with the side of his closed fist. It began to slide forward and as the weight on the floor began to rise, Pod stepped aside quickly to avoid its sudden ascent. A bit too sudden, Arrietty thought, as the floor weight clashed up against the pulley. The ventilator lay fully open, resting, it seemed, on the brick. You could walk out on it, Arrietty realized, into the sunlit world outside.

'Well, that's that,' said Pod, rubbing the side of his hand: the blow he had given on cast iron had been a bit severe. 'Is there any way of working this thing more slowly?'

'Well,' said Peagreen, 'you can keep a guiding hand on the twine and pull it aside, if you see what I mean. Depending on how far you want to let the whole thing go. If you want to stop it at a certain place, you can give it a couple of twists round this –' He put up a hand and touched a piece of metal in the wall. 'Sort of cleat, don't they call it?'

'I see what you mean,' said Pod. 'I never noticed that.'

'It comes in useful,' Peagreen told him. 'Especially for someone like me. I hardly ever open that grating fully . . .'

'How do you shut it?' asked Pod.

'You pull on the weight,' said Peagreen.

'I see,' said Pod. He seemed very impressed. 'What do you think of it, Homily?'

'Very nice,' said Homily uncertainly. 'But –'

'But what?' Pod asked her.

'Say you pull that weight right down till it reaches the ground, what's to prevent it going up again?'

'Because,' said Pod, 'by the time that weight's on the ground, the grating will be back in position: there'll be no more strain on the twine, like.'

He turned his back to the sill of the now empty gap and, with a hand on either side, swiftly hitched himself up into a sitting position. He did this, Arrietty noticed, with something of his old athletic manner. Proudly she watched him as, swinging both legs around on to the grating, he swiftly rose to his feet. To her loving eyes, he seemed, quite suddenly, to have found his youth again. Swiftly she turned as though to speak to her mother but was silenced by what she saw. Homily, too, had been gazing at Pod. She seemed to be smiling but her lips were trembling and her eyes looked suspiciously bright. Catching Arrietty's glance, she opened her arms and Arrietty flew into them. They clung together. Were they laughing or crying? It was difficult to tell.

CHAPTER TWELVE

In the end, they all climbed out on to the grating. The sun, by now, had moved slightly round towards the west but its rays still poured down on this south side of the house. Through a thin fringe of weeds, Arrietty could see the path along which they had traipsed (was it really only yesterday?) dragging Spiller's soap-box. Where was Spiller now, she wondered? Why had he disappeared? He would have liked this place. Or perhaps he already knew about it?

Pod, his legs apart, was staring down at the grating. 'You know, Peagreen,' he was saying, 'this thing isn't resting on the brick at all: it's held in this straight-out position by that weight coming up against the pulley . . .'

'All the same,' went on Pod, 'that brick's a bit of a safeguard: supposing, say, the twine broke, or something . . .'

'Heaven forbid . . .' muttered Homily.

'It's all right, Homily, I've got plenty of twine among our stuff. Fishing line,' he explained to Peagreen, 'good and strong. Stronger than this, I shouldn't wonder.' Another idea seemed to strike him. 'What sort of fish do you have in that pond?'

Peagreen hesitated: he was not a fishing man. 'Roach, they say, and chub. Wainscot once caught a trout. Minnows . . .'

'Minnows will do for us,' said Pod, 'there's nothing tastier than a fresh-caught minnow, the way Homily cooks it.'

Homily, thinking of that dark, draughty cavern behind the fireplace, said, 'But we've got the larder now, Pod. Seems to be everything that we might ever need in that larder. And most of it ready-cooked . . .'

'Now, Homily,' said Pod, 'let's get this straight once and for all: I don't want you depending too much on that larder. A bit here, a bit there – well that's all right. That's how we managed at Firbank. But remember when we lived in the boot? We had to use our . . .' he hesitated, '. . . our . . .'

'Imagination?' suggested Arrietty.

'That's it. We got to use our imagination, and get back to our old ways, as far as we can. Suppose those Witlesses moved out sudden, like? Suppose Mrs Witless took ill? Suppose I got caught, stranded on one of those shelves? Or Arrietty here – once she's learned to borrow? It's hard work, my girl, and dangerous work. Borrowers only borrow the things they can't live without. Not for the fun of it. Not out of greediness. And not out of laziness, neither. Borrowing for borrowers – and well you know it, Homily – is their only means of . . .' Again he hesitated, seeking the word.

'Subsistence?' murmured Arrietty tentatively.

'Survival,' said Pod firmly. He looked round at them all as though happy to have found the word for himself.

For a short while, there was a silence: it was a long time since they had heard Pod make such a long speech. And it seemed he had more to say:

'Now, don't get me wrong,' he went on, 'that walled garden, the kitchen garden, we can borrow

134

from that to our hearts' content. Compare us, say, with the pigeons, the field mice, the slugs, the snails, the caterpillars . . . I mean one pod of peas would give us a meal, like, and who's there to grudge us that? Not Witless, that's for sure. Nor Mrs Witless neither. And there'd be Spiller with his bow, keeping down the field mice. There's a mite of things to keep down in a kitchen garden . . .'

'Who's to grudge us a sliver of cheese, a pinch or two of tea, a drop of milk?' said Homily, 'or a bit of ham off the bone before they throw the bone away? Or . . .'

'I don't say we won't never borrow from the larder, Homily, all I'm saying is we got to watch it.'

'I *have* to depend on the larder for everything,' said Peagreen glumly, 'that's why I'm moving house.'

They all turned to look at him, and he smiled rather wanly. 'You see,' he explained, 'for me to get to the larder, I have to open this grating a crack, slide out sideways, and walk round the corner of the conservatory, and on along that same path as far as the larder window and then back again by the same route. It's the safest way for someone who can't run fast. There's always that box hedge for cover but it's very inconvenient sometimes, especially in winter: one can get snowed up.'

'I see your point,' said Pod. 'You want to be nearer the larder?'

'Yes,' said Peagreen. 'Not that I eat so much, but it's all that walking. I find it a waste of time. Of course,' he went on, 'it might be a bit shorter down that passage and across the old kitchen. But I have to take it slowly and there's not much cover. Once there used to be a great old table in the middle of that kitchen, but it's gone now . . .'

'Yes,' said Pod, 'there's a good bit of open floor to cover. I see your point,' he repeated. There was a short silence, then Pod said, 'Your new house –' and he hesitated. Arrietty guessed that her father longed to know where Peagreen's new house might be, just as she herself had longed to know, but manners forbade his actually asking. 'I mean,' said Pod, 'this new house of yours? You'll find it easier?'

'Very much easier,' said Peagreen. Suddenly his face lit up. 'Would you like to see it?'

'Oh, I would!' cried Arrietty, running towards him across the opened grating.

'It's a bit of a walk,' said Peagreen to Pod.

Pod still seemed to hesitate out of some kind of politeness: perhaps he did not want to appear to pry. 'Another day,' he said, 'I'd like to poke about here a bit longer.' He looked at the gap in the wall and down again at the grating. 'I want to get the hang of this thing . . .'

'Can *I* go, Papa?' cried Arrietty eagerly. Her legs already were over the side of the grating. Pod looked down at her.

'I don't see why not,' he said, after a moment, 'providing you're quick,' he added.

'We'll be as quick as we can,' she promised, and slid off the grating into the grasses, 'come, Peagreen!' For the moment, she had forgotten Peagreen's lameness.

'Oh, Peagreen –' called Pod, as the latter was preparing to slide off the edge of the grating, 'there's just one thing –'

'What's that?' asked Peagreen, pausing.

Pod jerked his head towards the long, window-like gap in the brickwork. 'All those books in there, have you read them?'

'Yes,' said Peagreen.

'Do you want to read them again?'

'Not particularly. Are they in your way?' he went on. 'I just left them there because they were too big to fit into my new place.'

'No,' said Pod, 'they're not in my way. Not at all,' he added in a satisfied voice.

'If so, now the grating's open, we can chuck them out into the grasses and move them away after dark. I've got a lot of smaller ones . . .'

'And where would we hide these?' asked Pod.

'No, no, leave them be. I might have a use for them . . .'

'Right,' said Peagreen, and slid off the grating into the grasses.

CHAPTER THIRTEEN

Arrietty did not speak as, matching her step to Peagreen's, they passed along the western side of the conservatory. Her feeling of relief and happiness seemed almost too much to bear: so they were going to stay – that much had become obvious! A new life and a freedom such as she had never dared to dream of; and it was just about to begin: it *had* begun!

Once round the corner, Peagreen said 'Excuse me,' and stooped rather gingerly to feel among the dried dock and nettles. He drew out a grimy piece of broken glass. 'I'm collecting these,' he said. He then took her arm and guided her across the path into the shelter of the box hedge. 'Safer to walk on this far side,' he said.

Arrietty stared with interest across the path at the ivy-clad wall of a part of the rectory she had not yet seen. The ivy was small-leaved and variegated, and clung stoutly to the dark red brick; its woody stems ran snake-like in all directions across the ancient surface. How easy, she realized, these root-like tentacles would be to climb. Could Peagreen's new house be on an upper floor? No, he had said that it was near to the larder. Then, a few steps ahead of them, she noticed a long cage-like erection firmly fixed, it seemed, to the old red bricks. As they came abreast of it, Peagreen halted. It consisted of several metal posts and cross bars, netted with torn and rusted chicken-wire. Inside it were what looked like several small dead trees, some of whose many branches had rotted away. In one corner stood a mossy-looking water barrel, full to the brim and with water flowing over. This was fed by a pipe running down from the roof. What could this place be? Some kind of fruit cage?

'It's the old aviary,' said Peagreen.

'Oh,' said Arrietty uncertainly: she was not quite sure what an 'aviary' might be.

'They kept birds in it,' Peagreen explained. 'All kinds of birds. Rare birds. I wish I had seen it in the old days . . .'

They stood looking at it for a little while longer. The ivy, Arrietty noticed, had spread itself like a tattered carpet over the whole floor of the aviary except in the very centre where a round stone trough stood up among the variegated leaves.

'The bird-bath,' Peagreen told her. 'Not as deep as it looks; it's raised up on a base. Come on, and I'll show you the larder window.'

A few paces further on, Arrietty saw a barred window set deep in the ivied wall. It was a latticed window and, from where she stood, peering hard at the bars, it seemed to her that one side of the window stood slightly ajar.

'It's open,' she said to Peagreen.

'Yes, they always leave it like that – to keep the larder aired. You can't quite see it from here, but they've got a bit of chicken-wire, from the aviary I suppose, tacked across the frame. Against the cats, when they used to have cats. I've untacked the bottom corner: you can sort of lift it. No one's ever noticed – not ever bothered, for that matter – seeing there are no cats here now.'

'I'm glad to hear that,' said Arrietty, 'my cousin Eggletina was supposed to have been eaten by a cat.

But it came out that she escaped in the end. But she was never quite the same afterwards . . .'

'It's understandable . . .' said Peagreen.

'Cats and owls,' Arrietty went on, 'I suppose those are the two things borrowers really are frightened of. As frightened as human beans are supposed to be of ghosts.'

'Don't say "human beans",' said Peagreen.

'Why not?' retorted Arrietty, 'we always called them that under the floor at Firbank.'

'It sounds silly,' Peagreen remarked. 'And it isn't correct.' He looked at her thoughtfully. 'I don't mean to be rude but you must have picked up a lot of odd expressions, living – as you say you did – under the kitchen.'

'I suppose we did,' said Arrietty almost humbly. It occurred to her that there might be quite a lot to be learned from Peagreen, steeped as he was in book-learning. And an Overmantel to boot. 'All the same,' she went on firmly, 'I believe that any expression which was good enough for my father and mother should be good enough for me.' She was eyeing him rather coldly. 'Don't you agree?'

Peagreen flushed. And then he smiled his gentle, sideways smile. 'Yes,' he said, 'I do agree. And I agree with something else . . .'

'Oh?'

'Something you didn't say: that I'm a rotten snob!'

Arrietty laughed. 'Oh, you're just an Overmantel . . .' she said airily. Then she laid a hand on his arm. 'Aren't you going to show me the larder?'

'I'll show you my house first.' He led her back beside the path until they stood once again in front of the aviary. 'That's where I'm going to live,' he said.

Arrietty stared in a puzzled way at the metal posts and the torn strips of rusted netting. 'Look up a bit,' said Peagreen. Arrietty raised her eyes and then she saw. A row of sun-bleached nesting-boxes were fixed to the ivied wall. Some were half concealed by tendrils of trailing leaves, others were fully exposed. In the front of each was a small round hole, a borrower-sized hole. 'The lids lift up,' Peagreen told her. 'You can put in all kinds of stuff from the top . . .'

Arrietty was breathless with admiration. 'How marvellous,' she breathed at last. 'What a wonderful idea!'

'It is rather,' Peagreen admitted modestly. 'And what's more, they're made of teak – a wood that lasts for ever . . .'

'For ever?' echoed Arrietty.

'Well, in a manner of speaking. Come rain or shine, it doesn't rot like other woods. The humans who built this aviary were not short of a few pennies.'

'Are rectors rich then?' asked Arrietty, still gazing admiringly at the nesting-boxes.

'Not nowadays,' said Peagreen. 'But from what I've heard and read, some of them used to be – horses, carriages, servants. The lot. And, of course, in the olden days, money went further . . .'

Arrietty knew about servants: Mrs Driver had been one. But she did not know much about money. 'What *is* money?' she decided to ask. 'I can never quite figure it out . . .'

'And you'll never need to,' Peagreen told her, laughing.

After a while, still staring bemused at the nesting-boxes, Arrietty said, 'Which one are you going to live in?'

'Well, the first will be my sitting-room, the next will be my bedroom in summer, the one after that I'll keep my books in and all my bits of paper. In the next one I'll keep my painting things, and the last one – the one nearest the larder window – I'll turn into my dining-room.'

This was a scale of living undreamed of by Arrietty: grandeur beyond grandeur – and all for one young borrower who lived alone!

'I suppose you must have a lot of furniture,' she said after a minute.

'Very little,' Peagreen told her. 'Nice rooms don't need much furniture.'

'What do you paint with your painting things?' asked Arrietty then.

'Pictures,' said Peagreen.

'On what you call your bits of paper?'

'Sometimes. But there's a roll of fine canvas on the top shelf of the library. Paper is very hard to come by. I try to keep it for writing.'

'Letters?' asked Arrietty.

'Poems,' said Peagreen, and he blushed. 'Most of the books I read are poetry,' he went on, as though to excuse himself, 'the smaller ones, up there,' he nodded towards the aviary, 'the ones I brought away.'

'Could you ever let me read a little of the poetry you write?' Arrietty spoke rather shyly.

Peagreen's blush deepened. 'It's not very good,'

he said shortly and he turned away somewhat hurriedly. 'Come along, now I'll show you the larder.'

He looked swiftly from right to left to make sure the coast was clear then, taking her by the sleeve, he pulled her across the path, moving as fast as he was able. He dragged her rather roughly through one of the many gaps in the wire netting into (what seemed to them) a forest of ivy leaves which met above their heads. 'Excuse me a minute,' he said then; and, pushing aside a frond or two of green and white ivy, he laid down his piece of glass on an almost hidden pile of other grimy pieces.

'What are you going to use those for?' Arrietty asked as he rejoined her.

'I'm going to wash them in the bird-bath, and put them over the holes in the nesting-boxes.'

'To keep out the draughts?'

'No, to keep out the wrens and blue tits and goodness knows what else. Field mice for instance . . .'

'Why did you hurry me so, across the path? You said all the human beans were out –'

'You can't take chances. At least, not out of doors: there might be a visitor, or an errand boy; or possibly a postman . . . Come on, we've got to climb the ivy. Just follow me –'

Arrietty found that climbing the ivy was almost as much fun as climbing the look-out bush. Peagreen was making for the last of the nesting-boxes, the one that was to be his dining-room. They went up beside it and, both a little breathless, rested on the slightly sloping lid. Arrietty looked down. 'You've got a good view from here of anyone coming along the path.'

'I know,' said Peagreen. He slid off the nesting-box on to a thick branch of ivy. 'Come along. We've got to go sideways now. It's quite easy . . .'

It took no time at all to reach the sill of the larder window. How clever of Peagreen, thought Arrietty, to have planned all this out! And how proud he looked as he lifted the loose corner of rusty wire, holding it back for her to pass through! He came in beside her and they stood together on the narrow indoor sill. 'Well, this is it!' he said.

It was a long, narrow room. On one side were wide slate shelves; along the other a row of wooden bins, with sloping lids, rather like the lids of the

nesting-boxes outside. In fact, Arrietty thought, they *were* rather like giant nesting-boxes except they were all joined together.

Peagreen followed the direction of her eyes. 'Yes, that's where in the olden days they used to keep the cereals – rice, dried beans, maize for poultry, flour – all those sort of things. And rock salt in lumps. All the stores that had to be kept dry. You see, that wall backs on to the old kitchen stove in the next room. It's quite warm in those bins. They used to be kept locked, but all the locks are broken now – except this end one just below us. That one, they can't *un*lock . . . Not that it matters, those bins are never used now. It's not like the old days: humans no longer store things in bulk. They just buy what they want when they want it.'

'With money, I suppose?' said Arrietty wonderingly.

Peagreen laughed. 'Yes, with money.'

'I still don't quite understand money,' Arrietty said in a puzzled voice. Then she turned her eyes to the wide slate shelves.

The upper ones seemed mainly to be stocked with bottled fruits, jams, pickles, ketchups and pudding basins of all sizes, tied round with cloths; these shelves above were narrower than the main shelf below them, on which many unrecognizable objects were laid out. Unrecognizable from where she stood because several of them were shrouded by clean white napkins, others by wire-mesh meat covers. Strings of onions hung down from hooks in the ceiling, also large bunches of bay and thyme. Between the main shelf and the stone-flagged floor, the space was filled by a honeycomb affair which

146

Peagreen explained later was a wine rack. Not for the best wines (those had been kept in the cellars), but the home-made wines, which the cooks used to make in season: elderflower, dandelion, parsnip, gooseberry and so on. There were none left now. The door at the far end of the room was held ajar by a weight exactly like the one attached to Peagreen's pulley, except that this one was even larger. What giant scales they must have used in those 'old days'!

Peagreen, edging past her, made his way along the sill and stepped down on to the slate shelf which lay almost flush with it. 'You see,' he said, putting out a hand to encourage her to follow him, 'how easy it is!' It was indeed easy, Arrietty agreed, and what fun it all was!

'Now,' Peagreen went on, 'let's see what Mrs W. has got under these covers . . .'

They lifted up the first wire-mesh cover (to Arrietty's surprise it was quite light) and peered beneath it: two partridges, plucked and dressed for the table. They dropped the cover rather quickly: neither of them liked the smell. Next, they lifted the corner of a white napkin: a crusty pie, gleaming and golden. 'No good to us,' said Peagreen, 'unless they've cut into it first.' All the same, Arrietty broke off the tiniest edge of pastry; light as a feather it was, and tasted delicious. She was aware suddenly of feeling very hungry: neither she nor her parents had touched the food which Spiller had brought them in the ashtray, and that now seemed a long time ago.

Under another cover, were the appetizing remains of a roast sirloin of beef. Arrietty ate up several small crispy bits which had fallen on to the dish.

They then found a large piece of cheddar cheese on a cheese board behind the sirloin. It looked deliciously moist and crumbly. Arrietty and Peagreen ate up the crumbs, carefully putting back the piece of butter muslin with which it had been covered. There was a glass jar of celery, crisp and scraped clean of its fibres. They broke off a little piece of this. Arrietty began to feel appeased. They bypassed the ham bone, although quite a lot of ham still adhered to it, but were tempted by a wire tray of freshly baked rock cakes, gleaming here and there with currants. 'We can't interfere much with cakes,' Peagreen advised her, 'there are exactly a dozen. She would be sure to wonder . . .' So they each dug out a currant and passed on to a row of small glass jars. They contained something pinkish and were topped with melted butter. 'Her potted meat,' said Peagreen, 'she sells it round the village and very good it is. But we can't touch these either, now the butter's hardened. Have you seen enough now?'

'What's in that brown bowl?' asked Arrietty, standing on tiptoe, but even then the sides were too high for her to see into it.

'Eggs,' said Peagreen, 'but they're no good to us either: you can't climb about carrying raw eggs.' He was making his way back among the various dishes towards the latticed window. 'Come on – I'll show you the way to climb down.'

Arrietty, following him, asked rather fearfully, 'Down to the floor?'

'Yes, we can go back by the old kitchen. And there's something else I want to show you . . .'

It was easy work climbing down the wine rack: a swift slide down on the wooden uprights, a short rest on the edge of the curved hole made to house each bottle; another slide or two and then they were on the floor. Climbing up might be harder, Arrietty thought to herself, but Peagreen showed her a dusty length of knotted rope attached to a nail below the lip of the shelf. Under the shadow of the windowsill, it had been hardly visible against the dark wood. 'You keep your feet to the uprights where they're built against the wall and sort of walk, and you're up in a minute. Rather like rock climbing but a lot easier . . .'

Arrietty remembered Pod's injunctions: 'A human bean could move that,' she pointed out (she was still determined to call them 'beans').

'They could, but they don't,' said Peagreen. 'They hardly ever look lower than the food shelves, except when they sweep the floor. And that's not often . . .' He was crossing the stone flagstones towards the locked bin which stood nearest the window. 'This is the thing I wanted to show you.' He went up to the corner where the front of the bin joined the white-washed wall. Arrietty came beside him. It was a dark corner, still in the shadow of the windowsill above. 'It's this,' said Peagreen, putting out a hand; and Arrietty saw that there was a crack in the plaster at floor level where the wood was joined on to the wall. 'It's always been there,' said Peagreen, 'but I widened it a bit: you can just slide through –' He proceeded to do so. 'Come on,' he called from inside the bin, his voice sounding curiously hollow. It was a bit of a squash, but she managed to creep in after him. If, by scraping away some of the wall plaster, he had widened the crack, he had not widened it very much.

Inside, it was very dark. She was aware of an empty, imprisoning vastness and a clean, half-familiar smell. But it was warm. 'Come and feel this back wall,' said Peagreen. She followed him and laid her hands on the smooth, unseen surface. 'It *is* warm, isn't it?' said Peagreen, in a whisper. 'She keeps a good fire up.'

'What did they store in here?' asked Arrietty. She also spoke in a whisper – something to do with the enclosure and vastness of the unseen space about them

'Soap,' said Peagreen, 'kitchen soap. In the old days, they used to make their own. Long soft blocks of it. They stored it in here to dry out. There's still a block of it there in a corner. Hard as nails, it is now. I'll show you later, when I get a bit of candle . . .'

'What are you going to use this place for?' asked Arrietty, after a moment.

'To keep warm in winter. I've got all summer to fix it up a bit. I'll get in a stock of candle ends and food will be no problem. If I can get hold of more paper, I'll most likely get on with my book.'

Arrietty was becoming more and more impressed. So he wrote poems, he painted pictures, and now he was writing a book! 'What's it about, your book?' she asked, after a moment.

'Well,' he said carelessly, 'I suppose it's a sort of history of the Overmantels. After all they've been in this house longer than any set of human beings have. Generation after generation. They've seen all the changes . . .'

Arrietty was silent again, her hands on the warm wall. She was thinking hard. 'Who's going to read your book?' she asked at last. 'I mean, so few borrowers can read or write.'

'That's true,' admitted Peagreen glumly. 'I suppose it depended on where you were brought up. In the old days, in a house like this, the human children had tutors and governesses and lesson books: the borrowers soon picked things up. My grandfather knew Greek and Latin. Up to a point . . .' he added, as though determined to be truthful. Then he seemed to cheer up a little. 'But you never know — there might be someone.'

Arrietty seemed less sure. 'A human bean I once knew,' she said slowly, 'said we were dying out. That the whole race of borrowers was dying out.' She was thinking of The Boy at Firbank.

Peagreen was silent for a moment, and then he said quietly, 'That may be so.' Then suddenly he seemed to throw such thoughts aside. 'But anyway we're here now! Come on, I'll take you back through the old kitchen . . .'

CHAPTER FOURTEEN

Once through the larder door, Arrietty stood still and looked about her. Peagreen came beside her and in a protective kind of way slid a hand under her elbow. Before them stretched a stone-flagged passage ending in what looked like an outside door. Beside this, a wooden staircase rose up, with bare, scrubbed treads, under which there seemed to be some kind of built-in cupboard. 'Those stairs lead up to their bedroom,' Peagreen whispered, 'and other rooms beyond.' Why were they still whispering? Because, thought Arrietty, they both felt themselves to be in some alien part of the house, a part in which the dreaded human beings lived out their mysterious existence.

Along the left-hand side of the passage hung a row of bells on coiled steel springs with, beyond them, some kind of cabinet. She knew what these were. Many a time at Firbank she had heard such bells, rung to summon Mrs Driver.

On the opposite side, facing the bells, were several doors, all closed. Immediately beside them, on their right, another door stood ajar and opposite it, on their left, a matching door which had no latch and was secured, Arrietty noticed, by a loop of wire fixed to a nail in the upright.

'What's in there?' she asked.

'It's the old game larder,' Peagreen told her, 'they don't use it now.'

'Can I look in?' She had seen that, in spite of the loop of wire, the door was not quite closed.

'If you like,' said Peagreen.

She tiptoed up and peered through the crack, and then she slipped inside. Peagreen followed.

It was a vast shadowy jumble of a place, lit by a grimy window just below a ceiling from which, she saw, hung row upon row of hooks. And something else – it looked like a longish log – hung, slightly on a slope, on two chains suspended on very stout hooks.

'What's that?' she asked.

'For hanging venison. You could hang a whole deer on that – with the legs hanging down each side . . .'

'A whole deer! Whatever for?'

'To eat – as soon as it got a bit smelly.' He thought a moment. 'Or perhaps they hung it the other way up with the four legs tied together. I don't really know: it was all before my time, you see. I only know they had a zinc bath underneath to catch the blood . . .'

'How horrible!'

Peagreen shrugged. 'They were horrible,' he said.

Arrietty shuddered and, turning her eyes away from the deer sling, glanced at several rows of musty antlers which hung against the wall. More dead deer, she supposed – used as hooks for hanging other game. She turned then to examine the jumble of objects on the floor: broken garden chairs, stained dressers, half-used pots of paint or distemper, an ancient kitchen stove which had lost a leg, slanting drunkenly to one side, old stone hot-water-bottles, two paint-splashed step-ladders -- one tall, one short – the top part of a grandfather clock, various bags

153

which seemed to contain tools, battered tins, cardboard boxes . . .

'What a mess,' she said to Peagreen

'A useful mess,' he replied.

She could see that. Her father would find it a gold mine. 'Are these the paints you use for your pictures?'

'No,' Peagreen laughed but he sounded rather scornful, 'there was an artist chappie staying here, left a lot of half-used tubes behind. And,' he added, 'quite a decent roll of canvas. We'd better get on now, we said we wouldn't be long . . .'

They slid out sideways. As they stood once again in the passage, Peagreen pointed out the various doors: 'That one, right at the end, used to be called "the tradesmen's entrance". It's the one the Whitlaces use now – the front door is hardly ever opened. That door beside the foot of the stairs was the servants' hall but the Whitlaces use it now as their sitting-room. The next one along was the butler's pantry, next to that is the one that leads to the cellar steps, and this one here –' he crossed the passage to the door opposite the old game larder, '– is the old kitchen.'

As Arrietty had noticed when she had first seen it, this door stood slightly ajar. 'What would happen if they closed it?' she asked, as she followed in Peagreen's wake. 'I mean if you wanted to get to the larder by way of the old kitchen?'

He paused. 'It wouldn't make any difference,' he said, 'you can see how cracked and worn these stones are – after years and years of cooks and kitchen-maids trotting backwards and forwards to the larders. Wainscot just took out a cracked piece of paving from below the door. Say the door's shut, you can crawl underneath it. A bit inconvenient at times. It depends what you're carrying . . .'

And Arrietty, looking down, could see the missing piece of stone had left a small pit.

They were in the kitchen now, almost as dark and gloomy as the game larder, lit only by a long narrow window set high in a farther wall. The floor seemed to go on and on, the stone flags patched up here and there with dingy-looking concrete. Immediately on her right, as she stood just within the doorway, she saw the great black stove. It seemed to be a slightly newer model of the one discarded in the game larder except, in this case, the surface gleamed and shone and gave out a heartening warmth. Beside it stood a roughly made table covered with oil-cloth, on which stood an earthen jar filled with wooden spoons. On one end of the stove stood a large copper stockpot. It, too, was polished and gleaming. A faint wisp of steam escaped from under the lid, and with it a savoury smell.

'It's better really –' Peagreen was saying, '– to go round this kitchen keeping close in to the walls. But as the human beings are out and, perhaps, your family waiting, do you think you could face the open floor?'

Arrietty looked across the vast expanse where, she realized, there was no hope of cover. Almost opposite, in the far distance it seemed, she saw the outline of a door. 'If you think it's all right,' she said uncertainly. Peagreen, she remembered, could not walk very quickly.

'Then come on,' he said, 'let's chance it, for once.

It's a longish walk if you have to stick to the walls . . .'

It seemed a longish walk anyway, and Arrietty had to fight an almost overwhelming instinct to run, in order to match her steps to Peagreen's. Never in her whole life had she felt so exposed as she did on this journey across the vast, disused kitchen, where only the stove and the wooden table created a kind of warm oasis.

As at last they approached the far door, she could make out some patches of cloth hanging loosely on its surface. Green baize? Yes, that was it: it was (or might have been) a padded, baize door like the one she remembered at Firbank. Yes, now she could see the rusty brass studs which once had secured the padding. Did all old houses have them, she wondered, to keep out the noise and smells from the kitchen? But, on this particular door, the baize was stained and motheaten, and some of it hung in tatters. She also noticed, as they drew closer, that the door swung slightly in the draught.

Arrietty stopped sharply in her tracks. She gripped Peagreen's arm. From somewhere far behind them, she had heard a sound, the fiddling of a key in a lock. Peagreen had heard it too. Both stood rigid as they caught the mutter of voices. A far door slammed to, and footsteps echoed loudly in the stone-flagged passage. Another door opened and the footsteps died away.

'It's all right,' breathed Peagreen, 'they've gone into the annexe. Come on! We'd better hurry –'

They had barely taken three paces when, once again, they froze. This time they heard the voice more clearly as the footsteps clattered out again. It was a woman's voice, calling back to someone: '. . . must just take a look at my stew.' And the footsteps came hurrying nearer.

Like a shot thing, Peagreen dropped to the floor, pulling Arrietty with him. 'Don't move,' he breathed in her ear, as they lay there prostrate. 'Not a muscle!'

Arrietty's heart was beating wildly. She heard the scrape of wood across the flagstones. The kitchen door through which they had sidled had been flung open more widely. Then the footsteps paused. It was a sudden, startled pause. They had been seen.

There were a few moments of complete silence, before the footsteps began cautiously to approach them. A thought flew through Arrietty's mind as she lay there, rigid with terror: Mrs Whitlace had seen something but, in this dim light and at that distance, she could not quite make out what it was . . .

At that moment there was a sudden hiss from the stove. Then a spitting sound, the clumsy bumping of a lid, and the acrid smell of burning fat. Lying there, unable to see or even turn her head, she heard the sudden rush of feet towards the stove, the sound of some heavy object pushed, with short gasps, across some uneven surface, followed by a sharp cry of pain. The hissing ceased immediately and Arrietty heard a faint whimper as the footsteps hurried away into the passage.

Peagreen sprang to his feet, more deftly than Arrietty would have believed possible. He seized her wrist, pulling her up beside him. 'Come,' he said, 'quickly, quickly!'

They reached the broken baize door which swung, rather drunkenly, to Peagreen's light touch and suddenly, almost magically it seemed, they were in the sunlight of the long main hall.

Arrietty, white and trembling, leaned against the outer jamb of the door.

'I'm sorry,' Peagreen was saying, 'I'm tremendously sorry. We should have gone around by the walls –'

'What happened?' asked Arrietty in a faint voice.

'She burned herself. Or scalded herself. Or something. It's all right. We're safe now. Whitlace will be seeing to her hand. It's all right, Arrietty. Neither of them would come along here . . . at least, not for the moment anyway.' He put a hand under her elbow and began to lead her down the hall. He still looked very distressed but, all the same, he tried to distract her, pausing at the foot of the great stairway. 'The drawing-room's up there,' he told her, 'they used to call it the saloon. And all kinds of other rooms. You can get to some of them from outside by climbing the ivy . . .'

But Arrietty did not seem to look at anything, her troubled eyes were gazing straight ahead. She was still aware of the acrid smell of burned stew. Yes, that was what these baize doors were for: to keep out such smells.

'And here's the front door,' Peagreen went on. 'I think you've seen it from outside. And there's the telephone, on the windowsill. With its paper and pad. I borrow my paper from there and the pencil when it gets down to a stub.'

Arrietty turned then, her eyes suddenly wide. 'Supposing it rang?'

'They'd let it ring,' Peagreen said. 'Come along.' He named several rooms on the left as they passed

by the doors: dining-room, gun-room, smoking-
room . . . 'All locked,' he told her.

'And what's that open door at the end?'

'Surely you know?' said Peagreen.

'How could I?'

'It's the library.'

Arrietty's face lost its sleep-walking expression.
'So we've come right round?' she said in a relieved
voice.

'Yes, we've come right round. And now you've
seen how your father can get to the larder without
having to go out of doors.'

'That's what I can't bear,' said Arrietty, as they
approached the open door. 'I can't bear the thought
of my father crossing that great, empty terrible floor
– with no cover anywhere!'

'He'll go at night – when they're safely upstairs
and asleep. That's what I always did. They never
stir once they've gone upstairs. Dog-tired, they are,
by then.'

Once inside the library, Arrietty relaxed. It was
strange to look down the long room from this
unfamiliar end. Through the glass doors, she could
see a strip of the conservatory, and into the garden
beyond. Arrietty made a mental note of this danger
zone. In future they would have to be careful to
keep on either side of it.

She paused for a moment to examine the middle
window seat: their future home! Were her parents
still inside, she wondered, or had Pod by this time
learned all the tricks of the grating? Peagreen, by
the fireplace, guessed her thoughts. 'They won't be
in there,' he said, examining the fire surround, 'the
loose tile's back in its place. And your father's a wise

man,' he went on, 'he wouldn't have left the grating open. They must be in the conservatory . . .'

As they came through the glass doors, Arrietty noticed that all the floor tiles were neatly back in place. Her mother was by the stove, holding the tin ashtray as though it were a very large tray. 'Oh, there you are!' she said, with evident relief. 'What an age you've been! We've kept a little food back for you. I was just going to put it away. Your father's very strict now about leaving things about . . .'

'Where *is* Papa?' asked Arrietty.

Homily nodded towards the garden. 'Out there: he's a bit worried about Spiller –'

'Hasn't Spiller turned up?'

'Not a sign of him.'

'Oh dear . . .' exclaimed Arrietty unhappily. She turned towards Peagreen, but found he was no longer beside her. He was limping across the library towards the door which led to the hall. 'Oh, Peagreen,' she cried, 'where are you going? Do come back!' Then she clapped her hand to her mouth, aware she had called out too loudly.

He turned and glanced at her, almost shame-facedly, and then his gaze flew to her mother. 'I'll be back later,' he mumbled and turned away again.

So that was it, Arrietty realized suddenly: he did not, at that moment, wish to face either of her parents. He had taken a risk with their precious child's safety and was keenly aware of it now. She watched him go without another word: she would reassure him later.

Homily was still talking away. 'If anything has happened to Spiller or his boat . . .'

'I know, I know!' cut in Arrietty, 'I'll go and speak to Papa.'

'Don't *you* disappear, too –' Homily called after her, as Arrietty made for the hole under the door.

Arrietty wove her way quickly through the weeds and grasses, and there was Pod on the path. He was standing quite still. 'Papa –' she called softly, as she emerged from the weeds. He did not turn.

'I'm looking at the moon,' he said. And, as Arrietty came beside him, puzzled because it was still daylight, Pod went on, 'Have you ever seen such a moon? And not a cloud in the sky! What a waste . . . what a waste!'

Arrietty never *had* seen such a moon. It hung pallidly in the sky, from which the colour was slowly draining, like a ghostly tennis ball.

'We couldn't have had a better moon,' said Pod. 'Not if we'd ordered it. Crossing the lawn to that river . . . all that unpacking. We'll need every bit of light we can get. And no rain. By tomorrow, the weather might change . . .'

Arrietty was silent. Then, after a while, she said, 'Peagreen has a truck.'

'Maybe,' said Pod, 'but a truck doesn't give light. And it's light we want. But where is Spiller?'

Arrietty pulled sharply on her father's arm. 'Look! I think . . . that's him, isn't it? He's coming now . . .'

Indeed, it was Spiller, coming round the corner of the house, dragging his soap-dish behind him! And, as if turned to stone, Pod awaited his approach. His relief, Arrietty sensed, was too great for words.

'Oh, there you are,' he said in a carefully composed voice as Spiller came beside them. 'What have you got in that?'

'Your tools,' said Spiller, 'and I made a new quiver.' Spiller's quivers were always made of short pieces of hollow bamboo, plenty of which grew on some marshy ground near the lake.

'You've been down to the boat?' exclaimed Pod.

'I brought the boat up here.'

'Up here! You mean this end of the lake?'

'It's there among the rushes. Thought it would be quicker unpacking. To have it nearer, like.'

'So that's what you've been doing all day!' Pod stared at him. 'But how did you know we had decided to stay?'

'He offered you a house,' said Spiller simply.

There was an amazed silence: he had known they would accept. Spiller, she realized, with his sharp wild instincts, understood them better than they understood themselves. And now, with the heavily laden boat so near, how much easier he had made their move!

'Well I never!' said Pod and a slow smile spread over his face. 'Nothing to do now but wait for the night . . .' He sighed a deep, happy sigh. 'Have you had anything to eat?'

'I sucked a robin's egg,' said Spiller.

'That's not enough. Better come inside and see what Homily can find.' He nodded towards the soap-box. 'You can push that thing into the weeds . . .'

When they had made their way in through the hole, Arrietty ran eagerly to her mother, seizing her by both hands. 'Oh Mother, wonderful news! Spiller's back! And Papa says we can move tonight – everything's quite near! And –'

163

But, just then, the telephone shrilled. Homily, about to speak, turned round in a startled way. She had been standing near the stove. All four of them froze into stillness, their eyes on the library door. The telephone rang out four times and then came the slow advance of heavy footsteps. None of the borrowers moved.

A man's voice said, 'Hello –' There was a short silence, before the deep voice went on: 'Not tomorrow, she can't.' Again there was silence while, in Arrietty's imagination, some unknown female voice must still be twittering on. Then Whitlace said, 'She's hurt her hand, see . . .' Another silence. Then Whitlace said (it *must* be Whitlace), 'Maybe the day after tomorrow.' Another small silence. An embarrassed grunt from Whitlace (he was not one for the telephone) and they heard him replace the receiver. The footsteps moved away.

'They're back,' said Pod, as soon as there was silence again. 'At least, *He* is.'

Homily turned a glowing face towards Spiller, 'Oh, Spiller!' she almost gushed. 'It's good to see you, that I must say!' She ran towards him but stopped in sudden confusion. Had she been going to kiss him, Arrietty wondered? Not very likely, she decided, remembering how often in the past her mother had disapproved of Spiller. All the same, with Homily, one never knew . . .

Pod was looking thoughtful. 'It might be safer,' he said at last, 'if we waited out of doors.'

'Waited for what?' asked Homily.

'For the night,' said Pod.

'Oh, that lawn!' exclaimed Homily. 'Crossing it once by daylight – that was bad enough, but crossing *twice* by night! Not sure if I can face it, Pod . . .'

'You won't have to,' said Pod, and he told her about the boat. She listened wide-eyed, then turned again towards Spiller. Was it going to happen now, Arrietty wondered, that kiss? But no – something impassive in Spiller's expression seemed to put her off. 'Thank you, Spiller,' was all she said. 'Thank you very much.'

Pod looked up through the glass panes. 'The light's fading already, as you might say. We won't have so long to wait. Now, Homily, you and Arrietty go outside. Take something to wrap round you. And sit quietly in the grass at the edge of the path. Spiller and I will join you later. Spiller, will you come with me and give me a hand? I've got to open the grating while we've still got a bit of light indoors.'

They all did as they had been asked. Quietly and with no fuss. Although it was a bit of a struggle to bundle one of Miss Menzies' feather quilts through the narrow hole under the door. But it was a mild and beautiful evening for so early in April and it was a joy to breathe in the soft air. As they settled themselves among the grasses, the coverlet round their shoulders, Arrietty looked up at the moon. It was becoming golden, and the sky around it turning a gentle grey. There were sleepy murmurs with a few sharp, quarrelsome high-notes as the birds, in the bushes opposite, began to settle in for the night. Arrietty slipped an arm below her mother's and gave it a comforting squeeze. Homily squeezed hers back. After that, they sat in silence, each busy with their very different thoughts.

By the time that Pod and Spiller joined them, the moon had become quite bright. 'But the shadows will be black,' he told them, as he squatted down. 'We must treat the shadows as cover.' Spiller squatted beside him, bow in hand and a quiver full of arrows at his back.

Pod, his hands linked upon his knees, was whistling softly, through his teeth. It was an irritating sound but Arrietty knew it of old: it meant that he was happy. All the same, after a while, she said, 'Hush, Papa . . .' and laid a hand upon his knee. She had heard another sound, a good deal farther away. 'Listen!' she said.

It was a faint squeaking; very faint, but gradually growing clearer. After a moment or two, she recognized the sound. 'It's Peagreen with his truck,' she whispered. They watched and waited until, at last, the tiny figure appeared in the middle of the path, indistinct in the strange half-light of dusk and brightening moon. He stood for a moment, undecided, by the door of the conservatory. He could not see them, half hidden as they were by the shadows of the grasses.

'Peagreen –' Arrietty called softly. He started and looked about, and then he came towards them. He seemed surprised to see them, sitting there in a row.

'We're moving in tonight,' Arrietty told him in a whisper.

'I guessed you might be,' he said, sitting down beside her. 'I saw Spiller passing the corner of the house, and I saw the size of the moon.' He kicked out a foot towards his truck, 'So I brought this thing along.'

'And very useful, too,' said Pod, leaning forward to see it better.

'It's yours, if you want it,' Peagreen said. 'Where I'm living now, I don't really need it.'

'Well, we could share it, like,' said Pod, and, still leaning forward to get a better view of Peagreen, he explained to him about the position of the boat and Spiller's selfless journey. 'With the grating open and the five of us to help, we can move that stuff within the hour.' He stood up and looked about him: in that strangely blended half-light, nothing looked very distinct. 'I don't see,' he said, turning round to them, 'why we shouldn't get going now. You see –' He broke off suddenly and dropped to the ground. An owl had hooted uncomfortably near.

'Oh, my goodness . . .' muttered Homily, clinging more tightly to Arrietty's arm. Peagreen remained calm. 'It's all right,' he said, 'but it's better not to move just yet.'

'Why did he say it's all right?' Homily whispered to Arrietty, in a trembling voice.

167

Peagreen heard her. 'You'll see in a minute,' he said. 'Keep your eyes on the top of that cedar tree.'

They all stared at the cedar tree, which was now lit up by the moon. Pod eased himself into a more comfortable position. After a while, he asked in a whisper, 'Are there many of them?'

'No,' whispered Peagreen, 'only that one, for the moment. But there's another one across the valley. This one will call again. In a minute or two, you'll hear the female answer . . .'

It was just as he said: the owl near them hooted again and, after a few tense listening seconds, they heard the distant reply: a faint echo. 'This can go on for quite a while,' said Peagreen. It did, a weaving shuttle of sound above the sleeping fields. Or were they sleeping? Had the night things begun to come out? Arrietty thought uncomfortably of foxes. 'It's a blessing,' whispered Homily, 'that we don't have to cross all that grassland.'

'There he goes . . .' said Peagreen. Had Arrietty seen that noiseless shadow, or had she imagined it? Pod had seen it: that was for sure. 'A tawny owl,' he said, 'but a big one.' He stood up. 'Now we can get going.'

Peagreen stood up, too. 'Yes,' he said, '*he* won't be back before dawn.'

'If that's his lady-love across the valley,' said Homily letting go of Arrietty's arm, 'I wish he'd move in with her.'

'He may,' said Peagreen, laughing, as he helped her to her feet.

CHAPTER FIFTEEN

Mr and Mrs Platter had also seen the moon. They were busy in the kitchen, preparing for their second night's 'vigil'. Mrs Platter had finished making the sandwiches and was sitting down waiting for the eggs, which were boiling noisily on the stove. Mr Platter, sitting opposite, was oiling a pair of wire-cutters. 'We can put the picnic in the cat-basket,' he said.

Mrs Platter blew her nose. 'Oh, Sidney,' she said, 'I've got a dreadful cold. I'm not sure that I'm fit to go.'

'There won't be any rain tonight, Mabel. You've seen the sky. And you've seen the moon.'

'I know, Sidney, but all the same . . .' She was going to add that she was not exactly built for sitting in a small boat, hour after hour, on a narrow wooden seat, but thought better of it; she knew it would not move him. Instead she said, 'Say you went on your own, I could have a nice hot breakfast ready for you in the morning?' Mr Platter did not reply: he was busily shutting and opening the wire-cutters. So Mrs Platter, greatly daring, went on, 'And I have a feeling that they won't be there tonight.'

Mr Platter carefully wiped the wire-cutters with an oily rag, and laid them down on the table beside the cat-basket. Then he sat back and looked across at her. His eyes were steely. 'Why should you think that?' he asked coldly.

'Because,' said Mrs Platter, 'they may have come and gone. Or –'

Mr Platter took up a blunt-nosed chisel, and ran a finger along its edge. 'We'll soon find that out,' he said.

'Oh, Sidney! What are you planning to do?'

'Take the roof off their house,' he said.

It was Mrs Platter's turn to stare. 'You mean go right up into the model village?'

'That's what I mean,' said Mr Platter, and he laid down the chisel.

'But you can't walk about in that village,' objected Mrs Platter, 'those silly little streets are too narrow: you couldn't get one foot before another!'

'We can try,' said Mr Platter.

'We'd be sure to break something. The public only view it from that concrete catwalk . . .'

'We aren't the public,' said Mr Platter. He laid both hands firmly on the table and leaned towards her, staring with a cold kind of anger into her dismayed face.

'I don't think, Mabel,' he said, 'that, *even now*, you begin to understand the real seriousness of all this: our whole future depends on our catching these creatures! And I shall need you beside me, with the cat-basket, open.'

'We managed all right before we had them . . .' faltered Mrs Platter.

'Did we?' said Mr Platter. 'Did we, Mabel? You know the Riverside Teas were falling off. And that most of the tourists were going to Abel Pott. Said his model village was more picturesque, or some such nonsense. Ours was far more modern. And, as you noticed yourself, there haven't been many funerals lately. And no new houses built since we finished the council estate. The only job on our list at the moment is clearing Lady Mullings' roof gutters . . .' There was something about Mr Platter's expression which really alarmed Mrs Platter: she had never seen him quite so disturbed. It could not be only because he had taken so much time and trouble in constructing the beautiful glass-fronted case in which he had hoped to exhibit such rare specimens: there was something coldly desperate about his whole attitude.

'We're not exactly in want, Sidney,' she reminded him, 'we've got our savings.'

'Our savings!' he exclaimed scornfully. 'Our savings! What are our puny little savings compared to the kind of fortune we had here in our hands?' He opened his hands widely, and then dropped them again. Mrs Platter looked more and more alarmed: their savings, to her certain knowledge, amounted to several thousand pounds. 'You get this into your head, Mabel,' he went on, 'no one in the whole world believes such creatures exist – not until they see them, with their own eyes, walking and talking and eating . . .'

'Not going to the lavatory, Sidney: you made them a little bathroom. But –' she repeated the word: '*but* you must remember that they may huddle in that back place all day. And never come out, like some of those animals in the zoo . . .'

'Oh, I'd think of something to make them come out – at least in front of the public. Something electric, perhaps. After midnight, I don't care much what they do so long as they're on show in the morning.'

'But how can we hope to find them, Sidney dear?' She still found his mood rather frightening. 'Say, they're not in the model village? Five or six inches high, they could slip into any corner.'

'We shall find them in the end,' he said slowly, stressing every word, 'however long it takes, because we are the only living people who know of their existence!'

'Miss Menzies knows of their existence . . .'

'And who is Miss Menzies? A foolish spinster lady who couldn't say boo to a goose!' He laughed. 'And even if she did, the goose wouldn't take any notice. No, I'm not frightened of Miss Menzies, Mabel, nor any of her ilk.' He rose from the table, and she was glad to see him calmer. 'Well, we'd better get going. It's a mild night . . .'

He put the wire-cutters and chisel into the cat-basket. Mrs Platter added the sandwiches and a bottle of cold tea. 'Would you like a piece of cake?' she asked him. But he did not seem to hear her, so, picking up her coat, she followed him quietly out through the front door.

In spite of the mild weather, the tranquil moon-light and the uneventful run downstream, the Platters' evening did not turn out to be a particularly pleasant one. First, they had to wait for Abel Pott to put his lamp out. 'Staying up late tonight,' muttered Mr Platter. 'Hope he hasn't got visitors . . .' Then, on the upper road behind Mr Pott's thatched cottage, they saw a figure on a bicycle. As it passed by, too slowly for Mr Platter's comfort, he recognized the tall headgear of a policeman. What was Mr Pomfret doing out so late, Mr Platter wondered?

'Perhaps,' said Mrs Platter, perched uncomfortably on her narrow seat, 'he takes a look round like this every evening . . .'

'Well, anyway,' said Mr Platter, as the bicycle passed out of sight, 'we can get on quietly with the wire cutting.'

Their boat was moored to an iron upright, against which the wire fencing had been stretched and nailed to a formidable tightness. At the first cut, the wire flew back with a loud ping. In the utter quietness of that peaceful night, and to the ears of the Platters, it sounded as loud as a pistol shot. 'Better we wait until his light's out . . .' whispered Mrs Platter.

Mr Platter sat down again, nervously tapping the wire-cutters against his knee, his eyes on that unwelcome light in Mr Pott's window. 'Say we had our little bit of supper now?' suggested Mrs Platter in a whisper. 'And it would leave us a bit more room in the cat-basket.'

Mr Platter nodded impatiently. But even the unwrapping of the sandwiches (cold fried bacon tonight) created a rustle and a stir in the uncanny moonlit silence. Mrs Platter had forgotten to bring a cup, so they drank their cold tea from the bottle. They would have preferred something hot, but Thermos flasks, only just invented, were expensive items in those days – bound in leather, with silver-plated tops. Mr and Mrs Platter had not yet heard of them.

And still the light glowed on. 'What can he be doing at this time of night?' Mr Platter muttered. 'He's usually in bed by eight-thirty at the latest. He *must* have visitors . . .'

But Mr Pott did not have visitors. Had they but

173

known it, he was seated quietly at his work table, his wooden leg stretched out before him, peering down in his short-sighted way at the delicate work in hand. This was the repainting of the tiny wicket gates, all of different shapes and sizes, which led into the miniature front gardens of his beloved model village. At Easter, he would reopen the village to the public and by that time every detail needed to be perfect.

At last, after what seemed hours to the Platters, the gentle lamplight was extinguished and, after another cautious wait, they both felt free to move. Mr Platter, fast and expert, soon freed the wire from the post. As it loosened, it did not ping so loudly, and he was able very soon to fold a section back.

'Now!' he said to Mrs Platter. And, taking the cat-basket from her, he helped her up the bank. It was slightly slippery from last night's rain but, at last, she was through the wire, and they could survey the miniature village by the light of the brilliant moon.

Mr Pott had set it on a slight slope, and the whole layout spread on the rise before them. The lines of the model railway glistened in the moonlight, and so did the slated roofs. The thatched roofs were a little dimmer but the tiny winding roads and lanes were snake-like chasms of blackest darkness. However, from where they stood, they could plainly see Vine Cottage, the house Miss Menzies had once fitted out for the borrowers. The question was: how best to get to it? 'Follow me,' said Mr Platter.

He chose roads wide enough to take the width of one foot, if each foot was placed carefully before the other. It was a finicky business but, at last, they stood beside the tiny house from where, six months ago, they had so heartlessly stolen the 'little people'. History was repeating itself, thought Mr Platter complacently, as he carefully inserted his chisel under the eaves of the roof. It came off surprisingly easily. Somebody must have 'been at it', Mr Platter decided as he stared down inside. He produced a torch from his pocket to see better.

The house was empty, abandoned. On the night they had captured the borrowers, it had been fully furnished: chairs, dressers, tables, cooking utensils, clothes in tiny doll's-house wardrobes. Now there was nothing, except the fixtures – a cooking stove and a tiny porcelain sink. Mrs Platter, peering down beside him, saw a scrap of white, beside the closed front door. She picked it out gingerly. It was a tiny apron, one which Homily had discarded in their rush to get away. She put it in her pocket.

Mr Platter swore. He swore quite loudly and rather rudely, which was quite unusual for him. He straightened up and stepped back angrily. There was a tinkle of breaking glass: he had put a careless heel through one of Mr Pott's miniature shop fronts.

'Hush, Sidney,' pleaded Mrs Platter in a hoarse whisper. She looked about her in a frightened way, and then she gave a gasp. 'Look! Abel Pott's put his light on again! Let's get out of here . . . Come, Sidney! Come quickly!'

Mr Platter turned sharply. Yes, there was the light – growing brighter every minute as Mr Pott turned up the wick. Mr Platter swore again and turned towards the river. In his disappointment and anger, all the houses between him and his boat seemed just a jumble to him now. He no longer bothered to seek out the roads. And Mrs Platter, feeling about for the cat-basket (it might, one day, be evidence against them), heard tinkles of breaking glass and sudden falls of masonry as Mr Platter made his clumsy way down the hill. She followed him, panting and crying and sometimes stumbling.

At last they reached the opened wire. 'Oh, Sidney –' sobbed Mrs Platter, '– he'll be out in a minute. I heard him unbolting the front door!'

Mr Platter, already in the boat, put out a hand; less to help her than to drag her in. She slipped on the mud and fell into the water. It was very shallow by the bank, and she soon climbed out again. But she had not been able to repress a slight scream. Mr Platter was fumbling for oars and took no more notice of her as she sat dripping in the stern. 'Oh, Sidney, he's coming after us! I know he is . . .'

'Let him come!' exclaimed Mr Platter fiercely. 'What do I care for old Abel Pott with his wooden leg. People have been found floating in the river before now . . .'

And with that, he began to row upstream.

Once safely back in their own house, Mrs Platter went straight through to the kitchen and pushed the large tea-kettle on to the hotter part of the stove. She raked up the embers beneath it until they began to glow red. Her cold felt much worse and she wondered if she had a temperature. She drove a hand into her coat pocket to find her handkerchief but pulled out Homily's rather grubby little apron instead. She tossed it on the table and felt in her other pocket. She found her handkerchief but it, too, was soaking wet.

'Would you like tea or cocoa?' she asked Mr Platter, who had followed her in. 'I'm going upstairs now to get into something dry . . .'

'Cocoa,' he said and picked up the little apron. He eyed it curiously. 'Oh, Mabel –' he called out just as she was reaching the door.

She turned back unwillingly. 'Yes?'

'What did you do with that other stuff they left behind upstairs?' He had the apron in his hand.

'Threw it away, of course, when I cleaned out the attic: there was nothing worth keeping . . .' and, before he could speak again, she had made her way towards the front hall.

Mr Platter sat down slowly. He was looking very thoughtful. He spread the small apron before him on the table, and stared at it musingly.

'Lady Mullings . . .?' he murmured to himself, and slowly, almost triumphantly, he began to smile.

CHAPTER SIXTEEN

Arrietty was to look back to that spring as one of the happiest periods of her life. Every day seemed full of excitement and interest, from that first night in their new home under the window seat when, worn out with carrying, they had slept at last in their own little beds among the cluttered piles of stacked furniture, to the week by week improvements instigated by Pod.

His inventiveness knew no bounds. He had his old tools and he constructed others and, as Arrietty

had foreseen, the jumble in the old game larder provided him with an almost endless supply of useful objects, more than even he could make use of or need.

The first priority was the construction of a kitchen within a kitchen for Homily. She hated cooking in that shadowy vastness where she said she felt as though she never knew what might be coming up behind her. First, he and Spiller and Arrietty moved the distant shelves nearer to the grill, replaced the pronged fork with a brass wheel (from the discarded grandfather clock in the game larder) set on a pivot so that Homily could turn it, varying the degrees of heat from the embers below. On the outer rim she could simmer; towards the spokes near the middle she could grill. A battered old tobacco tin, scoured out and hammered straight, once Pod had loosened the hinges and supplied it with a handle, provided a Dutch oven. He found two white tiles and constructed a small table to fit them. Homily was delighted with this: it was so easy to wipe down.

But how to wall it, this kitchen? How to enclose it in? This was Pod's great puzzle. There were plenty of strong old cardboard boxes in the game larder, tea chests, plywood and many odds and ends. But there seemed no way of introducing any large flat object through the very small openings which led into the chimney. The passage under the floorboards (now scrubbed and fresh-smelling) was far too narrow for any object large enough to serve as sides of a wall. The hard backs of two large atlases, such as Pod had seen on one of the library shelves, would have been ideal. But how to get them in? Except, perhaps, by climbing on the roof and dropping them down the chimney. But the getting of them up the side of the house on to the roof seemed too much labour to contemplate at this juncture. Besides, the chimneys themselves, where they emerged on the roof, might turn out to be too narrow.

It was Peagreen who solved the problem in the end. 'Supposing,' he said to Pod, 'you constructed a little cardboard shelter in some dark corner of the game larder? Then took it to pieces again, and I soaked the pieces in the birdbath and, when they had softened, we could roll them up, tie them with twine into . . . well . . . cylinders, you might say. We could then take those cylinders in through the grating and push them along the passage under the floor. Then build your little kitchen again round the fire in the old hearth. Keep a good cooking fire up for a day or two, and your walls would soon be stiff again . . .'

Pod was delighted, and very impressed. 'We'd have to flatten them out first, though,' he said.

'That'll be easy,' Peagreen told him, 'they'll be soaking wet. They'll almost flatten themselves out under their own weight of water. We can lay that book-cover down – the one that covers the hole to the steps – and walk about on it, say any of the cardboard started to curl up . . .'

Arrietty and Homily had been given the job of cleaning up the ancient hearthstones of the old chimneypiece, chopping and stacking the untidy piles of wood, sorting the tin lids and screw bottle-tops, on which it seemed the Wainscots had done their cooking. It was just a happy chance that Peagreen happened to be beside her when she was about to throw away a large charred tin lid contain-

ing something that looked like stiffened treacle.
'Don't throw that away!' he almost shouted. 'Let
me see it first . . .' Distastefully, Arrietty handed it
over and was surprised to see a slow smile spread
over Peagreen's face as he stooped to smell the
horrid-looking contents.

'It's some of Wainscot's resin mixture,' he told
her. 'It can be melted down again . . .' Triumphantly he carried the precious burden to a safe
corner. 'Your father will be pleased with this!'

The second brainwave came after the kitchen
partitions had been erected. The sides were glued
firmly together with the help of strong strips of
material cut by Pod from a dry – but grubby –
floorcloth, discarded by the caretakers. The little
room had no ceiling, so that any smoke from
Homily's fire would escape into the vast chimney
above. But Pod had made her a little door from a
small book called *Essays of Emerson*. He had removed
all the inside pages, glued the back of the book to
the cardboard wall, and had left the front cover to
swing to and fro against a small opening cut to the
right size.

All the same, for all Pod's cleverness and Peagreen's bright ideas, it did not look a particularly
cheerful kitchen. The cardboard walls, now they
stood erected, did not appear any too clean. There
were foot-marks on them here and there and, in
spite of Homily's efforts, they had collected grimy
smears when laid out to dry on the floor. One could
not wash so large an expanse of hearthstone with
drops of water collected, drip by drip, into an eye-
bath. One could only brush it, as thoroughly as one
could, with the heads of dried-up teazles.

It was then that Peagreen had his second brilliant idea. He remembered the roll of canvas on the top shelf of the library. It, too, formed a kind of cylinder. Tied and rolled, he could knock it to the floor. Pod would remove the loose tile in the fire surround and between them they could push the canvas through the gap.

No sooner thought of than achieved: Homily's kitchen became lined and shining white, and its enclosing walls even stronger. They pasted the canvas over the bookend, hiding it altogether, and now the little leather door looked what it was – a little leather door. 'And if ever the canvas should get a bit dingy with smoke,' Peagreen told them, 'there's plenty of whitewash in the game larder . . .'

'Maybe . . .' mused Pod, his eyes narrowing thoughtfully, 'later on, I'll fix some sort of a hood over the fire. But she'll be pleased enough with it as it is – for the time being . . .'

He smiled at Peagreen. Poets and painters might not be so 'good with their hands' (whatever that meant) but they certainly were good with ideas. 'Sure you won't need some of this canvas for yourself?' he asked.

'There's plenty over,' Peagreen told him, looking down in a satisfied way at the odds and ends on the floor.

Homily was unwilling to visit the Hendrearies until her kitchen was finished. 'The kitchen is the Heart of the Home,' she told Pod. 'I don't mind, for the moment, leaving all that stacked-up stuff in our living quarters. We can see to all that later at our leisure . . .'

*

And then, of course, there were the ghosts but, as Peagreen had prophesied, Arrietty soon got used to these. All the same, her attitude towards them differed a little from that of her parents and Peagreen: she never quite lost a sense of curiosity and wonder. Why should they suddenly appear and then, for no apparent reason, disappear and not be seen again for weeks? There seemed no logic in it.

She soon got used to The Footsteps. The first time she heard them was after the telephone had shrilled three times. Ready for flight into the conservatory, in case she heard the warning scamper of feet along the tiles of the front hall, after a short silence she heard instead a slow and ponderous tread which seemed, as she stood beside Peagreen in the library, to be coming down the main staircase. Who could it be? Not Mrs Whitlace's light, running steps, nor Mr Whitlace's slightly slower ones, unless, of course, he might be carrying something inordinately heavy? The footsteps grew louder as they seemed to cross the hall. She waited tensely for the lifting of the receiver and for some kind of human voice. But nothing happened beyond the sound of a dull kind of stumble, followed by a sudden silence.

She turned an alarmed face to Peagreen, and saw that he was laughing. 'Nobody's answered the telephone . . .' she whispered uneasily.

'Ghosts don't,' said Peagreen.

'Oh,' exclaimed Arrietty, 'was that . . .? Do you mean . . .?' She looked very scared.

'Those were The Footsteps. I told you about them.' He still seemed amused.

'But I don't understand. I mean, could they hear the telephone?'

'No, of course not,' said Peagreen. He was really laughing now. 'The telephone has nothing to do with it: it was just a coincidence.' He laid a hand on her arm. 'It's all right, Arrietty, there's nothing to be frightened about: the Whitlaces are out.'

Yes, Peagreen was quite right: the real danger lay with human beings – not with harmless noises, however unearthly they might seem. Feeling rather a fool, she walked off into the conservatory, which was filled with sunlight. But she never showed (or even felt) fear of The Footsteps again.

The second ghost was The Little Girl On The Stairs. Actually, during those first weeks, Arrietty did not see her. For one reason because she only appeared, slightly luminous, at night. And, for another, because Arrietty very seldom went into the front hall. On her rare visits to the larder, she preferred Peagreen's route along the ivy to the partly opened window. She really disliked that open, coverless trek across the vast kitchen floor and avoided it whenever she could. Pod had seen the vision regularly, on his nightly visits to collect old junk from the game larder. It was a little girl, dressed in her night clothes, crouched halfway up the curve of the main staircase. She seemed to be crying bitterly, although there was no sound. Pod had described her little nightcap, shaped like a baby's bonnet, tied neatly below her chin. She was there most nights, he thought, weeping for a favourite brother, 'who had somehow got himself shot . . .' Peagreen had told them. The faint, pale light she gave out helped him to find his bearings as he made his way through the darkness of the hall. He found her very useful.

Last, but not least, was The Poor Young Man.

On that first morning after their arrival at the rectory, having risen early, Arrietty had glanced into the library through the half-open glass doors which led into the conservatory. Although she had not taken it in at the time, she remembered now seeing something she had taken for a rolled-up rug, lying on the floor just in front of the fireplace. Then the squeaking wheels of Peagreen's trolley,

and the sudden appearance of Peagreen himself had made her forget all about it. She had never seen it since.

She remembered it again quite suddenly on the day when, the human beings being out, Peagreen – on the topmost of the library bookshelves – had manoeuvred the roll of white canvas so that it fell at the feet of Pod who had been waiting down below. She had turned away to the tap in the conservatory to get herself a drink of water and when she returned again to the doors of the library to see what was going on, Peagreen and Pod, one at each end of it, were carrying the roll towards the hole in the fire surround left by the missing tile.

But there was something between them and it. Again she took it for a rug, or a piece of rolled-up carpet, and went forward to see better. It was not a rug, or a piece of old rolled carpet; to her terror she saw it was a human being, stretched full length in front of the hearth. Asleep? Dead? She jumped back and screamed.

Pod, panting a little as he supported the back end of the roll, turned his head irritably. 'Oh, do be quiet, Arrietty! We've got to concentrate . . .'

Arrietty clapped her hand to her mouth, her eyes staring. 'Gently does it . . .' Pod was saying to Peagreen, who had not turned his head.

'Oh, Papa!' gasped Arrietty, 'whatever is it?'

'It's nothing,' said Pod. 'It's often there. You must have seen it. Lift your end up a bit, Peagreen. You've got the steps, remember. We've got to take it in a slant . . .' Then as if suddenly aware of Arrietty's distress, he turned his head towards her. 'It's all right, girl, no need to fuss – it's not a human being: a poor lad, they say, who shot himself. A kind of ghost, like. It won't hurt you. A bit higher, Peagreen, once you're inside the hole . . .'

Arrietty watched, dumbfounded, as Peagreen walked straight through the object on the floor. He and her father grew a little dim as they passed through the apparition, but her eyes could plainly follow the white gleam of the canvas.

At last, Peagreen emerged at the far side, and went on in through the hole. Pod, clearly visible again, followed. There was a lot of panting and grunting and a few muffled orders, and Arrietty was left alone with the ghost.

To her surprise, her first feeling was one of pity. They should not have walked through him like that. It showed – what did it show? – some kind of lack of respect: thinking of nothing but the 'job in hand'? But Peagreen – ? Well, she supposed that Peagreen, having lived at the rectory all his life, was so used to ghosts that he hardly noticed them.

Poor young man . . . She moved closer to look at his face. It was turned sideways, against the floor, and was very pale. Dark curls fell back against the boards. It was a beautiful face, the lips were gently parted and the long-lashed eyes seemed not quite closed. He wore a frilled shirt, knee-breeches and, looking back along the length of him, she could make out his buckled shoes. One arm was flung out sideways, the fingers curved as though they had held some object no longer to be seen. He looked very young. Why had he shot himself? What had made him so sad? But, even as she looked at him, her pity flowing over him, he began to disappear; to melt away into nothingness. It was, she felt, as though he had never been there. Perhaps he

187

never had? She was left staring at the floorboards and the familiar dark stain.

'Well, that's that . . .' said a cheerful voice. She looked up. It was Peagreen, appearing in the entrance to the hole and rubbing his hands in a satisfied way. 'I thought we might never get that great roll up the steps. But it was easy. One good thing about these old hearths is they do give one plenty of room.' He turned. 'Oh, here's your father. We'd better get the tile back now . . .'

Arrietty stared at Peagreen, her look was accusing. 'You shouldn't have walked through him like that –'

'But I didn't. Who? What do you mean?'

'That poor young man!'

Peagreen laughed. 'Oh, that! I thought you were referring to your father . . .'

'Of course I wasn't: you couldn't walk through my father.'

'No, I suppose one couldn't,' he moved towards her. 'But, Arrietty, that "poor young man" as you call him, wasn't really there at all: it was just a –' he hesitated, 'a photograph on air.' He thought a moment, 'Or on Time, if you prefer. We had to get that canvas through the hole . . .'

'Yes, I know. But you could have waited.'

'Oh, Arrietty, if we had to wait for ghosts to disappear or appear all the time, we'd never get in or out of anywhere in this house.' He half turned. 'Look, your father's struggling with that tile. I'd better go and help him –'

After that Arrietty was never frightened of 'the poor young man' again, but she was always careful to walk round him.

CHAPTER SEVENTEEN

The next excitement (as soon as Homily's kitchen was finished) was their long-delayed visit to the church.

'We can't put it off any longer,' Pod said to Homily, 'or Lupy will be offended. Spiller must have told them that we're here . . .'

'I don't intend to put it off any longer,' retorted Homily. 'Now my kitchen's finished, I'm ready to go anywhere.' She was very happy with her kitchen. 'And I'd like to see what sort of house they've got together. A church! Seems a funny kind of place to choose to live in . . . I mean, what is there to eat in a church?'

'Well, we'll see,' said Pod.

They chose a bright, clear morning without a threat of rain. The party consisted of Pod, Homily and Arrietty. Peagreen had excused himself, and Spiller was elsewhere. Homily had packed a few 'goodies' in a borrowing bag, so as not to arrive empty-handed and all three felt very cheerful. After all the days of gruelling work, this was an expedition – a welcome 'day off'.

It felt strange to be walking *away* from the rectory and down an unfamiliar path. Birds were building in the box hedge, and there was moss underfoot at edges of the gravel. Spiller had given them directions: 'When you see the vestry drain, that's your place.'

As they slipped through the palings of the wicket gate which led into the churchyard, Arrietty saw a little figure moving towards them on the edge of the path. 'Timmus!' she exclaimed and, leaving her more cautious parents standing, hurriedly dashed towards him. Yes, it was him – much thinner, a little taller, with a very brown sunburnt face. 'Oh, Timmus!' she exclaimed again, and was about to hug him but then she hesitated: he had become so still and so staring, as if he could not believe his eyes. 'Oh, Timmus, my Timmus . . .' she whispered again and laid an arm round his shoulders. Upon which, he stooped suddenly as though to pick up something on the ground. She stooped down beside him, her arm still about his shoulders.

'I thought I saw a grasshopper . . .' he mumbled, and she could hear a catch in his voice.

'Oh, Timmus . . .' she whispered, '. . . you're crying. Why are you crying?'

'I'm not crying,' he gulped. 'Of course I'm not crying . . .' Suddenly he turned his face towards her: it was aglow with happiness, but the tears were running down his cheeks. 'I thought I was never going to see you no more.'

'Any more . . .' said Arrietty from habit: she had always corrected Timmus's grammar.

'I was coming to find you,' he went on. 'I keep looking for you.'

'Right up to the rectory? Oh, Timmus, you'd never have found us, not in that great place: we're very hidden up there.' She had nothing to wipe his cheeks with, so she wiped them very gently with her fingers. 'And you might have got caught yourself!'

'What on earth are you two doing, crouched down there on the path?' Pod and Homily had come up beside them: 'How are you, Timmus?' Homily went on, as Arrietty and Timmus stood up. 'My, how you've grown! Come and give me a kiss.' Timmus did so: he was all smiles now. 'How did you know we were coming?'

'He didn't,' said Arrietty. 'He was on his way to the rectory to find us.'

Homily looked grave. 'Oh, you must never do that, Timmus, not on your own. You never know what you might find up at the rectory. A couple of human beans for a start! Is your mother in?'

'Yes, she's in,' he said. 'And my father, too.'

He led them to the drain beside the vestry wall. A lead pipe came out above it through a hole cut in the stones: there was plenty of room on one side of it for a borrower to squeeze past. Timmus went through first, agile as an eel. For the others it was stiffer going, but they soon found out the trick of it.

Inside, they found themselves beneath the stone sink, beside the rusty gas-ring. Here they paused and looked about them.

It was a largish room, and smelled faintly of stale cassocks. In the centre was a square table covered with a red plush cloth, against which several chairs were set. They were of the type usually found in kitchens. Exactly opposite to them, from where they stood, was a large oaken press set into the wall of the church. The original wall of the church, Pod realized; the vestry must have been added on at a much later date. The press was iron-studded and had a very large keyhole. On one side of the press stood a large, box-like piece of furniture which Pod learned later was a disused harmonium. This was piled, almost to the ceiling, with shabby hymn-books. On the other side of the press, was a tall old desk, on which stood an open ledger, an ink-well, and what he took to be a selection of old pens. To their right, a whole wall was taken up by cassocks and surplices hanging on hooks. To their left were floor-length curtains of faded mulberry plush. These hung on wooden rings, separating the vestry from the main church. In the far corner stood an ugly iron stove, usually described as a 'tortoise', whose pipe ran up through the ceiling.

They did not take all this in at first glance, because Timmus had run away from them across the flagstones. 'I'll just tell them you're here,' he called back, and disappeared into a dark, rectangular hole at the base of the harmonium.

'So that's where they live,' muttered Homily, 'I wonder what it's like inside.'

'Roomy,' said Pod.

After a few moments, Lupy appeared, wiping her hands on her apron – a thing, Homily noted, she would never have done in what might be called her grander days, when she had always been one to dress up smartly for visitors. She kissed Homily rather soberly, and then did the same to Pod. 'Welcome,' she said, with a gentle un-Lupyish smile, 'welcome to the house of the Lord . . .'

It was a strange greeting, Homily thought, as, equally soberly, she kissed Lupy back. At the same time, she noticed that Lupy had grown much thinner and had lost something of her bounce. 'Come in, come in . . .' she was saying, 'Hendreary and Timmus are lighting the candles. We've been expecting you this many a long day.'

Hendreary then appeared at the entrance hole, shaking out the flame of a match. Timmus came out beside his father; his brown little face was still aglow. There were further greetings and polite compliments as the visitors were ushered inside. Arrietty, Lupy declared, had become 'quite the young lady' and Homily herself was 'looking very well'.

The vast interior was ablaze with light, there were candle stubs in every type of container. These warmed the great room as well as lighting it and Homily, looking about her at the familiar pieces of furniture, thought these had gained elegance because of the ample space surrounding them: she hardly recognized the little snuff-box settee which once had been their own. What an age it had taken, she remembered, to pad and line it; but she felt very proud of it now.

She laid her small offering on one of the tables, and stiffly took a seat. Lupy bustled about and produced some sawn-off nutshells, which she carefully filled with wine. 'You can drink this,' she said, 'with a clear conscience, because it has not yet been blessed . . .' Homily again was puzzled by the oddness of this remark, but she took a sip of the wine.

'Or perhaps,' went on Lupy, 'you'd prefer gooseberry: my own make?'

'This is fine,' Pod assured her, taking a sip. 'Never *was* one for gooseberry wine – strong, gouty stuff . . .'

'Hendreary's very partial to it . . .'

'Hope it's partial to him,' said Pod. 'A bit too acid for me, like.'

Hendreary, Homily saw, was showing Pod round the premises. 'This,' he was saying, pointing out the entrance hole, 'is where the pedals used to be. Up there,' he raised his head to the heights above them, 'was where they had the bellows. but they took those out when they moved the broken harmonium to make room in the church for the organ. But we've still got the pipes: Lupy finds them useful for hanging the clothes to dry . . .'

'Hendreary looks very well,' said Homily, taking another delicate sip of wine. And Arrietty wondered why, when people had not met for some time, they must always tell each other they looked 'well'. To her, Uncle Hendreary looked more scrawny than ever, and his funny little tuft of a beard had become slightly grizzled. Did she herself look 'well', she wondered?

'He is, and he isn't,' Aunt Lupy was saying. 'With the boys away, he's finding the borrowing here rather heavy. But we manage,' she added brightly. 'Spiller brings us things, and the ladies are here twice a week . . .'

'What ladies?' asked Homily. She wondered if they were anything to do with 'the lord'.

'The ladies who do the flowers, and they always bring a little refreshment. And we have our ways with that. You see, they set their baskets down on the floor until Miss Menzies has laid the table. In fact, once they've finished the flowers they sit down to a very hearty tea.'

Arrietty jumped up from her chair. 'Miss Menzies?' she exclaimed. Only Timmus noticed her excitement.

'Yes, she's one of them. I know most of their names. There's Lady Mullings and Mrs Crabtree. And Mrs Witless, of course: she does most of the cooking; cakes, sausage-rolls – all those sort of things. And I must confess to you, Homily, that it's quite an entertainment to listen to their talk. I just sit here quietly and listen. Since we last met, Homily, I've learnt quite a lot about human beans. They come in all shapes and sizes. You wouldn't credit some of the things I've heard . . .'

Arrietty sat down again slowly and Timmus, on the arm of her chair, leaned against her. Something his mother had just said had obviously interested her: he wondered what it was. Her face was still a little pink.

'Does the lord live in the vestry?' asked Homily.

'Oh, dear me, no!' exclaimed Aunt Lupy – she sounded slightly shocked, 'the Lord only lives in the church.' Something about the way she pronounced the word 'Lord' warned Homily that it should be spoken as though it began with a capital letter. Lupy's normally loud voice had fallen respectfully to a note of awe. 'The vestry,' she said gently, as though explaining to a child, 'isn't really part of the church.'

'Oh, I see,' said Homily, although she didn't see at all. But she was determined not to reveal her ignorance.

'This church,' went on Lupy, 'by human standards, is a very small church. And the rector is inclined to be high. Because of this, we don't have a very large congregation . . .'

'Oh,' said Homily, but she could not quite see what the rector's height had to do with it.

'He does not use incense, or anything like that,' went on Lupy, 'but he does like lighted candles on the altar. And thank goodness for it, because we can always get hold of the leftovers.'

'So I see,' said Homily, looking round the brightly lighted room.

'Because of this, a great many of the locals go to the church at Went-le-Cray.'

'Because of the candles here on the altar?' asked Homily, astonished.

'Yes,' said Lupy, 'because the vicar at Went-le-Cray is very low.'

'Oh, I see,' said Homily again: a whole new world was opening before her. No wonder Lupy had said that human beans came in all 'shapes and sizes'.

'Of course, this "little" church – as they call it – is the more famous. It's far older, for one thing. And tourists come from all over the world to see the rood-screen . . .'

'Do they?' said Homily, wonderingly. She was feeling more and more puzzled.

'Of course, when we first came here, we went

through a few hard times. Yes, indeed. There was one week when we lived entirely on bull's-eyes –'

'*Bull's* eyes!' exclaimed Homily. Whatever was she going to hear next?

'They're those stripey sweets, shaped like pin-cushions – the choirboys always bring a few bags of them to suck during the sermons. The trouble with them is that when they get warm, they're apt to stick together . . .'

The choirboys or the bull's-eyes? Homily decided to keep silent.

'Little rascals, those choirboys. The gigglings, the goings-on in the vestry. And Timmus is beginning to pick up some of their expressions. And yet,' she went on, 'when they go into church, they sing like little angels; and look like them, too.'

Timmus rose from his seat and came beside his mother: he looked as though he wished to ask her a question. Lupy put an arm round him, affectionately but absentmindedly; she still had plenty more to tell Homily.

'Do you know, Homily, what were the first words we ever heard spoken in this church?' Homily shook her head. How could she know?

'A voice was saying "Come unto me all ye that travel and are heavy-laden and I will give you rest." We *had* travelled and we *were* heavy-laden –' Yes, thought Homily, glancing again about the room, heavy-laden with a whole lot of household objects which once belonged to us. 'Wasn't that wonderful? And we did find rest. And have done ever since. And the hymns they sing! You can't imagine!' With one arm round Timmus and the other held up as though to beat time, she broke out into a little air:

' "All things bright and beautiful, all creatures great and small . . ." Great and *small*, Homily. Although no one knew we were here, you will understand that we could not help but feel welcome, if you see what I mean.' She followed the direction of Homily's eyes. 'Yes, dear, I think there are one or two things here which once belonged to you and Pod. We never thought you'd need them again, going off in the night, like you did. But if there's anything you'd like to take away – just to help you start up life in the Old Rectory – just say the word: we'd only be too delighted. Anything we can do to help –'

Homily's astonished eyes swerved back to Lupy's face. She could hardly believe her ears. Lupy *offering* things! And, seemingly, with real sincerity. Although she did notice a little quiver about the lips, and a slightly nervous flutter of the eyelids. Homily looked round for Pod, but Hendreary had taken him out into the vestry. Some great change had taken place in Lupy, and Homily needed Pod to witness it. She turned back again to those eager, questioning eyes. 'Oh, Lupy,' she said, 'you're welcome to all that old stuff that came in the pillowcase. Up at the Old Rectory, we've got all we need now. And more.'

'Are you sure, dear? You're not just saying that?' Homily could hear the relief in her voice.

'Quite sure. It's a long story. I mean, there are some things that have happened to us since then that you'll hardly credit –'

'And the same with us, dear . . . What's the matter, Timmus?' She turned to him impatiently: he had been whispering in her ear. 'What are you saying? It's rude to whisper . . .'

'Could I take Arrietty into the church?'

'I don't see why not. If Arrietty wants to go?' And it might be a relief to get rid of two extra pairs of listening ears: there were still so many things she longed to recount to Homily.

As Arrietty and Timmus slipped away, Homily said, 'Timmus is very brown. I suppose he spends a lot of time out of doors?'

'No, very little, as a matter of fact. We never let him go out alone.'

'Then how –?' began Homily.

'All that brown? That's just a fad of his. I'll tell you about that later . . .' It was almost a relief to Homily to recognize a trace of Lupy's old impatience. Lupy leaned forward towards her. 'Now where had we got to? You were just going to tell me . . .'

'Ours is a long story,' said Homily, 'you tell me yours first.' Lupy did not need asking twice.

As Arrietty and Timmus crossed the vestry, Pod and Uncle Hendreary emerged from between the curtains which led into the church, each with his nutshell in hand. They were deep in conversation. 'Very fine,' Pod was saying, 'never seen carving like that, not anywhere. No wonder the – the – what-you-call-'ems come . . .'

'Tourists –' said Hendreary, '– from right across the world!'

'I can well believe it,' went on Pod as he and Hendreary, still talking, made their way into the harmonium.

Timmus and Arrietty slipped through the curtains and then, for a moment, Arrietty stood still. So this was the church!

The building was simple, with its pillars and arches, and its rows of orderly pews. If the human beans called this 'a little church' what, thought Arrietty, could a 'big church' be like? She almost trembled at the height and vastness. It had a strange smell and a strange feeling: it was a feeling she had never felt before. At the far end, behind the last row of pews, there was a pair of curtains very like the ones beside which she was standing. Beams of coloured light streamed in through the stained-glass windows. She felt more than a little afraid. Where did the Lord live, she wondered? She moved slightly closer to Timmus. 'What's behind those curtains at the end?' she whispered.

Timmus answered in his ordinary voice. 'Oh, that leads to the belfry chamber and the stairs to the belfry,' he said, cheerfully. 'I'll show you in a minute. And there are stone stairs to the belfry. But I don't use them myself.' His face suddenly filled with mischief. 'You can get out on to the roof,' he told her gleefully.

Arrietty did not answer his smile. Stone stairs! How could creatures their size get up stone stairs built for humans? Carpeted stairs had been another matter – in the days when Pod had still had his tape and hat-pin.

Timmus was pulling her sideways. 'Come on. I'll show you the rood-screen . . .'

She followed him across to the centre aisle. Here the stone flags had pictures engraved on them. Odd-looking pictures of stiff-looking people – right down the church, they went, in all shapes and sizes, as far as the curtains at the end. But Timmus was looking in the opposite direction. 'There it is,' he announced.

It was indeed a wonderful feat of carving, this rood-screen which divided the chancel from the nave. It rose from the floor at either side, with a wide arch in the middle. Through this arch, she could see the choir stalls which, unlike the pews, were set out lengthwise and, beyond these, facing her, she could make out the altar. Above the altar was a stained-glass window. Yes, there were the two branched candlesticks, which had once been stolen and since retrieved, and tall silver vases generously filled with flowers. The air was heavy with the scent of lilies of the valley.

Timmus was nudging her: evidently she was not

paying enough attention to the rood-screen. She smiled at him and took a few paces backwards down the aisle to study it from a wider angle.

The background (if anything so frail-looking could be called a background) was a delicate lattice of leaves and flowers, from among which peered a myriad little forms and faces: some human, some angelic, others devilish. Some were laughing, others looked very solemn. These last ones, Arrietty was told later, were most likely actual portraits of dignitaries of the time. At the very top of the arch was a larger face, very gentle and calm, with flowing hair. On each side of this a hand had been carved, the palms exposed, in a gesture which seemed to be saying, 'Look . . .' Or was it, 'Come . . .'?

Arrietty turned to Timmus. 'That bigger face up there, is that a portrait of the man who carved all this?'

'I don't know,' said Timmus.

'Or is it –' Arrietty hesitated, '– a portrait of the Lord?'

'I don't know,' said Timmus, 'my mother calls it the Creator.' He pulled on her sleeve. 'Now do you want to see the bell chamber?'

'In a minute,' said Arrietty: there was still so much to see in the rood-screen. A little gallery, she noted, ran along the top of it, with a quaintly designed balustrade. Halfway along the balustrade was the carved figure of a dove, with wings outstretched. It looked, thought Arrietty, as though it had just alighted there. Or, perhaps, was just about to take off. It was lifelike. The outstretched wings balanced and enhanced the outstretched hands just below them.

'It's beautiful . . .' she said to Timmus.

'Yes, and it's fun, too,' he told her and, as they turned aside to make their way down the aisle, he added suddenly, 'Would you like to see me run as fast as a mouse?'

'If you like,' said Arrietty. She realized suddenly that Timmus, who was not yet allowed out of doors alone, had only this church for a playground. She hoped the Lord liked little children. She rather thought he must do if Aunt Lupy had been right about 'all creatures great and small'.

She watched, smiling, as Timmus darted away from her towards the curtains of the alcove at the end. Yes, he could run: the little legs almost flew; and he fetched up panting before a low bench set just in front of the curtains. This bench, Arrietty noticed when at last she came up with him and had climbed up on a hassock, held neat piles of pamphlets about the church, a few picture postcards, and a brass-bound wooden collecting-box. There was an ample slit in the lid, almost long enough to take a letter. A notice, propped behind it, said 'THANK YOU'.

'Do you think –' Timmus was saying, still panting a little, '– that if I practised I could run as fast as a ferret?'

'Faster,' said Arrietty. 'Even rabbits can run faster than ferrets: ferrets can only catch rabbits by chasing them down their holes.'

Timmus looked pleased. 'Come on,' he said, and darting under the bench, he slipped through the gap in between the curtains.

The room inside was bare stone, but with a white, plastered ceiling. Three kitchen chairs were set along one wall and the staircase rose up along another. But what fascinated Arrietty most were the six round holes in the ceiling, through each of which protruded a long length of rope. A few feet up, along each rope, was a sausage-like piece of padding. So this was how they rang the bells! Since her family had been living in the Old Rectory, they had only heard a single bell and this was only for the services on Sunday. Each piece of rope ended in a 'tail' which lay in curves on the floor. It was thinner than the main rope.

Timmus leapt upon the first rope, clung there for a moment, then slid downwards so that he sat astride the 'tail'. 'Watch me,' he said, and eased off his shoes. As they tumbled off, Arrietty recognized them as a pair her father had made – some years ago now – for Timmus's elder brother. She looked down at her own shoes which were getting very shabby and had once belonged to Homily. She hoped that, when they were really settled in their new home, Pod would take up this trade again: he had been a wonderful shoemaker. All he would need was an old leather glove; and there must be plenty of those left in churches.

'Please look –' Timmus was begging. He was standing up now on the knot, his hands grasped the rope above his head. What was he going to do? She soon saw: if he could run like a mouse, he could climb like one, too. Up he went. Up and up, hands and feet moving like clockwork. Faster even than a mouse, more like a spider on a filament of web. Except the bell-rope was no filament: the coarse weave was heavy and thick, providing invisible footholds.

Arrietty watched, amazed, until at last he reached the ceiling. Without looking down, he disappeared through the hole. In just those few moments, Timmus had vanished from sight. Rooted to the spot, Arrietty stood there dumbfounded, craning her neck at the ceiling. Her neck began to ache but she dare not look away. What hours of practice this must have cost him! And she had thought that *she* could climb . . .

At last, the little face appeared, peering down at her through the hole. 'You see,' he called out, 'to get to the belfry, borrowers don't need stairs!'

He came down more slowly, perhaps a little tired by the effort, and sat himself comfortably astride the rope. 'You can get right up to the bells,' he told her, 'and there's a place where you can get right out on to the roof. There used to be six bellringers but now there's only one – except at Easter and a day they call Christmas.'

'Oh,' cried Arrietty, 'I know all about Christmas. My mother's always talking about it. And the feasts they always had. When she was a girl, there were a lot more borrowers in the house and that was the time – Christmas time – when she first began to notice my father. The feasts! There were things called raisins and crystal fruit and plum puddings and turkey and game pie . . . and the *wine* they left in glasses! My father used to get it out with a fountain-pen filler. He'd be up a fold in the table-cloth almost before the last human being had left the room. And my mother began to see what a wonderful borrower he might turn out to be. He brought her a little ring out of something called a cracker and she wore it as a crown . . .' She fell silent a moment, remembering that ring. Where was it now, she wondered? She had worn it often herself . . .

'Go on,' said Timmus: he hoped this might turn out to be one of her stories.

'That's all,' said Arrietty.

'Oh –' Timmus sounded disappointed. After a while he said, 'What's it like up at the rectory?'

'Nice. You could come and visit us . . .'

'They don't let me go out alone.'

'I could come and fetch you –'

'Could you? Could you really? Can you still tell stories?'

'I think so,' said Arrietty.

Timmus stood up, clasping the rope with his hands. 'Now, if you like, we could go and climb the rood-screen,' he suggested.

Arrietty hesitated. 'I can't climb as well as you,' she said at last. And then she added quickly, 'Yet.'

'It's easy. You can get about all over that rood-screen. I go up there to watch the human beans . . .'

'What human beans?'

'The human beans who come to church. They can't see you. Not if you stay quite still. They think you're part of the carving. That's why I brown my face . . .'

'What with?' asked Arrietty.

'Walnut juice, of course.' He swung the rope a little. 'Could you give me a bit of a push?'

Arrietty was bewildered. How quickly he went from one subject to another! 'What sort of a push?' she said.

'On me. Just give a push on me . . .'

Hand over hand, he was climbing up the tail rope

206

and once he had gripped it firmly between his feet and knees, Arrietty pushed him gently. This first bell-rope, she saw, hung lower than the others. Perhaps through constant use? The sausage-shaped pad looked frayed and shabby and had been cleverly reinforced by a piece of old carpet, neatly bound round with string. This, she supposed, was the bell they heard on Sundays.

'Harder!' cried Timmus. '*Much* harder!' So she gave him a massive shove. He leaned outwards from the rope and, by pushing with his feet and pulling

with his hands, he began to gain momentum. Backwards and forwards swung the bell-rope, farther and farther, higher and higher. Once he brushed the curtains which opened slightly. She became afraid he might hit the walls!

'Careful . . .!' she called in rising panic: the bell-rope was too long to be checked by its radius – it could go any distance within sight. 'Careful, Timmus!' she implored. '*Please* be careful . . .!'

He only laughed, lithe and confident. With a twist of his body, he made a circular swerve, brushing the other bell-ropes, so they too swung and trembled. The whole bell chamber became alive with movement. Supposing somebody came! Supposing the bells began to ring! Arrietty felt a sudden sense of guilt: this wild display was all for her benefit. 'Stop it, Timmus,' she begged him, almost in tears. She threw out her arms, as though to check him – a fruitless gesture at the speed he was going – and she had to dodge back swiftly as the bell-rope flew wildly past her through the gap in the curtains. She heard the sliding crash and the scrape of wood on stone. He had hit the bench. 'Oh, please don't let him be dead,' she cried out to herself as she rushed out through the curtains.

He wasn't dead at all: he was standing on the bench, surrounded by scattered pamphlets – the rope still held in his hand. He looked down on it in a bewildered way, then gently let it go. In her distress, Arrietty hardly noticed it as it sailed softly past her through the gaping curtains, and back to its usual place, curving and trembling as though it was alive.

There were pamphlets on the floor, the collecting-box was pushed sideways, and the bench was out of place. Not very much out of place, she noticed with relief. 'Oh, Timmus . . .!' she exclaimed and there was a world of reproach in her voice.

'I'm sorry,' he said and moved towards the edge of the bench, as if about to descend. It would have been a big drop.

'Stay where you are,' Arrietty ordered him. 'I'll get you down later. We've got to tidy this up . . . Have you hurt yourself?'

He still looked bewildered. 'Not much,' he said.

'Then collect all those papers together and put them back into piles. I'll pass you these ones on the floor . . .'

He did as he was told. He *was* moving rather stiffly but Arrietty, stooping to collect the scattered pamphlets on the flagstones, had no time to notice or look up. At least he could walk and bend.

On tiptoe, she passed her small collection of postcards and pamphlets up to him while he, perilously leaning over the edge of the polished bench stretched down to receive them. At last, all the papers were in place. The bench itself, alas, would have to remain crooked.

'Now, you'd better try to straighten up the collecting-box – if it's not too heavy . . .'

It was heavy, but he managed it after a struggle. Then Arrietty passed him up the card which said 'THANK YOU'. And that, at last, was that.

They walked back up the aisle very soberly. Neither of them felt very much like talking but, as they reached the rood-screen, Arrietty said, 'I don't think we'll climb that today.' Although he did not answer, Timmus appeared to agree with her.

CHAPTER EIGHTEEN

After that, Arrietty went down to the church quite often: it was because of the 'new arrangements' – arrangements which made Arrietty very happy and became a turning point in her life: she was to be allowed to 'borrow' and not only that, but joy of joys, to borrow out of doors!

It came about like this: her Uncle Hendreary had been finding the long walk to the kitchen garden increasingly tiring and Timmus was too young to be sent out alone. He would go with his father sometimes to help to carry, but he would dash about and 'run like a mouse' and this exercise, too, Hendreary found tiresome, being prone to odd twinges of gout. It had been different when the two elder boys had been at home: they had always undertaken to do what Aunt Lupy called 'the donkey work' but now that they had returned to their old home in the badgers' sett with Eggletina to keep house for them, seeking what they called their independence, the daily chores fell heavily on their father. 'I am not as young as I was,' he would say, and he would say it very often.

Pod could not help much: he had worked out a wonderful scheme for their living quarters under the window seat and the work this entailed took up all of his time. He was determined to divide up the fairly large space into three separate rooms: a little one for Arrietty, another for himself and Homily, and a bright, sun-filled sitting-room which would look out on to the grating. He would construct the partitions from the backs of the many odd books Peagreen had left behind. Montaigne's *Essays* in two volumes were the largest and these he had set up first, the smaller books he would use for doors. He kept back a good supply of the inside pages, with these he planned to paper the walls in vertical lines of news type. Homily thought the even lettering a little dull and uninteresting for the sitting-room: she would have preferred a touch of colour. 'You don't want a big room like this all *grey*. And that's what it'll look like if you don't look closely. Just *grey*: the print's so small-like . . .' But Arrietty and Pod persuaded her that this neutral shade would increase the feeling of space, and make a splendid background for the pictures Peagreen had promised to paint for them.

'You see, Mother,' Arrietty tried to explain, 'this room won't be furnished with bits and bobs – like the room under the floor at Firbank. I mean, now we've got all Miss Menzies' beautiful dolls'-house furniture . . .'

'Bits and bobs!' Homily had muttered crossly: she had been fond of their cosy room at Firbank. Especially fond of that beautiful knight from a chess set. She wondered where it was now.

But she would cook them splendid meals in her snow-white kitchen, well supplied with borrowings from the vegetable garden, and Spiller brought them an occasional minnow or freshwater crayfish from the stream, and – every now and again – a haunch of this or that, rich and gamey, but he would never say of *what*.

Pod hammered and sawed (and whistled under his breath), among the stacked furniture and general chaos under the window seat in the library. Peagreen would occasionally look in to inspect their work, and bring them some rare dainty or other from the larder, but he found it hard to tear himself away from his painting (which he was doing in secret so that each picture would be a surprise).

Everybody seemed happy, each with his own particular job, but perhaps the happiest of all were Arrietty and Timmus.

He would never 'run like a mouse' with Arrietty (except when danger threatened: they once had a very nasty encounter with a weasel). And, on their way to the kitchen garden, she would often tell him a story which would keep him enthralled. In those first early days of spring, there was little to borrow except brussels sprouts, parsley and winter kale, but as the weather grew warmer there were crowded rows of seedling lettuces which badly needed thinning: the borrowers thinned them. They also 'thinned' the tiny seedling onions and gathered sprigs of thyme. Then came the glorious day when Whitlace dug the first of the new potatoes and left in the soft earth a myriad of tiny tubors, some no larger than a hazel nut: with which he 'would not bother'. But Homily 'bothered' and so did Lupy. What a treat it was to serve up a whole dish of miniature new potatoes, flavoured with tender sprigs of early mint. And if Peagreen could produce a knob of butter from the larder! What a change from cutting off slices from tired old potatoes – potatoes so large that they had to be rolled along dusty floorboards into Homily's kitchen, as had been the case at Firbank.

Then came the promise of the first broad beans,

the scarlet runners, the strawberry-beds and raspberry canes breaking into leaf. And those mysterious fruit trees trained along the southern wall. Peaches? Nectarines? Victoria plums? They would have to wait and see. Oh, the bottlings and the dryings and the storings! Pod was hard put to it to find enough utensils. And yet the old disused game larder never seemed to fail him. With patient and persistent searchings, he could usually supply most needs.

Spiller would sometimes join them in the vegetable garden: with the aid of his bow and arrow, he kept down the larger pests. Pigeons were the greatest menace: they could strip a planting of early cabbage in less than a couple of hours. But they grew to detest the sting of his tiny arrows.

Borrowing for two families could sometimes be heavyish work. One brussels sprout was as big as a cabbage to Arrietty and Timmus and, besides all the other borrowings, they must always return with four, two for each household. All the same, in that warm and sheltered garden, there were quite long hours of fun and leisure: hide-and-seek among the parsley and, if it rained, they could shelter under the spreading leaves of rhubarb and play guessing games and such. They had, of course, to keep a sharp look-out for Whitlace. And there were rats among the compost. But Spiller saw to those. They, too, grew to know the 'ping' of that tiny bow.

On the way home, they would leave Arrietty's borrowings below the grating (where Pod would take them in), and then go on to the church. Sometimes Aunt Lupy would ask Arrietty to stay to tea, and Arrietty nearly always accepted: she was longing to catch a glimpse of Miss Menzies.

Although she had solemnly promised her father never again to speak to a human bean, there might be some way of letting Miss Menzies know that they were safe. But though the other ladies appeared on Wednesdays and Saturdays to do the flowers, Miss Menzies was never among them.

Aunt Lupy, Arrietty noticed, was getting quite fond of her ladies. She was very used to genteel human conversation, having become a Harpsichord by marriage and lived so long with her first husband inside that instrument in the drawing-room at Firbank. It was here (as Homily maintained) she had picked up grander manners than those rougher ways current below the kitchen. ('Although,' Homily would always add, 'Lupy was only a Rainpipe from the stables before she married Harpsichord.') The harpsichord was never opened because so many of the strings were missing. All the same, superior though it might seem, it had not been an easy life: they had to subsist entirely on what was left over from afternoon tea. And their borrowing had to be done at lightning speed, between the time the ladies left to change for dinner and the butler appeared to clear away the tea things. And there was many a day (as she once confessed to Homily) when there had been nothing to drink except water from the flower-vases, and nothing to eat at all. Aunt Lupy seemed doomed, Arrietty thought, (with a few exceptional interludes) to make a home inside some kind of musical instrument.

Arrietty liked to hear Aunt Lupy's stories about the human beans and picked up many kinds of interesting information with which she would regale her mother and father on her return to supper. For instance, *why* the old rector no longer lived in the rectory, but in a neat, compact villa across the lane. She learned that Mrs Whitlace came down to the church every evening to lock away the offertory box in the press in the vestry, and how that solid old press (set deeply into the stones of the original church) housed 'priceless treasures' (Lady Mullings' description): gold and silver altar plates, a jewelled chalice, exquisite candlesticks far more ancient than those which had been stolen from the altar and many other historic objects, described in an awed voice by Lupy but of which Arrietty had forgotten the names.

'Fancy!' Homily exclaimed as Arrietty reeled off as many as she could remember. 'Whoever would have guessed it!'

And Pod remarked, 'Sounds like the display cabinet at Firbank . . .'

'Should all be under lock and key,' Homily said sternly.

'They *are* under lock and key,' Pod explained patiently. 'I've examined those doors: the oak is that hard with age that no one could drive so much as a nail into it. Not even a human bean could —'

'Lady Mullings,' Arrietty told them, 'thinks all those things should be put in a bank.'

'In a *bank*!' exclaimed Homily, thinking of a grassy slope.

'Yes, it sounded funny to me, too,' admitted Arrietty.

'Is that the Lady Mullings who's a "finder"?' asked Homily, after a moment.

'Yes. Well, she is for other people. But Aunt Lupy says she can never find anything she mislays herself.

Aunt Lupy says she heard her telling Mrs Crabtree that she's lost the key of her attic and now she can't get at the things she laid aside for the jumble sale. And she's always leaving things in the church – umbrellas and handkerchiefs, gloves, and things like that . . .'

'I could do with a nice leather glove,' said Pod.

One afternoon, a little time later, Arrietty picked up courage to ask quite openly about Miss Menzies: why did she no longer come?

'Oh, poor thing!' exclaimed Aunt Lupy. 'She did come once to make her excuses. But she's been in dreadful trouble . . .'

Arrietty's heart sank. 'What . . . what kind of trouble?'

'Some vandals broke into the model village and knocked down all the houses!'

'*All* the houses?' gasped Arrietty, although she knew that Aunt Lupy was apt to exaggerate.

'Well, that's what it sounded like to me. Upset! I never heard a poor thing more upset. And it was nearly the end of Mr Pott. The brutes must have got in across the stream. They'd cut the wire and all. And there they both are – Miss Menzies and Mr Pott – working night and day to try to repair the damage. Poor things! They had wanted so much to get the place open for Easter. That's when the season starts . . .'

'When –' stammered Arrietty, '– I mean – how long ago did this happen?'

'Let me see . . .' Aunt Lupy looked thoughtful. 'About a week ago? No, it was more than that – more like two . . .' She wrinkled her brow, trying to remember. 'How long ago is it since you all first arrived here?'

'About two weeks . . .' said Arrietty.

'Well, it must have been about then. I seem to recall it was the night of a very full moon –'

'Yes,' Arrietty was leaning forward, her hands clasped so tightly in her lap that the nails dug into her palms, 'that was the night after we first arrived.' Her voice had trembled.

'What's the matter, child?'

'Oh, Aunt Lupy! Can't you see? If we'd delayed one night, just *one* night – and my mother wanted to – they'd have got us!'

'Who'd have got you?' Aunt Lupy looked alarmed.

'The Platters! They'd have taken the roof off, like they did before. And we'd have been in the house. Like rats in a trap, Aunt Lupy!'

'Goodness gracious me . . .' exclaimed Lupy.

'It wasn't vandals, Aunt Lupy, it was the Platters!'

'You mean those people who shut you up in the attic, and were going to show you in a showcase?'

'Yes, yes.' Arrietty was standing up now.

'But how do you know it was them?'

'I just know. My father was expecting them. I must go home now, Aunt Lupy.' She was searching round frantically for her empty borrowing bag. 'I must tell all this to my parents . . .'

'But you're safe now, dear. Those people don't know that you're here.'

'I hope not,' said Arrietty. She found her bag and stooped hurriedly to kiss her aunt.

'The Lord takes care of his own,' said Lupy. 'Thank you for the lettuce. Go carefully, child.'

*

But Arrietty did not go very carefully. She was in such a hurry that she nearly ran into Kitty Whitlace, who was approaching the wicket gate from the far side. Luckily Arrietty heard her singing and recognized the singer by the song and had time to slip under the edge of a flat gravestone.

'In a dear little town in the old County Down,' sang Kitty, as she approached the gate, 'You must linger way down in my heart. Though it never was grand, it is my fairyland –' she paused to unlatch the gate, and carefully relatch it, before she went on, '– in a wonderful world apart.' Arrietty, peering out from under the lip of the gravestone, saw that Kitty, as she strolled along, was swinging a very large key on the forefinger of her right hand. Ah, yes! She suddenly remembered that this was the hour that Kitty Whitlace always went down to the church for a last look round and to lock up the collecting-box in the solid old press for the night. Swiftly, she slid out from under the gravestone and between the palings of the gate.

Her mother and father looked grave when they had heard her story. They seemed shaken and appalled at the narrowness of their escape. There was no crowing by Pod about his unheeded warnings to Homily. Nor did she concede, as she half longed to, how right those warnings had proved. This was no time for cheap triumphs nor recriminations. They were safe now, and that was all that mattered. But what a near thing it had been!

'How desperate they must have been, those Platters!' Pod said, at last.

'And still are, I shouldn't wonder,' said Homily.

'Well, they won't find us here,' said Pod. He looked round in a pleased way at their sitting-room, which was now taking shape: the chairs and sofa were now unstacked and they were sitting on them.

Homily rose to her feet. 'I've got a bit of supper all ready in the kitchen,' she told them, and led the way down the steps to the passage under the floor.

Pod took one last look round. 'I'll cut a nice piece of glass to fit that grating,' he said. 'Peagreen's got plenty. And then come winter, when they turn the central heating on, we'll be snug as houses . . .'

Homily was very silent during supper, and a little absent-minded. When they had finished eating, she sat with one elbow on the table and, leaning a cheek upon her hand, stared downwards at her plate. Pod, looking at her across the table, seemed puzzled.

'Is anything on your mind, Homily?' he asked, after a longish silence. He knew how easily she could become worried.

She shook her head. 'Not really . . .'

'But there *is* something?' persisted Pod.

'Nothing really,' said Homily and began to gather up the plates. 'It's only . . .'

'Only what, Homily?'

She sat down again. 'It's only . . . well, I wish sometimes they'd never told us about that Lady Mullings.'

'Why, Homily?'

'I don't sort of like the idea of a "finder",' she said.

CHAPTER NINETEEN

There was no doubt that Homily very much enjoyed the snippets of human gossip with which Arrietty regaled her after visits to the church. Although the news of the Platters' invasion of poor Miss Menzies' model village had shocked and frightened her at the time, by next day, it had slid to the back of her mind, merging into a feeling of relief at their escape and the prospect of a safer and happier future.

Peagreen's pictures were a great success. They were the size of postage stamps and, as Homily said, 'went very well together'. Each painting was of a single object: a bumble bee with every glinting hair lovingly observed, its iridescent wings delicately transparent; blossoms of vetch, of speedwell and their familiar pimpernel; a striped fly; a snail emerging from its shell – all silver and gunmetal and whorling curves of golden brown, the head turned inquiringly towards them. 'Why,' she exclaimed, 'you could almost pick it up! Not that I would want to. And look at its eyes on stalks!'

Peagreen had stuck the fine canvas on to pieces of cardboard and, on the edge of each, he had painted a frame. It looked like a real frame: only by touching it did you find it was flat. (Some sixty years later, when repairs were being done to the house, these pictures were discovered by a human being; they aroused great wonder, and were put into a collection.)

'He says they're your Easter present,' Arrietty told her mother.

'What's Easter?' asked Homily wonderingly.

'Oh, I told you, Mother. Easter is next Sunday. And all the ladies will come and do the flowers for the church. Even Miss Menzies! I heard Lady Mullings say that, however busy she is, Miss Menzies would never miss helping with the flowers for Easter. Oh, Mother –' she sounded tearful, '– I wish Papa would let me speak to her – just *once*! After all, when you come to think of it, everything we have we owe to Miss Menzies – this lovely room, the chiffonier, the cooking pots, our clothes . . She loved us, Mother, she really did!'

'It wouldn't do,' said Homily. 'All our troubles started by you speaking to That Boy. And you might say he loved us, too . . .' She sounded sarcastic.

'He did,' said Arrietty.

'And much good it did us,' retorted Homily.

'Oh, Mother, he saved our lives!'

'Which wouldn't have been in danger, but for him. No, Arrietty, your father's right. Go down and *listen* to them as much as you like. But no speaking. No being *seen*. We've got to trust you, Arrietty. Especially now, when you've got all this newfangled liberty . . .' Seeing the expression on Arrietty's face, she added more gently, 'Not that you and Timmus aren't doing a very good job. And your Aunty Lupy thinks so, too . . .'

Some days before, Aunt Lupy and Uncle Hendreary had come to tea. It had taken a good deal of persuasion. The rectory was foreign ground to them and they did not know quite what to expect. Nowadays neither of them went much out of doors: the church was their territory and there they felt at home. And, although Aunt Lupy was thinner than

221

she used to be, she did not much care for that scramble through the stone wall and the rough passage alongside the drainpipe: there was always the fear of getting stuck. However, Pod and Arrietty went to fetch them. Pod helped Lupy through the hole, and guided her courteously along the path, through the paling of the wicket gate and up to the opened grating. Arrietty stayed down in the church with Timmus – both of them delighted to miss the boredom of a grown-up tea party.

Once she was safely inside, Lupy was astonished at the grandeur of their doll's-house furniture. Homily, as polite as Pod on this occasion, took no credit for it. 'All *given*,' she trilled gaily, 'there's nothing here we chose ourselves. Nor made, for that matter – except the walls and doors.'

Aunt Lupy had looked round wonderingly. 'Very tasteful,' she said at last. 'I like your wallpaper.'

'*Do* you?' exclaimed Homily with feigned surprise, 'I thought it a bit dull.' Though, in reality, she had grown to admire it herself.

'I'd call it refined,' said Lupy.

'Oh, would you? I'm so glad. Of course there's a lot of good reading on it, if you bend yourself sideways . . .' The fact that neither Lupy or Homily could read was gently ignored.

If there was a gleam of envy in Aunt Lupy's eye when Homily brought out the doll's tea-service, she suppressed it quickly. That it was a little out of proportion did not seem to matter: Miss Menzies had searched high and low for cups small enough to suit such tiny fingers and a teapot that would not be too heavy for a tiny hand to hold. But, large as the cups were, they were very pretty with their pattern of wild forget-me-nots, and Homily remembered always only to half-fill the teapot.

After tea, Lupy was taken to see the kitchen. She expressed some surprise at the long walk under the floor. 'I wouldn't like to have to carry *our* meals all this distance,' she said. 'At home, I have only to slip back from the gas-ring.'

'Yes. Very convenient,' agreed Homily politely. For some reason, she did not explain to Lupy that they never carried meals 'all this distance' but ate them comfortably at the tiled table in front of the kitchen fire.

'And in winter,' went on Lupy, 'they light up that big coke stove in the corner of the vestry. And what's more they keep it in all night.'

'Very cosy,' said Homily.

'And useful, for soups and stews and things like that.'

'Well, you were always a good manager, Lupy.'

By this time, they had reached the steps and Homily paused for a moment. Pod had gone ahead to light the candles and she wanted to give him time. Lupy was staring up the steps, mystified and very curious. 'It looks very dark up there . . .'

'Not really,' said Homily: she had seen the gleam of candlelight. 'Come along, I'll show you . . .' and she led the way up into the chimney.

Lupy looked around with something like horror at the great draughty space, the soot-darkened walls. She could not think of anything to say. Was this really their kitchen? Ah, there was a glint of light in the far corner . . .

'Better take my hand,' Homily was saying. 'Careful of the sticks. The jackdaws drop them down . . .'

Stooping, she picked up two recent ones and threw them on to the neat pile.

When at last they reached the little door marked *Essays of Emerson*, Homily held it aside for Lupy to enter first. There was no mistaking the pride on her face, lit up as it was by the glow from two bright candles: the fire burning merrily (remade up by Pod), the shelves, Miss Menzies' cooking utensils, the spotless cleanliness . . .

'It's very nice,' Lupy said at last. She sounded rather breathless.

'It is rather,' Homily agreed modestly. 'No draughts in here . . . just a bit of fresh air from above.'

Lupy looked up and glimpsed the distant sky. 'Oh, I see, we're in some kind of chimney . . .'

'Yes, a very large one. Sometimes the rain comes in. But not in this corner. But sometimes below that far wall, there's quite a little pool.'

'You should keep a toad,' said Lupy firmly.

'A toad! Why?'

'To eat up the black beetles.'

'We have no black beetles,' retorted Homily coldly. How like Lupy to mention such a hazard! She felt deeply affronted. All the same, as they made their way back towards the entrance, she glanced at the pile of wood on the shadowy floor a little fearfully.

CHAPTER TWENTY

'Where are you going, Sidney?' asked Mrs Platter, as Mr Platter got up from the breakfast table, making his way rather lackadaisically towards the back door.

'To catch the pony,' he said in a bored voice (once they had employed a boy to do these chores). 'I'll need the cart this morning. I'm not going to bicycle all the way to Fordham: that hill coming back just about kills you . . .'

'What are you on to at Fordham?' There was a note of hope in Mrs Platter's question. They had not been doing so well lately: people were not dying as often as they used to and, now the council estate was finished, nor did they seem to be building many houses. She hoped he was on to a good job?

'It's that Lady Mullings,' he told her, 'and hardly worth the journey. Some of her windows got stuck with the rain last winter – wood swelled up, like. And she's locked herself out of the attic, and lost the key . . . We had a box of old keys somewhere. Where did you put it?'

'I didn't put it anywhere. It's where you always keep it: on one of the bottom shelves of your workshop.' She stood up suddenly. 'Oh, Sidney –!' she exclaimed.

He looked surprised at the sudden emotion in her voice. 'What is it now?' he asked.

'Oh, Sidney!' she exclaimed again. 'Don't you see? This may be our last chance . . . Lady Mullings might get her "feeling". Take the little apron!'

'Oh, that,' he said uncomfortably.

'You ought to have taken it weeks ago. But there you were – going on about not knowing quite what to say to her. Feeling foolish, and all that. You should have taken it when you did her gutters.'

'It's not my line, Mabel – psychic or physic, or whatever they call it. It's such a silly little bit of a shred of a thing – who was I going to say it belonged to? It takes a bit of thinking about. I mean, how to bring the subject up, like, when all we was talking about was gutters. And I've got to bring up gutters again: she hasn't paid my bill yet . . .'

Mrs Platter went to a drawer in the dresser, and drew out a small beige envelope. She laid it firmly on the table. 'All you have to say to her, Sidney, is: "Lady Mullings, if it isn't too much trouble, could you find out who the owner of this is and where they are living now?" That's all you have to say, Sidney, quite casual, like. They are only *words*, Sidney, and what are words with our whole future at stake! Just hand it to her, as though it was your bill, or something. That's all you have to do.'

'I'll hand her my bill, too,' said Mr Platter grimly. He picked up the envelope, looked at it distastefully, and put it in his pocket. 'All right, I'll take it.'

'It's our last chance, Sidney, as I said before. It was you yourself who told me she was a "finder" and all about the church candlesticks and Mrs Crabtree's ring. If this fails, Sidney, we might just as well go to Australia.'

'Don't talk nonsense, Mabel!'

'It isn't nonsense. And I don't see much future for us here, unless – I say, *unless* – we can get back those tiresome creatures and show them in a showcase

226

just as we had planned. As you have always said, there was money in them all right! But your brother's getting on now, and in the same line of business. And you remember what he said in his last letter? That he wouldn't have minded taking on a partner? That was a broad hint if ever there was one. And –'

'All right, all *right*, Mabel,' Mr Platter interrupted, 'I said I'd take the envelope,' and he made, more hurriedly this time, for the outside door.

'It's all washed and ironed and folded –' Mrs Platter called after him. But he did not seem to hear.

The door was opened for Mr Platter by Lady Mullings' stiff and starched old house-parlourmaid and he was ushered into the hall. 'Her Ladyship will be down in a minute,' he was told. 'Pray take a seat.' Mr Platter sat down on one of the straight-backed chairs beside the oak chest, took off his hat and placed it on his knees and his tool-bag beside him on the floor. Mr Platter had always been a 'front door caller', by reason of his status as undertaker, and comforter of the bereaved (no common handyman he!) but he was always willing to oblige his more favoured clients with small repairs in the hope of another funeral or a building contract to come. When at last Lady Mullings appeared, she seemed to be in a hurry. She flew down the stairs, hatted and veiled, and pulling on her gloves. At the same moment, her gardener appeared from the back premises carrying two large buckets filled to overflowing with a variety of spring flowers.

'Oh, Mr Platter, I am so relieved to see you, we

are in a dreadful pickle here –' Mr Platter had risen and she was shaking him warmly by the hand. 'How are you? And how is Mrs Platter? Well, I hope. We can't get into the attic and it's so tiresome. All the stuff for the jumble stall is locked up in there and the church garden-party's on Easter Monday. And those new windows you put in last spring seemed to have hermetically sealed themselves during the winter. And there are one or two other things –' she was opening the front door. 'But Parkinson will explain to you . . .' She had turned to the gardener. 'Those look wonderful, Henry! Are you sure you can manage them as far as the church? We don't want any more bad backs, do we?' As the buckets were being carried through on to the pavement, she turned back to Mr Platter. 'I am so sorry, dear Mr Platter, to be in such a rush. But yesterday being Good Friday and tomorrow Easter Sunday, we have only this one day in which to decorate the whole church. It's always like this I'm afraid. It's the fault of the calendar . . .'

Mr Platter almost leapt forward to catch her before she closed the door. 'One moment, my lady–'

She hesitated. 'Only one, I'm afraid, Mr Platter. I'm late already –'

Mr Platter almost gabbled as he brought two beige envelopes out of his pocket. 'Should I take the liberty of adding the account of today's little jobs on to the account for the guttering?'

'Didn't I pay you for guttering, Mr Platter?'

'No, my lady, it must have slipped your memory.'

'Oh, dear, I *am* so sorry. What a juggins I am getting in my old age! Yes, yes. Add today's account on to the other one. Of course, of course. Now, I really must be . . .'

'It just occurs to me, my lady, that I might not be here when you get back from the church.' He only just stopped himself from holding on to the door.

'Then send it through the post, Mr Platter. Oh, no, I have my cheque-book. When you've finished here, why not come along to the church? I shall be there most of the day. It's only a step –'

'Very well, I'll do that, my lady.' He was pushing one beige envelope back into his pocket but the other one he was holding out towards her. This was the difficult moment but he was determined to get it over with: you never knew with these people. By the time he had got to the church, she might have gone off somewhere else – to tea with Miss Menzies or something. He couldn't go chasing her around the village. 'There's just one thing, if you'll forgive me detaining you just a bare second longer –'

Lady Mullings looked down at the envelope. 'Not another account, Mr Platter?'

Mr Platter tried to smile – and almost managed it, but the hand which held the envelope was trembling slightly. 'No, this is something quite different, something I promised my wife to do.' He had rehearsed this approach all the way down to Little Fordham: it was a manoeuvre he had once heard described as 'passing the buck' and he had decided to use it.

Lady Mullings seemed to hesitate. She liked men who tried to please their wives and, in all the long years she had known Mr Platter, he had always been so kind, so tactful, so obliging. She glanced up the road and was reassured to see her gardener plodding along towards the church with the buckets. She turned back to Mr Platter and took up the envelope. It felt soft. What could it be? Perhaps Mrs Platter had sent her a little present? A handkerchief, or something? She began to feel touched already.

'It is something my wife cares very much about,' Mr Platter was saying. 'She knows your great gift, my lady, of being a "finder" and she begs you that, when you have time and it isn't too much trouble, you might be able to tell her who is the owner of this little thing in the envelope and where that owner is living at present. Please don't bother to open it now,' as he saw Lady Mullings was about to do so, 'any time will do.'

'I'll do my best, Mr Platter. I never promise anything. Sometimes things happen, and sometimes they don't. I don't really have "a great gift", as you so kindly put it. Something just seems to work through me. I am just an empty vessel.' She felt in the little basket containing her picnic luncheon, took out her handbag and placed the envelope, almost reverently, inside. 'Please give my warmest regards to Mrs Platter, and tell her I'll do my very best,' and, smiling very kindly at Mr Platter, she closed the door gently behind her.

As Mr Platter picked up his tool-bag, he felt extremely pleased with himself. He felt he had 'handled' Lady Mullings very successfully, all due to his own foresight and hard thinking as he had driven along in his cart. What he did not take into account (and it would never have occurred to him to do so) was Beatrice Mullings' own character: that it was one which was incapable of thinking ill of others. And that, since the death of her husband

and her two sons, she had devoted her life to her friends. Any call for help, however trivial, took first priority over all the other, more mundane, duties of her daily life. She would have no curiosity about the contents of the beige envelope, only that the object it contained was somehow dear to Mrs Platter, and that news of its owner's whereabouts must mean a great deal to her.

Mr Platter was really smiling now, as he went off to the nether regions in search of Parkinson (Miss Parkinson to him). It was as he feared. She had found a hundred extra jobs for him besides the windows and the door of the attic. Well, perhaps not a hundred but that's what it seemed like. Would he ever get home to his luncheon? He knew Mrs Platter was preparing Lancashire hot-pot: one of his favourites.

CHAPTER TWENTY-ONE

Arrietty had risen very early on that same Saturday morning. Aunt Lupy had impressed upon her that she must take Timmus off with plenty of time to spare before all the flower-arranging ladies invaded the church. 'The whole place gets awash with them,' Aunt Lupy had explained the night before, 'not just the ones we know: all sorts come – and they run about every which way, gabbling and arguing, strewing the place with petals and leaves, coats and picnic baskets all over the pews. Calling out to each other as if they were in their own houses. What the good Lord thinks about it, I just can't imagine. And it's a dreadful day for us: not a step dare we venture outside the harmonium. Food, water . . . everything has to be got in. And there we're stuck, hour after hour, in almost pitch darkness – you dare not light a candle – until at last they decide to go. And even then you don't feel safe. Someone or other is bound to come back with an extra bunch of flowers or to collect some belonging or other they've carelessly left behind. So you must take Timmus off early, dear, and don't bring him back until late . . .'

The vestry was indeed a wonderful sight when Arrietty entered through the hole that morning. Flowers in buckets, in tin baths, in great vases, in jam-jars – all over the floor, on the table, on the desk . . . everywhere. The curtains which led into the church proper were drawn back and even beyond these she could see pots of flowering shrubs, and tall budding branches of greenery. The scent was overpowering.

Timmus was waiting for her at the entrance to his home, his round little face alight with happiness: he had a treasure! Spiller had made him a miniature bow and a tiny quiver of miniature arrows. 'And he's going to teach me to shoot,' he told her ecstatically, 'and how to make my own arrows . . .'

'What are you going to shoot at?' Arrietty asked him. Her arm was round his shoulders, and she couldn't resist giving him a hug.

'Sunflowers. That's how you start,' he said, 'the nearest you can get to the heart of a sunflower!'

Aunt Lupy came out then and drove them off. 'Get along, you two. I've just heard a carriage drive up to the lychgate –'

And, indeed, the evening before, Arrietty having supper with her parents had heard the clip-clop of horses' hooves as pony-carts and carriages, one after another, had driven up to the church: delivering these flowers, she thought, as she and Timmus picked their way through the jungle of scented blooms – flowers from every garden in the parish. Suddenly the day began to feel like a holiday.

'Do you know what?' Arrietty said, when once they were out and hurrying along the path – at the same time keeping an eye out for whoever might have arrived in the carriage.

'No. What?' asked Timmus.

'After we've been to the vegetable garden, we're going to have lunch with Peagreen!'

'Oh, goody,' said Timmus. Peagreen had been giving him reading lessons and teaching him to

233

write. Twice a week, Peagreen would come to Homily's parlour with sharpened pencil stubs and odd bits of paper and, being a poet and an artist, he could make these lessons a delight. He would always stay to tea and, sometimes, would read aloud to them afterwards. But Timmus had never been invited into any of Peagreen's nesting-boxes: these Peagreen kept strictly for working in solitude at his painting or writing.

'Oh, goody!' said Timmus again, and gave a little skip: he had always longed to climb the ivy. And this sunny Easter Saturday, minute by minute, began to seem more and *more* like a holiday. He had not even brought a borrowing bag because his mother (as she had explained to Arrietty) had 'got everything in'.

So there was not very much to do in the kitchen garden but to play games and explore and tease the ants and earwigs and see who could get closest to a resting butterfly. The sunflowers were not out yet, so Timmus shot at a bumble-bee, which made Arrietty very cross. Not only because she loved bumble-bees but because (as she told him), 'You have only got six arrows and now you've lost one!' She made him promise not to start shooting again until Spiller had given him a lesson.

When the church clock struck twelve, Arrietty pulled up three tiny radishes and a lettuce seedling, and they began to make their way towards the house. They had to hide once when they saw Whitlace trundling a wheelbarrow along the path, filled with rhododendrons: he was heading for the church. Arrietty felt a sad little pang because she realized that her beloved Miss Menzies might be at the church by now but that she, Arrietty, would not be there – even to watch her from a distance.

Peagreen soon managed to cheer her up, however: he was delighted with the radishes which Arrietty had washed in the bird-bath, and the tiny lettuce went beautifully with the delicious cold food he had borrowed from the larder. The spring sunshine was so warm that they were tempted to eat out of doors but decided, in the end, that they would feel more at ease eating in Peagreen's dining-room, with the open lid of the nesting-box propped up by a stick. Peagreen's dining-table was made from the round lid of a pill-box, like the one Arrietty remembered at Firbank, but Peagreen had painted it carmine. For plates he had set out small-leaved nasturtiums, the roundest he could find, with a larger one in the centre of the table on which he had arranged the food. 'You can eat the plates, too,' he told Timmus, 'nasturtium goes well with salad.' Timmus thought this a great joke.

After luncheon, Timmus was allowed to go climbing among the ivy, with orders to freeze should anyone come along the path, and strictly forbidden to put even one foot inside the opened larder window. Peagreen and Arrietty just talked.

Arrietty described to Peagreen how sometimes she and Timmus would watch church services from the rood-screen. Timmus, being small, had his own comfortable little perch on the carved vine leaf, with the solemn face of a mitred bishop to lean back against, and from below he looked exactly like part of the carving. She herself, not wanting to brown her face, usually climbed up into the gallery which ran across the top. Here she could squat down behind the dove and peer out from below the spread wings. Weddings she liked best: weddings were beautiful. Funerals they liked next best: sad, but beautiful too. Except for that dreadful one at which Mr Platter had officiated as undertaker, and her heart had gone cold at the sight of that hated face. On that occasion, having raised her face once, she had never dared raise it again. In fact, it cured her of funerals.

At one point, she asked Peagreen why he never went down to the church. 'Well, it's a bit of a step for me,' he told her, smiling. 'I used to go more often before –' he hesitated.

'Before the Hendrearies came?'

'Perhaps you could say that,' he admitted rather sheepishly. 'And there are times when one prefers to be alone.'

'Yes,' said Arrietty. After a moment she added, 'Don't you like the Hendrearies?'

'I hardly know them,' he said.

'But you like Timmus?'

His face lit up. 'How could anybody not like Timmus?' He laughed amusedly. 'Oh, Timmus could go far . . .'

Arrietty jumped up. 'I hope he hasn't gone too far already!' She thrust her head out through the round hole in the nesting-box, and looked along the ivy. At last she saw him: he was hanging upside-down just above the larder window, trying to peer inside. She did not call out to him: his position looked too perilous. And, after all, she realized, he was obeying her to the letter: he had not 'set a foot inside'. She watched him anxiously until, with a snake-like twist, he reversed his position and made his way upwards among the trembling leaves. She drew in her head again. There was no need to worry. For one who could climb a bell-rope with such speed and confidence, ivy would be child's play.

When, at last, Timmus rejoined them, the clock was striking five. He looked very hot and dirty. Arrietty thought she had better take him home. 'But the church is full of "ladies",' protested Peagreen.

'I mean to *my* home. I'll have to clean him up a bit before his mother sees him.' She sighed happily. 'It's been a lovely afternoon . . .'

'How long will those women stay in the church?' asked Peagreen.

'I've no idea. Until they've finished the flowers, I suppose. I thought that, at about six o'clock, I'd climb that high box tree. You can see everything from there. All the comings and goings . . .'

'Do you want me to come with you?'

'Do you want to?'

'Yes. I'll feel like a climb by then.'

When Arrietty and Timmus reached home, they found Homily bustling towards the kitchen. As they walked across it, Arrietty noticed that the long dark hearth looked curiously neat. 'Somebody's restacked the wood pile,' she said to her mother, as they entered the bright kitchen.

'Yes, I did,' said Homily.

'All by yourself?'

'No, your father helped me. I got an idea in my head about black beetles . . .'

'Were there any?'

'No, only a couple of wood-lice. They're all right – clean as whistles, wood-lice are. But your father's thrown them out of doors, we don't want a whole family. Timmus, just look at your face!'

This was something Timmus could not do. So Homily washed it gently, and his little hands as well. She had always had a soft spot for Timmus. She brushed down his clothes and smoothed back his hair. There was nothing she could do about the walnut juice.

At six o'clock, when Arrietty climbed up the tall bush, she found Peagreen already there. 'I think they've all gone now,' he told her, 'they've been coming out in twos and threes. I've been watching for ages . . .'

Arrietty put herself in a side-saddle position on a slender branch, and they both stared down at the empty path in silence. Nothing stirred in the churchyard. After about twenty minutes, both became a little bored. 'I think I'd better get Timmus now,' Arrietty said at last, 'he's waiting just beside the grating. I don't want him running out . . .' She was disentangling her skirt which had caught on a twig. 'Thank you for watching, Peagreen.'

'I've rather enjoyed it,' he said. 'I like to get a good look at a human being now and again. You never know what they're going to do next. Can you manage?' he asked as she started to climb down.

'Of course I can manage.' She sounded a little nettled. 'Aren't you coming?'

'I think I'll stay here and see you both safely in.'

When Arrietty and Timmus reached the vestry, they found it tidy and clean. The tablecloth was back on the table and the ledger on the desk, and the curtains leading into the church were demurely drawn to. But instead of the smell of stale cassocks there was a lingering fragrance of flowers. It drew Arrietty to part the curtains slightly and peer into the church. She caught her breath.

'Come and look, Timmus,' she whispered urgently. 'It's lovely!'

Every windowsill was a bower. But the sills being high and she so far below, she could only see the tops of the flowers – all the same, they were a riot of scent and colour. Timmus pushed past her, dashed straight through the curtains, and ran sharply to the right. 'You can't see from where you are –' he called back at her. He was making for his perch on the rood-screen. Of course! Arrietty stepped forward about to follow him when something or someone touched her on the arm. She swung round swiftly. It was Aunt Lupy, a finger to her lips, and looking very alarmed. 'Don't let him shout,' she whispered hurriedly, 'there are people still here!'

Arrietty looked down the seemingly empty church. 'Where?' she gasped.

'In the porch at the moment. Another whole hand-cart of flowers has arrived. They'll be bringing them in, in a moment. You'd better come inside with me . . .' She was pulling rather urgently at Arrietty's arm.

'What about Timmus? He's on the rood-screen . . .'

'He'll be all right. So long as he keeps still. And he will, because he'll see them from there.'

Arrietty turned unwillingly and followed her aunt under the table, whose hanging cloth gave them good cover. It was the Hendrearys' usual route when any kind of danger threatened and only meant one quick dash at the far end.

'Did Miss Menzies come?' Arrietty whispered, as they passed under the table.

'She's here now. And so's Lady Mullings. Come on, Arrietty, we'd better hurry. They may be coming in here for water . . .'

But Arrietty stood firm in her tracks. 'I *must* see Miss Menzies!' She tore her arm away from her aunt's urgent grasp, and disappeared under the hanging folds of the tablecloth, but not without having noticed her aunt's expression of dismay and astonishment. But there was no time to lose. As she sped along beside the foot of the rood-screen, she was aware of the great bank of flowers edging the chancel. Plenty of cover there! She glanced up at Timmus's perch. *That* was all right: to all intents and purposes, he had become invisible. But even as, breathlessly, she climbed up the side of the rood-screen towards the little gallery, she could hear Lady Mullings' voice (really annoyed for once) saying, 'Twelve huge pots of pelargonium, what on earth does she think we can do with them at this hour?'

Arrietty sped along the gallery and took cover under the spreading wings of the dove. She stared down. The great west door was wide open and the sun was streaming in from the porch. She saw Lady Mullings come in and move a little aside to let two men pass her, each carrying a large pot filled with a bush-like plant which, to Arrietty's eyes, resembled a striped geranium.

'Twelve, you say!' cried Lady Mullings despairingly. (How human voices echoed when the church was empty!)

'Yes, ma'am. We grew them special for the church. Where would you like them putting?'

Lady Mullings looked round desperately. 'Where do you suggest, Miss Menzies?' Arrietty craned forward over the edge of the gallery. Yes, there at last was her dear Miss Menzies, standing rather listlessly in the doorway to the porch. She looked somewhat pale and tired and, though very slim at the best of times, she seemed to have got a good deal thinner. 'Somewhere right at the back, don't you think?' she said faintly.

Then Kitty Whitlace entered in a rush, looking equally aghast. 'Whoever sent all these?' she exclaimed. She must have seen the cartload outside.

'Mrs Crabtree, wasn't it kind of her?' said Lady Mullings weakly. Then, pulling herself together, she added in a more normal voice, 'I think you know Mr Bullivant, Mrs Crabtree's head gardener?'

'Yes, indeed,' said Kitty. She made as though to put out her hand but, looking down at it, saw it was far from clean. 'I won't shake hands,' she added, 'I've just been carting all the leftover leaves and dirt and things away in the wheelbarrow . . .'

As the men went out for more pots, Kitty wheeled round to Lady Mullings. 'Now, you two ladies sit down. You've done quite enough for one day. I've

241

got the wheelbarrow outside and can give the men a hand with the pots. We'll have them all in in no time.'

'We thought we'd put them all at the back by the bell-chamber,' said Miss Menzies, as she and Lady Mullings slipped gratefully into the nearest pew, 'and sort of mass them all up against the curtains.'

'*Mass* them!' exclaimed Lady Mullings enthusiastically. 'What a wonderful idea! Build them up into a kind of pyramid of glorious pink against those dark curtains . . .' She jumped to her feet, very agile for a lady of her somewhat generous proportions. 'Now that is what I call a real inspiration!'

Miss Menzies rose, too, but a little more reluctantly, but Lady Mullings, now in the aisle, turned eagerly towards her. 'No, my dear, stay where you are. You've been overdoing things – anyone can see that – what with the model village and now the decorations: we ought not to have let you come. And yet we all know that you are the only one, the only truly artistic one, who can make such a show of the windowsills. Now, my dear,' she leant over the edge of the pew, her face alight with the prospect of her own turn at creation, 'take my bag, if you wouldn't mind, and sit back there quietly in your corner. I know exactly what to do!'

Miss Menzies was not reluctant to obey. As she sank back into her corner of the pew, her head against the wall, she heard Lady Mullings, hurrying towards the back of the church, say to Kitty Whitlace, 'Now, Kitty dear, the next thing is to find something to prop them up on . . .' Miss Menzies closed her eyes.

Arrietty, from her perch on the top of the rood-screen, stared down at her pityingly. How wicked it had been of those Platters to destroy those little houses and give her so much work! Perhaps she and Mr Pott had been up all night in their desperate attempt to be ready for Easter Monday? Then she turned her gaze towards Miss Menzies' windowsills and saw (as she had not been able to see from below) what Lady Mullings had meant. Each windowsill had been lined with moss (perhaps with earth below?) out of which the spring flowers seemed to be growing naturally. All in their right groups and colours: grape hyacinths, narcissi, late primroses, some bluebells, clumps of primulas . . . Each windowsill was a little garden in itself. And what was even better, Arrietty realized, was that, sprayed occasionally with water, Miss Menzies' little borders would last all week. How glad she was to have torn herself away from Aunt Lupy and reached the roodscreen just in time!

There was so much to watch. There was Lady Mullings removing all the pamphlets and the collecting-box from the bench in front of the far curtains, sweeping them aside, as it were, as though they were so much rubbish, and setting up plant pots along its length. Heavy as they were, she seemed to be given strength by the joy of her newly discovered talent. 'Just four along here, Kitty, and a space in the middle, and two standing higher up in the space. Now, what can we find to stand them up on?' Her eyes alighted on the collecting-box and she grabbed it up from the floor. 'Ah, this will do –'

'No, Lady Mullings, we can't use that. It's the tourists' collecting-box and people will be coming

243

all next week – in their hundreds, I shouldn't wonder. What about a hassock?' She took the collecting-box from Lady Mullings and set it once again on the floor. When she brought out a rather dusty, sawdust-filled hassock from the back pew, Lady Mullings looked at it rather distastefully.

'It's a bit clumsy,' she said, 'and how are we going to hide the front of it? I know –' she exclaimed (it was her day for inspiration), '– we can drape it with a bit of pink aubretia, hanging down. There's some round the bottom of the pulpit.'

As she hurried down the aisle to fetch it, Kitty Whitlace tried to protest again. 'It's the two Miss Forbes's aubretia . . .' she pointed out.

'It doesn't matter,' Lady Mullings called back to her, 'I'll only take a little bit.' Nothing could stop her now.

At that moment something else caught Arrietty's eye. In the long patch of afternoon sunshine which streamed in from the west door, there lay a dark shadow. It was the shadow of a man. Why, oh why, did she have this sudden sense of foreboding? Was it perhaps because this shadow kept so still, thrown by a figure that was neither coming in nor intending to move away? A kind of 'watching' shadow? Her heart began to beat more heavily.

Lady Mullings came bustling back down the aisle, a clump of aubretia in her hand. Perhaps it had left rather a bald-looking patch at the foot of the pulpit, but she could see to that later by spreading the rest of it along. As she passed the open door, she glanced carelessly sideways to see who was standing on the threshold. 'Oh, Mr Platter,' she exclaimed, scarcely

pausing in her step, 'I had forgotten all about you! Do come in. I shan't keep you a minute. Take a look round the church. It's really worth it. The flowers are quite wonderful this year. *And –*' she called back to him gaily, as she hurried on, '– you're our first visitor . . .'

Mr Platter took off his hat and entered rather dubiously. He and Mrs Platter were very 'low church' (in fact, he had been brought up 'chapel') and he was not at all sure he approved of all these light-hearted goings-on on the eve of such a solemn feast as Easter. However, he was not a bad gardener

245

himself, and, hat in hand, he made a slow but professional inspection. He quite liked the aubretia at the foot of the pulpit, but did not care much for those ashen-coloured roses below the lectern. The things that took his fancy most were the two long rows of variegated plants arranged along the foot of the rood-screen. Quite a herbaceous border, you might say! He sat down quietly on the front pew in order to study them better and while away the time until Lady Mullings should be ready to attend to him.

Arrietty peered down at him, her heart still beating heavily. From where she was stationed, she could not see Timmus and she hoped he was keeping still. She need not have worried. Mr Platter did not raise his eyes. He was not interested in rood-screens. After a while, he brought out an envelope, drew out a piece of paper, uncapped his fountain-pen and made a few jottings. He was adding to the list of extra jobs which Miss Parkinson had thrust upon him and wondering, in view of all the hours he had put in, whether or not he dare add a few inventions of his own.

Lady Mullings, down at the end of the church, was saying, 'Now we need something to top up the pinnacle. A few hymn-books would do . . .'

'A good idea,' Kitty Whitlace replied, 'I'll run and get them.' And hurried up the church towards the vestry. Aunt Lupy who, at that moment, had been peering out of her 'front door', heard her footsteps and darted back inside.

Lady Mullings, standing back to admire her handywork, did not notice when another person entered the church; someone who looked around vaguely for a moment, then tiptoed up the side aisle. But Arrietty noticed, and also noticed that Mr Platter started slightly when he felt the figure take her place quietly beside him on the front pew. 'Mabel!' he gasped, in a sort of whisper.

'I thought something must have happened to you,' she whispered back, 'so I hopped on my bicycle.'

'They gave me a whole lot of extra jobs,' he told her, still in a whisper. But Arrietty could hear every word.

'They would,' hissed Mrs Platter. 'That Parkinson! Did they give you anything to eat?'

'They brought me something on a tray. Not much. Not what she and Cook were having in the kitchen.'

'I had a lovely hot-pot,' said Mrs Platter. She sounded almost wistful.

'I know.' He was silent a minute. 'What have you done with the bicycle?'

'Put it in the back of the pony-cart. I'm not going to bicycle back all the way up that hill . . .' Leaning more closely towards him, she put a hand on his arm. 'What I really wanted to know, Sidney, what really brought me down was – did you give that package to Lady Mullings?'

'Of course I did.'

'Oh, thank heavens for that! What did she say?'

'She said she'd do her best.'

'It's our only chance, Sidney. It's our last chance!'

'I know that,' he said uncomfortably.

CHAPTER TWENTY-THREE

Lady Mullings almost flung herself down beside
Miss Menzies in the pew beside the west door.
'Well, that's done!' she exclaimed in a voice both
exhausted and satisfied.

Miss Menzies, startled, opened her eyes. 'Have
you finished? How splendid!' She blushed, 'I'm
afraid I must have nodded off . . .'

'And I don't blame you, my dear, after having
been up all night! Would you care to take a look at
it? I always value your opinion . . .'

'I'd love to,' said Miss Menzies, although it was
the last thing that she felt inclined to do at that
moment.

She followed Lady Mullings out of the pew and
down to the back of the church. It was indeed a
startling erection, a beautiful burst of colour against
the darker curtains and, facing straight down the
aisle, adding a focal point to all the lesser decorations.

'It really is quite lovely,' exclaimed Miss Menzies
with genuine admiration. 'I can't think how on
earth you've managed to prop it all up –'

'With this and that,' said Lady Mullings modestly, but she was looking very pleased.

Kitty Whitlace was on her knees, tidying up the
pamphlets which somehow seemed to have scattered
themselves about the floor. She made a neat pile of
these and another one of the postcards, and set them
in an orderly fashion beside her rescued collecting-
box. Then she sat back on her heels and looked up

at Lady Mullings. 'What are we going to do with this lot?' she asked.

'Oh, dear! Yes . . . well, I see. Oh, I know! Just leave them where they are for the moment. I've a small card-table at home, which I can bring down later. With a pretty piece of brocade on top, we could set it by the west door.' She turned to Miss Menzies. 'Well, my dear, I really think we've all done enough for today. Where did you leave your bicycle?'

'Up at the rectory.'

'I'll ride it down for you,' said Kitty, 'or better still, I'll walk up with you and make you a nice pot of tea. You look as though you need one. And I've got my cakes to see to . . .' These were cakes she was baking for the garden-party on Monday.

'Actually,' said Lady Mullings, 'I don't think there *is* any more to do. Except perhaps tidy up the pulpit.' She looked round the church. 'It all looks quite lovely, better even than last year –' She broke off abruptly, staring up towards the chancel. 'Oh, dear, there's Mr Platter! And Mrs Platter too. I'd forgotten all about him again. He's such a *quiet* man. Miss Menzies, dear, where did I leave my handbag?'

'In the pew. I'll get it. I've left mine there, too.'

In the end, they went together. Lady Mullings sat down. 'I'll just make sure I did bring my cheque-book.' She felt about in her handbag. 'Yes, here it is. And Mr Platter's bill –' She drew out a beige envelope. 'No, it isn't: it's the other thing he brought me. Do sit down for a minute, Miss Menzies, I really am a little curious to see what's inside . . .'

She slid a thumb under the flap of the envelope and drew out a very small, neatly folded piece of

249

cambric. 'Oh, dear!' she exclaimed in an exasperated voice, crumpling the envelope and content together in her lap, 'I do wish people wouldn't send me things like this!'

'Why – whatever is it?' asked Miss Menzies.

'Washed and ironed! I can never do anything with things that have been washed and ironed. It leaves no trace whatever of the original owner. You see, dear,' she went on, turning to Miss Menzies, 'to get my "feeling", or whatever you might like to call it, it has to be from something that has recently been handled or worn, or close in some way to another human being. I couldn't get any "feeling" from this, except perhaps of soap-suds and Mrs Platter's ironing-board.'

'May I see?' asked Miss Menzies.

'Yes, of course,' Lady Mullings passed it to her, 'it's some kind of doll's apron . . .'

Miss Menzies, unfolding the scrap of material, gave a sharp gasp. 'Mr *Platter* brought you this?' Her voice sounded almost fearful with astonishment.

'Yes. He, or rather Mrs Platter, wanted to locate the owner.'

Miss Menzies was silent for a moment, staring down at the little object on the palm of her hand. 'Mr Platter?' she said again, in a tone of tremulous wonder.

'I must admit I was a little surprised myself. When you think of Mr Platter, it does seem a little out of character.' She laughed. 'I suppose I should feel flattered . . .'

'You *have* found the owner,' said Miss Menzies quietly.

'I don't quite understand –'

250

'I am the owner. I made it.'

'Good gracious me!' exclaimed Lady Mullings.

'I remember every stitch of it. You see these little stroked gathers? I thought I'd never get a needle fine enough . . . Mr Platter! I mean, how did he . . .? It's quite extraordinary!'

'I suppose you made it for one of your little model figures?'

Miss Menzies did not reply: she was staring into space; never had a face looked more bewildered. Mr Platter? For some reason, she thought of the cut wire, the trampled streets, the broken shop-fronts, the general devastation in her model village. What thoughts were these? Why had they come to her? Mr Platter had a model village of his own (one might almost say a *rival* model village, if, as she was not, one was of a jealous disposition) and, as Lady Mullings had remarked, he was 'such a quiet man' – always courteous, so good at his job, so scrupulous in his building, such a comfort to those who found themselves bereaved. Miss Menzies tried to resist these bad, unworthy thoughts which, somehow of their own accord, had crept into her mind.

'Well, my dear,' Lady Mullings was saying, 'I think we've solved Mr Platter's little problem.' She picked up her bag and gloves. 'Now, if you'll excuse me, I'll go and settle up with him.'

Arrietty, in her eyrie, had not quite heard the confidential exchanges going on half way down the church: she had been too much taken up by trying to overhear the Platters. She *had* heard Miss Menzies' first, sharp repetition of Mr Platter's name, and thought perhaps the Platters had heard it too, because both had turned their heads warily to

251

glance behind them. Even then Arrietty did not pay too much attention. All her anxiety now was concentrated on Timmus: would he be wise enough to keep absolutely still?

Then she noticed that Lady Mullings had eased herself out of her pew and, handbag in hand, was coming up the church towards the Platters. She held her breath: something was going to happen!

Mr Platter rose when she approached and so did Mrs Platter, with whom Lady Mullings shook hands. 'Ah, Mrs Platter, how very nice to see you! Come to see the decorations, have you? We're rather proud of them this year . . .' Mrs Platter mumbled some reply, but her face looked oddly anxious as the three of them sat down again.

Mr Platter produced his accounts, which took a little explaining. Lady Mullings listened amiably, nodding her head from time to time. She completely trusted him. When she had written out his cheque and received his receipt, she rose to her feet. Mr Platter rose too.

'And that other little matter,' he said. 'I don't suppose you've had time –'

'Oh, the little thing you brought me – what a scatterbrain I am! I didn't *need* any time, Mr Platter: I find it belongs to Miss Menzies. She made it.' She turned to Mrs Platter. 'Here it is. Perhaps you'd like to give it back to her yourself? She's sitting down there by the west door . . .'

Mrs Platter did not seem to hear her. She was staring at the rood-screen. There was the strangest expression on her face and her mouth had fallen open. Lady Mullings, envelope in hand, looked puzzled. What was the matter with the woman?

'Well, here it is,' she said at last, and put the envelope down on the seat. Mrs Platter turned towards her then, her face still looking curiously dazed. But Lady Mullings saw that she was trying to pull herself together. 'No. Please –' she stammered, '– *you* give it to her. And thank you. Thank you very much. It was –' and her eyes flew back to the rood-screen.

Well, thought Lady Mullings as she made her way back towards Miss Menzies, I suppose there is rather a lot to look at in that rood-screen. Perhaps Mrs Platter had never seen it before? Perhaps it had rather shocked her, brought up (as Mr Platter had been) to a more austere form of worship. And, now she came to think of it, some of those medieval faces (although beautifully carved) did appear rather devilish . . .

Belongings were collected, and goodbyes said. Lady Mullings left by the west door, and Kitty and Miss Menzies came up the church to leave by the vestry, which gave them a short cut to the wicket gate. Mr Platter, too, was standing up as though preparing to leave, but Mrs Platter was still sitting down. It looked, as Kitty and Miss Menzies passed them – bidding them goodnight – as though Mrs Platter was gripping Mr Platter by the sleeve.

The church became very silent. Mrs Platter looked round cautiously. 'Don't go, Sidney . . .' she whispered urgently.

He pulled his arm away from her grip. 'Oh, come on, Mabel. We've played our trump card – and we've lost. I'm tired and I'm hungry. Is there any of that hot-pot left?'

'Oh, forget about the hot-pot, Sidney! This is

serious —' Her voice seemed to be trembling with some kind of excitement.

'What is?'

She pulled on his sleeve again. 'Sit down and I'll tell you —' He sat down unwillingly. 'One of them *yawned*!'

'Well, what of it?' He thought she was referring to one of the ladies. But Arrietty, up above, understood immediately and went cold with fear.

Mrs Platter was pointing with a shaking finger at the rood-screen. 'One of those creatures up there – it *yawned*!'

'Oh, don't be silly, Mabel,' he attempted to stand up again. 'You're just imagining things . . .'

'Sidney, it *yawned* I'm telling you! You don't imagine a yawn. I saw the flash of its teeth –'

'Which one?'

Mrs Platter began to gabble. 'Well, you see that long kind of face, that one with a hat on – some kind of bishop something – there just by the edge of the arch. And you see there's a smaller face, just below its ear, sort of leaning against it – ? Well, that's the one that yawned!'

Mr Platter leaned forward, peering hard in the direction of her pointing finger. 'Oh, Mabel, it couldn't have, it's carved out of wood!'

'It could be carved out of rock for all I care, but it yawned!'

From where Arrietty crouched, she could not see Timmus, except for one little leg which overhung the vine leaf. This was because the eaves of the gallery stood out a little on either side of the rood-screen. To see the whole of Timmus, she would have to lean right over. This, at the moment, for fear of

254

being 'seen', she did not dare to do. Oh, why had
she left him so long climbing about in the ivy? Of
course he had yawned: he had tired himself out . . .

'It's one of *them*, Sidney, I know it is!' Mrs Platter
was saying. 'And *one* would be better than none.
Could you reach it, do you think?'

'I could try,' said Mr Platter. He rose to his feet
and, rather gingerly, approached the massed blooms
at the foot of the rood-screen. He leaned over,
stretched up an arm, and rose up on tiptoe. 'It's no
good, Mabel, I can't reach it.' He had very nearly
overbalanced into the flowers. 'I'd need something
to stand on.'

Mrs Platter looked around but could see nothing
movable. Then her eye lighted on the two shallow
steps leading into the chancel. 'Why don't you try
from the other side?' she suggested, 'that's higher:
you could put your hand round the edge of the arch,
like . . .'

Arrietty was filled with a sudden anger: these two
awful human beings were talking as though poor
little Timmus had neither eyes nor ears.

Mr Platter went up the two steps and disappeared
on the far side of the rood-screen. Arrietty, watching
from above, saw the bony hand come out and feel
its way along the smooth edge of the arch. '*Inwards*
a bit more, Sidney, you're nearly there –' said Mrs
Platter, watching excitedly. 'That's the bishop's
face. Can you stretch a bit more? And then go
lower –'

Arrietty decided to stand up and lean farther
over: those dreadful feeling fingers were approaching the little leg. At last, they touched it. She heard
Mr Platter give a strangled gasp as though he had

255

been stung by a wasp, and the fingers flew away again. 'It's *warm*!' he cried out in a frightened voice. Arrietty realized then that Mr Platter had only been trying to humour Mrs Platter and had never believed that Timmus was alive.

'Of course it's warm!' Mrs Platter's voice had risen almost to a scream. 'Grab it, Sidney! Grab it! Quickly . . . quickly!' But the little leg had been withdrawn. The groping fingers, now in a panic of hurry, spun frenziedly about the vine leaf. It was empty. The prey had gone.

Mrs Platter burst into tears. As Mr Platter emerged in a crestfallen way from behind the rood-screen, Mrs Platter gasped out, 'You nearly had it! You actually touched it! How could you be so silly . . .!'

'It gave me a shock,' said Mr Platter and Arrietty, crouched back in her old position, could see he was looking pale. His eyes roved despondently over the rood-screen, but with little hope that among the myriad strange figures and faces he might see the one he sought.

'It's no good looking there,' gasped Mrs Platter, feeling for her handkerchief. 'It's down among those flowers. Or *was*. These creatures can move, I tell you!'

'Did it fall?'

'Fall! Of course it didn't fall. It nipped along to the edge of the screen, and slid down it into the flowers. Like greased lightning, it went!'

Mr Platter looked down at the flowers. 'Then it must be in there still,' he said.

'There's no "*must*" about it, Sidney. It could be anywhere by now –'

Mr Platter still stared down at the flowers, as if hoping to detect some kind of faint stir among the leaves and blossoms. He seemed to have got over his sudden attack of nervousness. Stooping, he put down a careful hand into the mass of colour. He felt about for a moment, and then withdrew it. He had discovered that, although the display had looked like a growing border, the cut stalks of each clump were set in some sort of container filled with water

– jam-jars, tins, vases of all shapes and sizes – among which any creature small enough could move with ease. Well, that was that.

Sighing, he sat down beside his wife. 'We'll just have to watch and wait,' he said.

'What's the point of that, Sidney? It may have run out already.' She turned her head towards the open west door, where the sunlight seemed to be fading, 'and the light will be going soon . . .'

'If you didn't see anything run out – and you didn't, did you?'

'No, of course I didn't.' But she wondered about those moments when she had been wiping her eyes.

'Then it stands to reason that it must still be in there somewhere.'

'But we can't sit here all night!' Was he really thinking of another 'vigil'?

He did not reply immediately: he seemed to be thinking hard. 'There's only one other thing we can do,' he said at last, 'that is to remove all these pots and vases one by one. You starting at one end and me at the other.'

'Oh, we can't do that, Sidney – supposing somebody came in . . .?'

Even as she spoke, they heard voices in the porch. Mrs Platter sprang to her feet. 'Sit down, Mabel, do!' hissed Mr Platter, 'we're not doing anything wrong.' Mrs Platter sat down again obediently but, all the same, both of them turned round to see who had come in.

It was Lady Mullings, followed by Parkinson who was carrying a small folding card-table. 'Just prop it up beside the door,' Lady Mullings was saying. 'And do ask Mrs Crabtree to come in –'

'She'd like to, but she's got the dog, my lady.'

'Oh, that doesn't matter on this sort of day, as long as she's got it on the lead. We won't be staying more than a minute or two, and I do want her to see her pelargoniums . . .' and she made off swiftly in the direction of her cherished flower arrangement. She did not even glance at the Platters sitting so quietly at the other end of the church. All her attention was centred elsewhere.

Mrs Crabtree was an extremely tall, elderly lady, dressed in shabby but very well-cut tweeds. The little dog was a young wire-haired terrier, and was pulling at the lead. 'Oh, come on, Pouncer,' she was saying irritably, as they made their way into church, 'don't be a fool! Walkies, after . . .'

'I'm here, dear,' called Lady Mullings, in her pleasant, rather musical voice, 'down by the bell-chamber.'

The Platters had half turned in their seats again to take note of the newcomer. Arrietty was watching, too. Mrs Platter seemed especially interested in Mrs Crabtree's frail right hand, as she hauled her unwilling little dog down the aisle. 'Just take a look at those diamonds,' she whispered to Mr Platter. Mr Platter said, 'Hush . . .' and turned away abruptly: the less attention they drew to themselves the better. But Mrs Platter went on staring.

The two ladies stood in silence for a moment before Lady Mullings' masterpiece. 'It's magnificent,' said Mrs Crabtree at last, 'quite magnificent!'

'I'm so glad you think so,' replied Lady Mullings, 'I did so want you to see it before the light failed . . .'

'I do congratulate you, my dear.'

'Well, you must take some of the credit, my dear

Stephanie: it was you and Bullivant who grew the flowers.'

What persuaded Timmus to bolt then always remained a slight puzzle to Arrietty. Was it because he had overheard the conversation between Mr and Mrs Platter about moving the rood-screen flowers pot by pot? Or was he taking advantage of the unexpected distraction caused by the sudden entrance of two ladies and a dog? Or was he banking on the dimness of the aisle in this fading, pew-shadowed half-light? But there he was, barely more than a shadow himself, streaking down towards the bell chamber, as fast as his little, flailing legs would carry him!

She guessed his destination: under the curtain, on to the bell-rope, up through the hole in the ceiling, and then – *safety*!

But Mr Platter, facing forward, had seen him run out from among the flowers; Mrs Platter, looking backwards, had seen him chasing down the aisle, and Arrietty, watching so intently from her perch above the rood-screen, of course had seen every stage of his panic-stricken dash. And now (oh, horror of horrors!), the dog had seen him! Just as Timmus was about to chase round the far end of the collecting-box, which still was standing on the floor, the dog gave a joyous yelp and pounced, his lead freed in a second from Mrs Crabtree's frail and inattentive hand. He had not been named 'Pouncer' for nothing.

The collecting-box slithered along the floor, pushing Timmus with it. Arrietty saw two little hands come up and grip the top and, with an agile twist, the slim little body followed. Mrs Crabtree groped down for the lead and jerked the dog aside but not before Timmus, lithe as an eel, had slipped down through the slot. Was it only Arrietty, in the short sharp silence which followed the dog's first yelp, who heard a shifting and clinking of coins in the bottom of the collecting-box?

Lady Mullings came out of her dream. 'What was all that about?' she asked.

Mrs Crabtree shrugged. 'I don't know: he must have seen a mouse or something. I'd better take him home . . .' She patted Lady Mullings on the shoulder. 'Thank you, my dear, for showing me: you've worked wonders. I can have a good look at all the rest of the flowers after the service tomorrow – the light will be better then.'

As Mrs Crabtree went out, Kitty Whitlace came in, humming 'County Down' and swinging the key on her first finger as usual. Her cakes had turned out beautifully, she had put Miss Menzies to rest on the sofa, where she had fallen asleep again, and tomorrow was Easter Day. Kitty Whitlace was feeling very happy.

Not so Mr and Mrs Platter. A certain amount of anxiety still gnawed at their vitals. Neither could withdraw their gaze from the collecting-box. Both were standing up now. What must be their next move?

'At least, we know where it is,' whispered Mr Platter.

Mrs Platter nodded. After a minute, she said, her voice a little uncertain, 'It's a very young one.'

Mr Platter gave a grim little laugh. 'All the better: it'll last us longer!'

Kitty Whitlace and Lady Mullings had set up the card-table, spread with the piece of brocade, and Kitty had arranged the pamphlets, the picture postcards, and the visitors' book in a neat row towards the front. The collecting-box she tucked under her arm.

Arrietty shuddered as she heard the rush of coins to one end of it, hoping Timmus would not be hurt. Perhaps it contained a few of those rare pound notes which might act as buffers. American tourists could be very generous at times . . .

'I expect you'll be wanting to lock up now,' Lady Mullings was saying, glancing once more around the church. 'Oh, Mr and Mrs Platter, I didn't see you! I *am* so sorry. It's all so beautiful that I suppose you're like the rest of us – almost impossible to tear oneself away.' Mr Platter nodded and smiled weakly. He didn't know quite what to say. Out of the corner of his eye, he could see Kitty Whitlace hurrying towards the vestry, the collecting-box under her arm. She returned almost immediately, swinging an even larger key, and went towards the door.

They all filed out. They had to: they could not keep her waiting. Mr and Mrs Platter came last. They walked like two people in a dream (or was it a nightmare?). Cheerful goodnights were said and see-you-tomorrows, and each went their separate ways. Mr and Mrs Platter walked reluctantly towards where they had tethered their pony-cart. Kitty Whitlace locked the church door.

CHAPTER TWENTY-FOUR

Neither spoke as Mr Platter untethered the pony
and Mrs Platter – in her awkward way – climbed up
on to the seat. Her bicycle lay safely in the back on
top of Mr Platter's tool-bags. 'Where now?' she said
in a dispirited voice as Mr Platter, reins in hand,
took his place beside her.

He did not reply at once: just sat there staring
down at his hands. 'We've got to do it,' he said at
last.

'Do what?'

'Break into the church . . .'

'Oh, Sidney, but that's a felony!'

'It's not the first felony we've had to commit,' he
reminded her glumly. 'We know exactly where that
creature is –'

'Yes. Locked up, in a locked box, in a locked
cupboard, in a locked church!'

'Exactly,' said Mr Platter, 'it's now or never,
Mabel.'

'I don't like it, Sidney,' she looked round in the
gathering dusk, 'it'll be dark soon and we won't be
able to put a light on.'

'We can borrow a torch from Jim Sykes at the
Bull. He's got a good one, for going round the
cellars . . .'

'The Bull!' exclaimed Mrs Platter; the face she
turned towards him looked almost stupid with
surprise. Mr Platter had never been one for visiting
village pubs.

'Yes, the Bull, Mabel. And what's more, we're

going to stay there up to near on closing time. We'll have a nice glass of stout, a couple of roast-beef sandwiches, and some oats and water for the pony, and leave the cart there till we're ready for it. We're not going to leave that cart and pony parked outside the church – Oh no! It'd be evidence against us.'

'Oh, Sidney,' faltered Mrs Platter, 'you think of everything . . .' But she was feeling very nervous.

'No, Mabel, there was one thing I didn't think of.' He picked up the reins. 'When I took all my locksmith's tools down to Lady Mullings's to open up her attic, I never thought I'd need 'em again for a tricky job of this size. Giddup, Tiger!' And the pony trotted off.

When next they reached the church porch, night had completely fallen but, low above the yew trees, a pale moon was rising. Mr Platter threw it a glance, as though measuring it for size. They had come down on foot, Mrs Platter carrying the box of keys and Mr Platter his tool-bag and the torch.

'Now, you hold the torch, Mabel, and pass me the box of keys. I took a good look this afternoon at the key that woman was using and I'll be blowed if I hadn't got one almost exactly like it. Most of these old church locks were made the same –' he was feeling about among the keys. 'I took it when they modernized the church at Went-le-Cray. Got antique value some of those old keys have . . .'

He was right – on all counts. After a bit of initial fumbling, they heard the lock grind back, and the heavy door squeaked open. 'What about that?' said Mr Platter in a satisfied voice.

They went inside, Mrs Platter on tiptoe. 'No need for that,' Mr Platter told her irritably, 'there's no one to hear us now.' But there was somebody to hear them.

As soon as Kitty Whitlace had locked the west door and silence reigned again in the church, Arrietty had climbed down from the rood-screen and had run to the harmonium, to break the dreadful news. Her Uncle Hendreary had his foot up on the sofa (as Pod had prophesied, he was becoming a martyr to gout) and her Aunt Lupy was busy preparing a little supper. The candles were all lighted again and the room looked very cosy. 'Oh, there you are!' Aunt Lupy had exclaimed, 'I couldn't get on till you came: I'm making a sparrow's-egg omelette. Where's Timmus?'

And then Arrietty had had to tell them. It had been a dreadful evening. There was nothing anyone could do. For almost the first time, Arrietty had realized the utter helplessness of their tiny race, when pitted against human odds. She had stayed on and on, trying to comfort them, although she knew her own parents must be getting worried. At last she said (thinking of Timmus's terror and loneliness), 'It will only be for one night. When Mrs Witless opens the press in the morning, he'll be out and away in a moment!'

'I hope you're right,' Aunt Lupy had said, but she did wipe away her tears and Arrietty, although she did not fancy the idea of the long walk back in the dark, now felt she might leave for home. It was then that they heard the squeak and scrape of the main door into the church.

'What's that?' whispered Aunt Lupy, and they all froze.

'Someone's come into the church,' said Hendreary, very low. He rose from his couch and, limping badly, blew out the candles one by one. They sat in the darkness, waiting.

A voice had spoken sharply, but they had not heard what it said. Footsteps were approaching the vestry. They heard the sudden rattle of the curtain-rings, and a strange light was flashing about. The borrowers drew together on the sofa, clasping each other's hands.

'Did you bring the key-box, Mabel?' Oh, that voice! Arrietty would have recognized it anywhere; it even haunted her dreams. She began to tremble.

'Shine the torch into my tool-bag, Mabel.' The voice was very close now. They could hear the sound of heavy breathing, the clank of metal, the shuffling of boots on the flagstones. 'And take the cloth off that table . . .'

'What are you going to do now, Sidney?' It was Mrs Platter. She sounded nervous.

'Nail that tablecloth up over the window. Then we can switch on the light. We might as well work in comfort, seeing as we've got all night, and the place to ourselves, like . . .'

'Oh, that will be better. I mean, a bit of light. I don't like it in here, Sidney. I don't like it in here at all!'

'Oh, don't be silly, Mabel. Take that other end –' The borrowers heard the sound of hammering. Then Mr Platter said, 'Draw those other curtains tight together, the ones leading to the church.' Again there was a rattle of curtain-rings, and the electric light flashed on. 'Ah, that's better. Now we can see what we're doing . . .'

The borrowers could now make out each other's faces, and very frightened faces they were. However, the sofa was well back from the glow which seeped in from their entrance.

There was silence. Mr Platter must be studying the lock. After about five minutes, he said in a pleased voice, 'Ah . . . now I think I see!'

The oddest sounds were heard as the operation got under way: squeaks, tappings, scrapings and, 'Pass me that, Mabel; no, not the thick one, the fine one; now that thing with a blunt end; put your finger here, Mabel; press hard; hold it steady; now that thing with a sharp point, Mabel,' and so on. Mabel did not say a word. At last, there was a long, loud, satisfied 'Ah . . . !' and the faint squeak of hinges: the door of the press was open!

There was an awed silence: the Platters had never seen such treasure. Mr Platter's amazement was such that he did not make an immediate grab for the collecting-box which stood humbly on the middle shelf.

'Jewels, gold . . . all those stones are *real*, Mabel. The rector must be mad. Or is it the parish?' He sounded very disapproving. 'Stuff like this ought to be in a museum or a bank or something . . .' Arrietty listening was again surprised by the word 'bank' – a bank, to her, was something with grass growing on it. 'Oh well,' Mr Platter went on sternly (he sounded genuinely shocked), 'I suppose it's their look out. Glad I'm not a churchwarden!'

There was a pause, and the borrowers guessed

267

that Mr Platter had picked up the collecting-box because they heard the faint clink of loose money.

'Careful, Sidney,' warned Mrs Platter. 'We don't want to damage it. I mean that creature inside. Set the box down here on the table.'

The borrowers heard a chair being pulled out, and then a second chair. Again there was silence (except for a little heavy breathing) while Mr Platter picked his second lock. This one did not take so long. Arrietty heard the rustle of paper money and the clink of coins as fingers felt about inside the box.

Mrs Platter broke the sudden shocked silence, 'It's gone! Look, Sidney, how he's piled up the half-crowns, and the florins, made a kind of staircase to get out, to reach the slot in the lid –'

'It's all right, Mabel, don't panic. He may have got out of the box but he couldn't have got out of the cupboard. He's in there all right, hiding among all that stuff.'

Again Arrietty heard the scrape of chairs, and the shuffle of footsteps on stone. 'Oh, goodness,' exclaimed Mrs Platter, 'here's a five-pound note – dropped on the floor!'

'Put it back, Mabel. I'll have to lock that box up again and place it back just where it was. But, first, we've got to take everything out of this middle shelf. You stand by the table and I'll pass things out to you. We'll get to him in the end. You'll see . . .'

Aunt Lupy began to cry again, and Arrietty put her arms round her – not so much, this time, to comfort her as to prevent her from breaking down into a storm of audible sobs.

The only sound they heard from the vestry was the faint clank of metal on wood. There were a few

'Ohs' and 'Ahs' of awestruck admiration when it seemed that Mr Platter had handed his wife some particularly beautiful object. Otherwise, they worked in methodical silence.

'He doesn't seem to be here . . .' said Mr Platter in a puzzled voice, 'unless he's behind that ivory thing at the back. Did you look inside all the chalices?'

'Of course I did,' said Mrs Platter.

There was a short silence. Then Mr Platter said, 'He's not on *this* shelf, Mabel . . .' He sounded more puzzled than desperate.

Then everything happened at once. A sudden shriek from Mrs Platter of 'There he is! There he is! There he goes . . .' and from Mr Platter, 'Where? Where? . . . Where?'

'Through the curtains into the church –'

'After him, Mabel. I'll put on the lights –'

Arrietty heard the sharp clicks, one after another: all lights in the church were controlled from the vestry and it was as though Mr Platter had run his hand down the whole set. There was a clashing of curtain-rings and Mr Platter, too, was gone.

She heard the panting voice of Mrs Platter echoing down the church. 'He was on the *bottom* shelf . . . !'

Arrietty ran out into the vestry. Yes. There was the cupboard wide open and the middle shelf bare. It was on the bottom shelf, the one at floor level, where Timmus must have been hiding: the shelf where the candlesticks were kept. Some of these were so tall and ornate that they nearly touched the shelf above. Timmus must have slid over the outer edge of the middle shelf on to a candlestick on the shelf below. Perhaps, thought Arrietty, in a strange old cupboard like this the edges of the shelves did not quite meet the backs of the doors when closed. There must have been a little space. Timmus had used it.

Now, if he could reach a bell-rope in time, he would be safe. She ran up to the curtains where Mr Platter had dragged them aside and peered round the edge of one into the church, but started back at the sound of a crash and a cry of pain. She knew what it was: someone, trying to get to the curtains leading to the belfry, had knocked over one of Mrs Crabtree's heavy flowerpots, on to somebody else's foot. Cautiously, she went back to the curtain and stared into the church. All the lights were on and there at the far end was Mr Platter hopping about and gripping his foot in both hands. Mrs Platter was nowhere to be seen. Arrietty guessed what had happened. Timmus had dashed under the curtains into the bell chamber. And Mrs Platter had dashed after him and in her clumsy haste had knocked over one of the precious pelargoniums. Plant, plant-pot, shards and earth must now lie strewn on the ground below Lady Mullings' cherished arrangement, completed with so much pride only a few hours before.

Then came a sound, so deep and resonant, that it seemed to fill the church, pass through its walls and throb into the still night air. A lingering sound. A sound which could be heard (by those who were still awake) in every house in the village. The sound of a church bell.

It was then that Mrs Platter began to shriek. Shriek after shriek. Even Aunt Lupy came out, followed by a limping Hendreary, to see what had happened. All they could see from the vestry steps was an empty church, ablaze with light. But the shrieks went on and on.

And the bell shuddered out again.

CHAPTER TWENTY-FIVE

Kitty Whitlace was upstairs making up a bed for Miss Menzies when she heard the bell (she had managed to dissuade Miss Menzies from cycling 'down those lonely lanes at this hour of the night' and Miss Menzies had, as last, agreed). Kitty, trembling, and white as the sheets she had been smoothing, dropped the pillow and the case into which she had been inserting it, and stumbled down the stairs into the little sitting-room.

'Did you hear that?' she gasped.

'Yes,' said Miss Menzies. She had risen from the sofa on which Kitty had left her reclining. Whitlace had gone to bed.

'There's someone in the church!'

'Yes,' said Miss Menzies again.

'I left everything locked – everything. I must go down!'

'Not by yourself,' said Miss Menzies quickly. 'You must go and wake up your husband and we had better telephone Mr Pomfret. I'll do that, if you like?'

'You know where the lights are in the hall?' said Kitty.

'Yes, I think so.' Miss Menzies did not sound too certain. She knew the reputation of this house and did not much fancy feeling her way in the dark.

'All right then,' Kitty was saying, 'I'll go and wake up Whitlace. It takes a bit of doing once he's gone right off . . .' and she rushed upstairs again.

Mr Pomfret (who, by the sound of his voice, had

also been asleep) said he would come at once and that no one was to go into the church until he arrived on his bicycle. 'You never know. I've got my truncheon but tell Whitlace to bring a stick . . .'

As Miss Menzies walked back through the empty old kitchen, firmly leaving the light on in the hall, she rather hoped there *would* be someone in the church even if they *were* a bit violent. She felt she would die of shame if, after her last interview with Mr Pomfret, this late night call on a possibly weary policeman should turn out to be a false alarm. The bell rang out again. For some reason, this seemed to reassure her.

They waited for Mr Pomfret by the lychgate. Whitlace had pulled on a few clothes and was armed with a broom handle. There was someone in the church all right if the light from the windows was anything to go by. But even this was slightly dimmed by the brilliance of the moon.

'You're sure you didn't leave the lights on by mistake?' Miss Menzies asked Kitty anxiously.

'There weren't any lights. It was still daylight when I locked up. And what about the bell? There it goes again . . .'

'But not so loud.' As the sound died away, Miss Menzies went on to explain, 'A bell can go on quite a long time on its own momentum.'

'That's right,' said Whitlace. 'Once it's on the swing, like . . .'

Mr Pomfret arrived quietly and propped his bicycle against the wall. 'Well, here we are,' he said. 'Got your stick, Whitlace? We men better go first . . .' and led the way towards the church. Kitty Whitlace felt in her pocket to make sure she had brought the key. A great beam of moonlight lay across half the porch and Kitty could see that there seemed to be another key in the door. She pointed this out to Mr Pomfret and showed him her own. He nodded sagely, before trying out the one in the door. But the door had been left unlocked and opened easily (with its usual grinding squeak) and they all followed Mr Pomfret in. The bell tolled out again, even more quietly this time, as though on a dying fall.

The church looked empty, but somebody had been there all right. They saw the overturned flowerpot and, after the sound of the bell had died away, they heard a strange noise, a kind of regular gasping; or was it more like a grunting? Mr Pomfret went straight towards the back of the church, slid behind Lady Mullings' flowers, and (rather dramatically) flung back the curtains leading into the bell chamber. Then he stood still.

The three others coming up behind saw the tableau framed, as on a stage, by the drawn-back curtains.

A largish lady seemed to have fallen to the floor, her hat askew, her hair awry. One leg stuck out before her, the other one seemed doubled somewhere underneath. It was Mrs Platter. It took him quite a minute to recognize her. She was sobbing and gasping, and seemed to be in pain. The bell-rope he saw was moving with a kind of steady indifference but the 'tail', like a frenzied snake, was threshing about the floor. Mr Platter, trying to keep clear of it, was rushing back and forth, hopping at times from one foot to the other. Mr Pomfret did not know very much about bells, but he had heard grim stories

274

about the tail ends of bell-ropes: they could whip your head off as likely as not. Mrs Platter seemed relatively safe: she was the centre of the storm.

The great bell sounded again, quite gently this time. The main rope was moving more slowly and the threshing 'tail' began to lose its impetus, until as last it settled down, like an exhausted serpent, in curls and whorls upon the floor.

They did not rush forward to assist Mrs Platter. They walked rather gingerly as if they feared the tangled serpent might revive and come alive again. It was Whitlace who ran a steady hand down the main rope, making sure that it was still; and then, quietly and matter-of-factly, he tidied up the 'tail'. 'You got to know about bells,' he told them, in a voice which sounded rather irritated, 'these were all set up for the ringers on Easter Day . . .'

But none of them listened. They were busy hoisting Mrs Platter up on to a kitchen chair. She was still sniffing and gasping. Miss Menzies produced a handkerchief and then, very gently, raised what seemed to be the injured foot on to a similar chair.

'It's broken,' sobbed Mrs Platter, 'I may be lame for life . . .'

'No, my dear,' Miss Menzies assured her (she had felt the ankle carefully: it was not for nothing Miss Menzies had been a Girl Guide). 'I think it's only a sprain. Just sit there quietly and Mrs Whitlace will get you a drink of water.'

'Of course I will,' said Kitty Whitlace in her cheerful way, and made off down the aisle towards the vestry.

'I'm bumps and bruises all over,' complained

Mrs Platter. 'And my head! Cracked it on the
ceiling . . . feel as though it's coming in half . . .'

'Good thing you were wearing that thick felt hat,'
said Whitlace. 'Might have broken your neck.'
There was little sympathy in his voice, and he still
looked offended: his bells, his precious bells . . . set

up so carefully! And what on earth did these people think they were doing, trying to ring them in the late hours of the night? And how had the Platters got into the church in the first place? And why?

Perhaps, by now, they were all thinking the same thoughts (Mr Pomfret certainly was) but they were too polite to voice them. Well, no doubt all would be explained later . . .

A sudden sound from the other end of the church caused Mr Pomfret to turn his head. It had been more an exclamation than a scream, and it seemed to come from the vestry. Mrs Whitlace? Yes, it must be she! As the whole group turned and stared up the aisle, Kitty Whitlace appeared between the curtains, holding them apart. 'Mr Pomfret,' she called, in a voice which it seemed she was trying to control, 'could you please step up here a minute?'

Light-footed Mr Pomfret was up the aisle in an instant: he had sensed the urgency in her tone. The others, though equally curious, followed more slowly. What were they going to witness now?

Mr Platter, bringing up the rear, was talking excitedly. But they did not quite hear all he said: it was too much of a gabble. Something about hearing intruders in the church . . . sense of duty . . . valuable stuff here . . . bit of a risk . . . but he and his missus had never lacked for courage . . . door locked . . . they had had to break in . . . intruders gone. But –

At this point he seemed to run out of steam: they were in the vestry now. And all Mr Platter had been saying somehow did not quite *do*: not with the cupboard doors standing wide; the rare and lovely pieces laid out haphazardly on the table; and, on

277

the floor, open for all to see, Mr Platter's familiar tool-bag. They all knew it well: there was hardly a house in the village where, sometime or another, Mr Platter had not done 'a little job'.

'Do you recognize these tools?' asked Mr Pomfret.

'I do,' replied Mr Platter with icy dignity, 'they happen to be mine.'

'Happen?' murmured Mr Pomfret and took out his note-book. Then another thought seemed to strike him. He looked sharply at Mr Platter. 'Your good lady – she must have thrown all her weight on that rope. Now, why would she do that, do you think?'

Mr Platter thought quickly. 'To raise the alarm. In the Middle Ages, you see . . .' But this did not quite *do* either – somehow. Mr Pomfret was writing in his note-book. 'We're not living in the Middle Ages now,' he remarked drily. 'I'm afraid, sir, I'll have to ask you to come down to the station.'

Mr Platter drew himself up. 'Not a thing has gone out of this church. Not a thing. So what are you going to charge me with?'

'Breaking and entering?' murmured Mr Pomfret, almost under his breath, as though he were speaking to himself. He was writing in the note-book. He looked up. 'And your good lady, will she be fit to come?'

'We're neither of us fit to come. Can't you leave it till the morning?'

Mr Pomfret was a kind man. 'I suppose I could,' he said. 'Say eleven-thirty?'

'Eleven-thirty,' agreed Mr Platter. He did look very tired. He glanced down at his tools, and around at the table. 'I think I'll leave this stuff here for tonight. No point in taking tools and bringing 'em down again: I've got to put these locks right, anyway.'

'A rum go,' said Mr Pomfret, shutting his note-book. He turned to Mr Platter, suddenly changing his tone. 'What were you doing, *really*?'

'Looking for something,' said Mr Platter.

'Something of yours?'

'Could be,' said Mr Platter.

'Oh, well,' Mr Pomfret put his note-book in his pocket. 'It's as I said, there'll be quite a bit of explaining to do. Goodnight all.'

After Mr Pomfret and Whitlace had departed and Miss Menzies and Kitty were tidying up the vestry, Arrietty heard Miss Menzies say in a thoughtful voice, 'I think, Kitty, the less we say about this evening in the village, the better. Don't you?'

'Yes, I do. The talk would be dreadful and most of it lies. Well, there's all the stuff back but I can't lock the cupboard . . .'

'It doesn't matter, just for one night.'

Dear Miss Menzies, thought Arrietty, protector of everyone, but all the same she wished they would go. She was longing to see Timmus, who she knew would not appear until the church was empty and the west door safely locked, although she guessed what must have happened down, almost, to the last detail. Mrs Platter had seen Timmus making his way up the rope, had nearly grabbed him with one hand, while twisting the other round the rope. Her weight had turned the bell right over and they both had sailed up to the ceiling. Timmus had been carried smoothly through the hole while Mrs Platter, after a painful crack on the head, had slithered to the floor.

At last Arrietty heard Miss Menzies say, 'Kitty dear, I think we'll leave the rest for the morning. I shall be here to help you. Oh dear, I don't know quite what we can do about Mrs Crabtree's plant . . .'

'Whitlace will re-pot it,' said Kitty.

'Oh, splendid! Let's go, then. I must admit I'm rather longing for bed – it's been quite an evening . . .'

Arrietty, back on the sofa, smiled and hugged her knees. She knew, once the door had closed behind them, Timmus would arrive back, safe and, she hoped, sound.

CHAPTER TWENTY-SIX

Much later that night, when Arrietty had climbed in through the partly opened grating and tumbled into their arms, Pod and Homily forgot the anxious hours of waiting and the dark unspoken dreads. There were tears but they were tears of joy. The church clock had struck two without being heeded before she had answered all their questions.

'Well, that's finished Platter,' said Pod at last.

'Do you think so, Pod?' quavered Homily.

'Stands to reason. The church broken into – at that hour of the night! Locks of the cupboard picked, cupboard bare, and all those vallyables out on the table . . .'

'But he tried to say there were intruders – or whatever they call them.'

Pod laughed grimly. 'Intruders wouldn't be using Sidney Platter's tools!'

Then next morning there was Peagreen to tell – and Spiller, too, if she could find him. By a happy chance, Arrietty found them together. Peagreen, among the ground-ivy near the path, had risen early to sort out his pieces of glass and Spiller, though bound on some other errand, had paused to watch him. Spiller, as Arrietty remembered, was always curious but would never ask a direct question. Both were suitably impressed by her story. As it went on, Arrietty and Peagreen sat down more comfortably on the dry ground below the ivy leaves. Even Spiller condescended to squat on his haunches, bow in hand, to hear it to the end. His eyes looked very bright but he did not speak a word.

'There's just one thing . . .' said Arrietty at last.

'What's that?' said Peagreen.

Arrietty did not reply at once and, to their surprise, they saw her eyes had filled with tears. 'It may seem silly to you, but . . .'

'But what?' asked Peagreen gently.

'It's Miss Menzies. I'd like to tell her we're all right.' The tears rolled out of her eyes.

'You mean –' said Peagreen in a tone of amazement, '– that *she* saw all this!'

'No, she didn't see anything. But I saw her. Sometimes, I was close enough to speak to her . . .'

'But you didn't, I hope!' said Peagreen sharply. He looked very shocked.

'No, I didn't. Because . . . because . . .' Arrietty seemed to swallow a sob, '. . . I promised my father, very gravely and sacredly, never to speak to any human being again. Not in my whole life.' She turned to Spiller. 'You were there that night. You heard me promise . . .' Spiller nodded.

'And your father was absolutely right,' said Peagreen. He had become very stern suddenly. 'It's madness. Utter madness. Every borrower worth his salt knows that!'

Arrietty put her head down on her knees and burst into tears. Perhaps her early rising after the strain of the past night had begun to take its toll. Or perhaps it was the angry tone of Peagreen's voice. Would anyone, ever, begin to understand . . .?

They watched her helplessly: the little shoulders shaking with the sobs she tried to quench against her already damp pinafore. If he had been alone,

Peagreen would have put out a hand to comfort her but, under Spiller's bright and curious eye, something made him hesitate.

Suddenly Arrietty raised an angry tear-stained face towards Spiller. 'You once said *you'd* tell her,' she accused him, 'that we were safe and that. But I knew you wouldn't. You're much too scared of human beans – even lovely ones like Miss Menzies. Let alone *speak* to one!'

Spiller sprang to his feet. His thin face had become curiously set. It seemed to Arrietty that the fierce glance he threw at her was almost one of loathing. Then he turned on his heel and was gone. Gone so swiftly and so silently that it was as though he had never been there. Not a leaf quivered among the ivy.

Between Arrietty and Peagreen there was a shocked silence. Then Arrietty said in a surprised voice, 'He's angry.'

'No wonder,' said Peagreen.

'I only said what was true.'

'How do you know it's true?'

'Oh, I don't know. It stands to reason. I mean . . . well surely *you* don't think he'd do it?'

'If he promised,' said Peagreen, 'and given the right time and place.' He gave a grim little laugh. 'And be gone again before she could say a word. Oh, he'll do it all right. But he's a law unto himself, that one. He'll choose his own moment . . .'

Arrietty looked troubled. 'You mean I should have trusted him?'

'Something like that. Or not been in too much of a hurry.' He frowned. 'Not that I hold with any of this – this mad idea of talking to human beings.

283

Foolhardy and stupid – that's what it is! And hardly fair on your father . . .'

'You didn't know Miss Menzies,' said Arrietty and, once again, her eyes filled with tears. She stood up. 'All the same, I wish I hadn't said all that . . .'

'Oh, he'll get over it,' said Peagreen cheerfully, and stood up beside her.

'You see, *really* I do rather like him . . .'

'We all do,' said Peagreen.

'Oh, well,' sighed Arrietty in a mournful little voice. 'I think I'd better be getting home now. I came out so early, and my parents may be wondering. And –' she dashed a quick hand across her eyes and tried an uncertain smile, '– to tell the truth, I'm getting rather hungry.'

'Oh,' said Peagreen, 'that reminds me.' He was feeling in his pocket. 'I hope I haven't broken it. No, here it is.'

He was holding out a very tiny egg – creamy pale with russet freckles. Arrietty took it gingerly, and turned it over between her hands. 'It's lovely,' she said.

'It's a blue tit's egg. I found it this morning in one of my nesting-boxes. Odd, because there wasn't a sign of a nest. I thought you might like it for breakfast . . .'

'It's so lovely. Just as it is. It seems a pity to eat it.'

'Oh, I don't know,' said Peagreen, 'today is a sort of egg day . . .'

'How do you mean?'

'Well, today's the day the humans call Easter Sunday . . .' He watched her thoughtfully as, very

284

carefully, she wrapped the egg up into her pinafore.
'You know, Arrietty,' he went on after a moment,
'as a matter of fact, the less Spiller says the better;
this human being . . . this Miss . . . Miss?'

'Menzies.'

'There's one thing that she must *never* find out —
and I really mean NEVER — and that is where we
are all living now.'

'I only wanted her to know we were *safe* . . .'

Peagreen looked back at her. He was smiling his
quizzical, one-sided smile.

'Are we?' he said gently. 'Are we? Ever?'

It was not until a few years later, at the time of
the First World War, it occurred to Arrietty that
those words of Peagreen's, spoken so quietly on
that sunlit morning, might have a wider meaning:
that they referred to others as well as themselves.
What was the hymn so beloved of Aunt Lupy?
The one that the family had heard at their first
('heavy-laden'), weary arrival at the church?
Something about 'all creatures great and small'?
And there was another one, wasn't there, which
spoke of 'all creatures which on earth do dwell'?
All creatures! That was the point. ALL creatures . . .

Dependent as they were on snippets of conversation overheard by Aunt Lupy, the borrowers
never discovered *exactly* what happened to Mr
Platter. Some said he had gone to prison; others
that he had only been fined and cautioned; and
then (many months later) that he and Mrs Platter
had sold their house and departed for Australia
where Mr Platter had a brother in the same line

of business. Anyhow, the borrowers never saw the Platters again. Nor were they much spoken of by the ladies who came on Wednesdays and Fridays to do the flowers in the church.

COME BACK SOON
Judy Gardiner

Val's family seem quite an odd bunch and their life is hectic but happy. But then Val's mother walks out on them and Val's carefree life is suddenly quite different. This is a moving but funny story.

AMY'S EYES
Richard Kennedy

When a doll changes into a man it means that anything might happen . . . and in this magical story all kinds of strange and wonderful things do happen to Amy and her sailor doll, the Captain. Together they set off on a fantastic journey on a quest for treasure more valuable than mere gold.

ASTERCOTE
Penelope Lively

Astercote village was destroyed by plague in the fourteenth century and Mair and her brother Peter find themselves caught up in a strange adventure when an ancient super-stition is resurrected.

THE HOUNDS OF THE MÓRRÍGAN
Pat O'Shea

When the Great Queen Mórrigan, evil creature from the world of Irish mythology, returns to destroy the world, Pidge and Brigit are the children chosen to thwart her. How they go about it makes an hilarious, moving story, full of totally original and unforgettable characters.